Hugh Miller started his
pathologist, but his oth
flexible work pattern.
a stills photographer a
John Grierson. He ma
teaching films, and th
marketing of professio
books on magic and gambling.
Hugh Miller has been a full-time writer for eight years, and his more recent novels include, *Ambulance*, *The Dissector* and *The Saviour*. This is his first Futura Spectacular.

Other Futura Spectaculars:

STORM ISLAND by Ken Follett
FOXBAT by Peter Cave
CAPRICORN ONE by Bernard L. Ross
FATHOM by Marc Hammond
THE MOSCOW HORSE by John Denis

Hugh Miller

Terminal 3

Futura Publications Limited
A Futura Book

A Futura Book

First published in Great Britain by
Futura Publications Limited in 1978

ISBN 0 7088 1426 3

Printed in Great Britain by
Hazell Watson & Viney Ltd
Aylesbury, Bucks

Futura Publications Limited
110 Warner Road
Camberwell, London SE5

For Lesley, James and Rachel

ACKNOWLEDGMENTS
My thanks to Commander John McLean for technical guidance and for his help in fictionalising details too unwieldy for inclusion in an entertainment. Further information from Roy and Graham Maver is gratefully acknowledged, and I must also thank Derek Chapman, whose grasp of space technology eased my task considerably.
In particular I am indebted to Anthony Cheetham, whose original idea forms the basis of this novel.

I would remind you that extremism in the defence of liberty is no vice. And let me remind you also that moderation in the pursuit of justice is no virtue.

—Barry Goldwater

The moral powers of the vegetarian, the pacifist, and the nationalist have been so refined away from the source of much power – infantile violence – that their moral powers exhibit a leanness, a keenness, and total ferocity which can only hint at worlds given up.

—Norman Mailer

ONE

Eight times the man called Sherman had called for a delay in take-off and eight times the Dulles flight controller had complied. The 747's four colossal Pratt and Whitney power plants whined like leashed animals as the delays piled up. The final security check on the jumbo's twelve toilets took fifteen minutes, and by the time Sherman and his partner Bradley had given the all-clear, several economy class passengers were circulating a rumour about a fault in the plumbing.

As the plane finally began to taxi towards runway nine the security officers on the terminal gates eased away from their posts, merging with the crowd and making casually for the rendezvous points where they would be discharged for the evening. Twelve men and six women had been involved in the operation and not one of them had spotted anything suspicious. The back-up scan of all passenger baggage on Flight 898 had produced nothing interesting either, except for one holdall, belonging to a New York housewife, that had turned out to be full of metal hair rollers and bundles of foil-wrapped indigestion tablets. In the airport manager's office a senior government policeman put down the telephone and told his relieved assistant that it would be OK to make that dinner date after all. The Israeli VIPs were off their hands now, taxiing out to the strip that would aim them for London. All members of the Washington security force could start patting themselves on the back.

'Nothing bigger than a matchbox got on that plane without clearance,' the tall officer rumbled, then winked. 'Leastways, that'll be the story, if we're ever asked.'

On the airport approaches five unmarked cars were radioed simultaneously to drop surveillance and return to standard duties. Up in the observation lounge a neat little blonde in a suede suit turned from the window and made her way towards the coffee shop, slipping on the safety catch of her pocketed Browning automatic as she went. Three of her colleagues down on the apron, concealed behind specially placed pallet trucks, began dismantling their Ingram SMGs before breaking cover. As the controller gave Speedbird 898 the final clearance for take-off, a man who looked like a weary commuter shuffled into the observation lounge refreshment area and unbuttoned his jacket, letting the three members of his unit know they could concentrate on their coffee and forget about terrorists, at least for tonight.

The blonde had bought doughnuts as well as coffee, for she had not eaten all afternoon. With half a mouthful of soggy dough she leaned towards her acquaintance opposite, a girl with the same security rating, and confessed she had been worried once or twice during the last twenty minutes of the operation.

'That kid,' she said, 'over in the far corner, the one who looks like a Chicano or something.' The boy, about eighteen, was still gazing out over the runways, his nose almost touching the glass. 'Maybe it's the way he stands. Tentative, you know? Anyhow, he hardly blinked while they were loading up. I got the feeling he was going to do something. Then he took the little radio out and jammed it to his ear.'

The other girl rolled her eyes. 'A plane freak. I had some bad moments with a couple of them downstairs. They just wander around listening to the short wave squawk and staring at the aircraft. Creepy.'

'Yeah.' The blonde finished one doughnut and picked up another. Her boss had taken a stool near the door and was flipping casually through a notebook. She bit through the sugary crust and used the cover of her hands to mumble to her companion, 'Beasley's whacked. He's been up here since this morning. If anything happened now he'd just fall off that stool.'

'But nothing's going to happen.' The other girl sounded disappointed. 'I bet nobody even knew the commission would take that flight.'

'Can't be too careful, though,' the blonde said, through a small spray of crumbs.

'Yes you can. This operation's been so careful I'm dreading the next one. The boredom could give me wrinkles.'

Late sun on the runway cast streaking highlights across the surface of the Boeing as it roared forward for take-off. The dark-skinned youth by the observation window went on watching. The everyday miracle of jumbo technology was still enough to hold the attention of airport staff, several of whom paused to look as the craft approached lifting speed. Sixteen massive wheels spread the seven hundred and fifty thousand-pound weight, equivalent to nine and a half wartime Lancasters with full bomb load. The JT9D turbofans produced a thrust sufficient to take the forty-four first-class and two hundred and eighty economy-class passengers up to the long-range cruise speed in five minutes. At a height of thirty-five thousand feet, the plane would hold a speed of five hundred and eighty miles per hour, with fuel reserves to tackle a maximum journey of over six thousand miles. But the catalogue of technical prodigies did nothing to suppress the plane's most striking feature. Even for those in the know it was an unusually beautiful giant, a huge, breathtaking wonder.

The youth turned abruptly from the window as Flight 898 cleared the runway and soared towards the darkening cloud. He crossed the hall and entered a telephone booth by the coffee shop, closing the door tightly. With a coin ready in his hand he dialled a New York number and waited for the connection to go through.

Less than a minute later a telephone rang in a Fifth Avenue attorney's office. It was answered by a young man in an expensive suit who did not identify himself.

'Yes?'

'They're in the air,' his brother told him.

He put down the receiver and sat with his hand over it for a few seconds, then picked it up again. Carefully, working from an open pad on his desk, he dialled the international exchange prefix, then the double-four UK code, and finally a London number. He waited impassively for two minutes until a deep male voice answered from the other end, then he delivered his message clearly.

'They are coming to you,' he said, and dropped the receiver back in its cradle.

*

In the twelve years he had been with Pan American, Harry Turner had flown practically everything from Sikorsky amphibians and Lockheed Lodestars to Convairs and 727s. He had been making the scheduled Washington to London run for five months, and it was beginning to pall. In jumbos, as he had said more than once, he was no longer a pilot but a machine minder. His Second Officer, Bob Fields, was inclined to agree. A flying ballroom that could be manned by just two pilots and a flight engineer was dandy technology, but the tedium was something else.

During take-off, with its ever-present risk of engine failure, the tension was always enough to keep the crew on peak alert. John Mitchell, the Flight Engineer, kept unblinking eyes on the readouts flashing across his main console. The ratio between increasing ground speed, runway length, wind speed and direction, aircraft payload and available engine thrust produced tight procedural requirements that were transferred instantly from computer to pilot action. On lift-off, even the sharp noise-abatement climb was predicted by the electronic sensors and matched by Harry Turner's fist clamped around the appropriate lever. Beside him, Bob Fields fed verbal confirmation of every procedure to ground control, until they were levelling-off at thirty-five thousand feet and throttling to an initial cruise speed of five hundred and fifty miles per hour. As they cleared the perimeter of Washington, John Mitchell activated the flight corridor monitor, which ensured the craft a minimal sideways drift and kept the height constant. Manual control was gradually taken away from the pilots, and over the northern end of Chesapeake Bay the inertial navigation system took over completely, heading the plane for London.

Harry Turner confirmed his position and co-ordinates to Dulles control, bade them goodnight,. and sat back in his chair, yawning and scratching his chest.

'All set for another night of adventure in the air, boys,' he grunted into his mike, and turned to grin at Mitchell, whose control area was set at right angles behind the pilots' seats.

'There could be some trouble yet,' Bob Fields said, glancing up darkly from his altimeter.

Harry squinted at him. 'How come?'

'The dinner menu for our special guests. I had a look at it earlier. I don't think it's really kosher.'

'Hah!' Turner eased his right leg forward and rubbed the calf gingerly. He was a Korean vet and a souvenir wound had left him with a touch of arthritis. 'They're a mean looking bunch.'

'A scared looking bunch,' Bob corrected. 'Did you see the two goons they brought with them? Israeli heavies look even worse than Chicago heavies, if they're a sample. They were all jumpy. Six marked men.'

'You adore drama,' Harry observed. He was fifteen years older than his second officer and inclined to be paternal. 'They're just politicians, doing what their kind do all the time. They're nothing special to be scared about.'

'Not much.' In certain quarters of the Pan Am administration Bob Fields was known as The Whizz. At thirty he displayed the professional maturity of a senior pilot, the social skills of an advanced seducer and, occasionally, the conversational arrogance of a television interviewer. He held lengthy opinions on most topics, and he was never above drawing facts from thin air to pad out his authority. Right now, he was on home ground, folding his arms and staring at Harry. 'They've just clinched a deal to protect their border with enough ground-to-ground and ground-to-air hardware to flatten the Arabs if they put a foot wrong.' He leaned forward for emphasis, jerking his thumb towards the first-class seating area. 'Those men are a living, breathing symbol of murderous aggression, as far as a lot of people are concerned. I mean, how does it look to all those guys talking about maintaining the tempo of peace moves? And the Syrians are going to have a ball, aren't they? All along they've been saying Israel can't be trusted an inch.' He shook his head with exaggerated sadness. 'Our guests are standard terrorist targets, which is why the airport was under a double security net tonight—'

'And why we've got a couple of taut-faced CIA crewcuts on board, in addition to the Israelis,' Mitchell put in. He swung in his seat to face Bob. 'It's like a circus out there. I dropped my clipboard coming aboard and that Bradley guy nearly jumped me.' He was older than the other two, almost fifty, but his mild manner and quiet voice always suggested the deference of a junior. 'I'm kind of sorry for those diplomats.'

'No need to be.' The Captain eased off his headset and put it down. 'For one thing, nobody makes them do their job. For another, the danger's past. If there ever was any.' He ran his fingers through his wiry black hair and cast challenging eyes at Bob. 'If there's to be any trouble, it'll be on the Arab-Israeli border, nowhere else.'

'Maybe,' Bob mumbled.

'We have a very clean passenger list,' Turner said patiently. 'Families, business men. The plane's been combed so thoroughly we know the colour of everybody's underwear. Unless one of those security guys runs amuck with his shooter, everything's fine. Or maybe you'd like to make a small bet on us having a skyjack?'

Bob Fields shook his head. 'I'm not saying you're wrong. All I'm saying is, you just never know with these political things. And this one's big. We're transporting people who are probably on a dozen death lists already.'

The Captain returned his attention to his instruments and sighed heavily. 'Drama,' he groaned, and John Mitchell began to laugh.

In the forward economy-class cabin, Kay Morgan was having security problems of her own. A leaky coffee pot had joined forces with a full milk jug to produce three large stains on the front of her stewardess's uniform, much to the amusement of a fat male passenger who kept nudging his neighbour and pointing to the escaping dribbles of coffee and the damp patches widening on Kay's dress. Finally, realising she was stranded in mid-aisle with a situation that was growing worse by the second, she put both containers on the floor and marched forward to the galley, where the Senior Steward, O'Malley, showed her no sympathy and told her to get changed, fast, for she had to take over in the first-class lounge.

Kay was twenty-two, and until a week before she had been proud of her job and excited at the prospects. Now, in the wake of several minor accidents and feeling things would never get any better, she would cheerfully have walked out, if such a thing had been possible. The trouble, she believed, was her hands. She could normally be both elegant and dexterous, carrying out the tasks of a stewardess with as much efficiency as the rest of them, but when one thing went wrong, just one small thing, then her hands went out of control and her confidence vanished. It had all started with a broken cup. Since that day, she had not completed one trip without at least two accidents. She had dropped butter on a passenger's silk dress, poured vermouth over another, slipped and knocked the dinner flying across the lap of a senator, of all people, in addition to a myriad lesser disasters involving crockery, glassware, collapsing paper cups and, now, leaking coffee.

'I'll do something *terrible* up there,' she moaned as Jo Hampton helped her get changed in the narrow galley. 'I just know I will. Oh, God, when we get back to Washington I'm going to walk off this plane and never set foot on another one, ever.' Kay showed signs of retaining her schoolgirl weakness for grand tragedy, which had attended her at proms and amateur drama rehearsals and after boring dates for as long as any of her friends could remember.

'You'll be fine,' Jo snapped, jerking up the zip on the back of Kay's dress. 'Everybody goes through the accident phase. You're no worse than the rest of us. Just take your time and be methodical, like they taught you.'

'But why *me*?' Kay turned wide, pained blue eyes on her colleague. 'I've only been in the job a short time. What about you, or any of the others, for that matter? I mean, it's like some kind of punishment. I make goofs all over the place, so what happens? I get sent up to the penthouse. It doesn't make sense . . .'

'Oh yes it does.' Tight-lipped, Jo Hampton stood back and checked that everything was in order. She patted a soft wave of honey-coloured hair at the side of Kay's cap and nodded approvingly. 'You're the pretty one, honey. There's a very fancy crowd up there tonight so cabin services are putting on a special show.'

It was no comfort to the girl. Her looks, as she was well aware, had probably helped to swing her the job in the first place, and they could be relied upon to see her through emergencies that might floor another woman. But now she could only believe that her cute face and provocative figure were getting her into more trouble than she liked to handle. 'I'll make a fool of myself,' she whined, and nervously stepped through the door to the first-class seating area.

'This way.' O'Malley was waiting for her and led the way up the spiral staircase to the lounge. Kay gripped the handrail at the top and looked around her. The four Israelis were seated at a table by the stairwell and their two-man guard reclined, rather too casually, on the curved seats around the far end. 'Come on, come on,' O'Malley hissed. 'Move it around.' He went behind the small fitted bar and began rattling glasses and bottles. Kay stepped forward to the table and tried to smile confidently.

'Bring me a large whisky,' one of the men said, before she had time to open her mouth. He looked like a Jewish John Wayne, Kay thought. The man opposite, smaller and with a less aggressive voice, asked if he might have the same. The other two said nothing.

Kay gave the order to O'Malley and jerked her head fractionally towards the two guards. 'What about them?'

'They're working,' O'Malley whispered, and narrowed his eyes significantly.

'How come there's nobody else up here?'

'Special circumstances.' He held up a glass at eye level and poured in the whisky like a chemist preparing a delicate compound. 'Now don't ask any more questions. Just do your job.'

Kay did her job for another hour, without one mistake. The Israelis didn't talk very much, and when they did it was in sharp grunts or whispers. The two guards began to look as if they had fallen asleep. Eventually, when the drinking seemed to be at an end, O'Malley told Kay he was going downstairs for a while. 'Just stay here,' he instructed her. 'If they want anything, give it to them.'

Five minutes after O'Malley had gone, one of the guards stood up, stretched, and sauntered over to the bar. He was very tall, and when he smiled it somehow made Kay feel good.

'I think I would like something to drink,' he said. His accent, Kay noticed, was almost American, with a trace of something like Dutch. 'Have you anything refreshing with no alcohol?'

Kay suggested a chilled fruit juice, and when the man nodded she uncapped a bottle of grapefruit cocktail and poured it. The accident she had been expecting occurred just then. The glass slipped through her fingers as she passed it to the big Israeli and it hit the bar, spattering both of them with sticky citrus juice.

'Oh, dear . . .' Kay began to turn crimson as she dabbed at the man's jacket and shirt with a napkin and tried, simultaneously, to mop up the spreading puddle on the bar. The four diplomats had stopped muttering and they were watching her. So was the other guard, and to make things worse he was laughing. 'I'm terribly sorry . . .'

'Please, it is no trouble.' The man had produced his own handkerchief and was helping her to wipe his sopping shirt front. As his jacket swung aside, Kay saw the black leather holster slung at his left armpit. That made her even more nervous.

'Having trouble, miss?'

The voice, coarse and startling, had come from the top of the stairs, and everyone looked there at once. Sherman, the squat, bull-necked CIA man who had been running the crew ragged before take-off, was standing with his hands on his hips, staring at the frozen tableau.

'Oh . . . Ah, it's all right,' Kay stammered.

Sherman continued to stand there, focusing his grim attention on the guard now. The man's partner unwound himself from his seat and stood up. 'There is no trouble,' he said. The hostility in his voice was unmistakable.

Sherman, without moving his eyes, said, 'Just attend to your own job, friend.' He came forward and stood beside the bar. 'Let me have a beer, will you?' Up close he was impressively ugly, with leathery skin and hard blue eyes that jutted from under the slab of his forehead.

The guard at the far end of the lounge took a couple of steps forward, while his partner continued to mop thoughtfully at his shirt. 'Should you be here?'

Sherman swung round. 'I told you to mind your own store . . .'

'My job is to ensure there is no disturbance in this part of the aircraft.' The contrast between the two men was striking. The Israeli was lithe and sinuous, and when he moved he was like a cat, silent and graceful. His voice was soft, too, menacingly soft. 'I believe you should not be here.'

Sherman reached and took the glass of beer Kay was holding out to him, then used it to gesture with. 'You're a bodyguard. You're guarding those gentlemen, right?' He nodded towards the diplomats, who were now ignoring him. 'My brief is the total security of a United States plane, and that takes in passengers and crew. I move where I want to.' He sipped his beer. 'I'm going back downstairs when I finish this, but there's every chance I'll be back, because I do my work thoroughly. Just get used to me.'

By stages the tension eased. Both Israeli guards returned to the seats at the end of the lounge, and the quartet around the table resumed their guarded discussion. Sherman told Kay he hoped everything would go smoothly for her, then he finished his beer and went back down the spiral stairs. Kay washed the sticky mess from her fingers and dress, then sponged the top of the bar. Allowing for the delay in take-off, she estimated they had just over five hours to go before they reached London. Silently she prayed for the remainder of the trip to be dull and uneventful.

O'Malley came back a few minutes later, wearing a fresh white jacket. His first name was Philip, but most of the girls called him Phyllis behind his back, and he displayed some of his habitual touchiness when he saw the marks on Kay's uniform.

'You'd better take a break,' he snapped discreetly, 'before you set fire to yourself or something.' He touched the damp surface of the bar with a fingertip and made a face. 'Come back and relieve me in an hour. And for God's sake clean yourself up.'

Feeling tacky, dishevelled and miserable, Kay straightened her cap and made for the stairs. She glanced across at the guards and the one she had splashed smiled and waved. The other just stared at his hands. As she passed the table she noticed the diplomats were arguing. She had no idea what they were saying, but two of them sounded angry, terribly angry. Somehow, that made her feel better. She picked her way carefully down the carpeted steps, thinking how weird it was that people's lives should have such different ways of getting them down. For all she knew, those men were fretting and fighting about the fate of millions. Kay just dreaded the prospect of dropping another glass.

TWO

By 3.30 a.m. UK time, when Pam Am flight 898 from Washington was almost twelve hundred miles into its journey, activity at Heathrow was building steadily to the frenetic pace normal to the running of an important airways junction. Total efficiency, the smooth kind that took care of every expected and unexpected contingency with regimented ease, was a long lost dream. But they coped. That morning, Thursday, 24th November, 1977, Air Traffic Control were preparing to cope with four JAL diversions from Brussels in addition to the usual throughput.

As he sat down at his desk to prepare the revised schedules, Senior Controller Mike Evans eyed the growing chaos. 'The shit,' he said, 'is approaching the fan on a priority corridor.' One or two of his staff smiled.

It was essential to reduce the density of traffic coming their way, and as usual the smaller craft had to be the focus for the thinning. Divert signals were sent out to four freighters on approaches from Glasgow, Manchester, Castle Donington and Cambridge. Simultaneously, land-line calls to Prestwick, Coventry and Leeds-Bradford were put through to make arrangements for taking the diverted planes. Three deputy controllers fed all confirmed re-routings to the computer, while four of their colleagues contacted the JAL flights from Brussels and a late charter from Turin, passing on approach co-ordinates. A BAC Trident from Glasgow, carrying no passengers and destined to be an early shuttle from Heathrow, was advised to hold for a time until one of the Brussels flights had landed, as runway space, even at that hour, was scarce. As Mike Evans started his second cup of coffee, he was told that a delayed take-off, a winter holiday charter for Tunisia, would be delayed for at least another hour. That, he confided to one of his assistants, was all they needed.

Lines of authority and execution crossed and re-crossed as

separate bodies with individual headaches tried to attain a semblance of geared unity. A panic in the main freight storage bay, caused by the discovery of three ruptured oil drums and a broken crate of electrical components, reverberated through Airport Security, the fire safety unit, Freight Handling and even Catering, where two drivers waved mugs of hot tea at each other and argued about who had dumped the drums in the first place. Passengers for the delayed flight to Tunisia were haranguing baggage staff and anybody else they could collar, while Catering, Transport and Customs were making arrangements to handle the growing list of upheavals. The VIP lounge was being cleaned and polished in preparation for the arrival, in approximately five hours' time, of the Israeli Foreign Minister, who was coming direct from his London hotel to greet his subordinates on the Arms Commission.

On the northern perimeter, walking with his head bowed against the swirling rain, a security patrolman called Jenkins stopped suddenly and peered towards the fence. A hundred yards away, on the bleak Osterley Park link road that ran close to the double-wired security fencing, he had seen a light blinking. Jenkins had walked that stretch for over five years, and he had never seen a light on the road before, not at that hour. He was a tall man, very fit for his fifty years and particularly proud of his eyesight. The light had vanished, but he did not doubt for a moment that he had really seen it. He started to move nearer the fence, which was rooted in concrete on the edge of deliberately pitted ground overgrown with scrub grass. He stepped with great care, and as he moved he saw the light again.

'The cheeky buggers,' he murmured, freezing to the spot, tightening his fingers around his non-regulation nightstick, donated by a sympathetic constable living nearby in Ealing. By blinking rapidly a few times Jenkins could see them clearly, silhouetted against the distant lights from West Drayton – three people, climbing the tall wire, one of them already over the top. Jenkins took a long deep breath, automatically remembering all the obstacles between him and heroism. There was the wife, the nice little home, his garden and his weekend bowls. The job was steady and boring, but it was safe; it looked after him and his. The thing to do now was to get on the radio and summon assistance. On the other hand, a commendation for initiative never did any harm, and these looked like youngsters, easy meat for a man who had once been an amateur middleweight contender.

He started to run through the tough grass, his stick at shoulder height. The stretch of ground suddenly felt very remote from the bright, populated safety of the main complex, a quarter of a mile behind him. There was a sound off to his right and Jenkins stopped, peering again, wiping rain from his eyes with his sleeve. It was McKenna, another patrolman. He had spotted the intruders as well, and he was signalling frantically for Jenkins to come in closer, so they could reach the fence together. Jenkins started moving again, veering towards his mate, glad of the company.

They stopped ten feet from the wire and McKenna switched on his torch. The white beam picked out two young men and a girl, standing with their backs to the fence. All three wore jeans and combat jackets and they carried canvas holdalls. The girl, who had an appealingly delicate face, looked scared, but the two men were almost casual. They grinned like schoolboys caught stealing apples, shifting their feet and shrugging at one another.

'What the hell do you think you're doing?' Jenkins moved in close, brandishing his stick.

'Nothing,' one of the men said, and widened his grin. He was taller than the other, but apart from the height difference they looked very similar, swarthy-skinned and moustached, with straight black hair.

'Don't be so flaming cute,' McKenna shouted. 'What are your names?' He was keeping the torchlight in their eyes and reaching for his two-way radio.

'We are students,' the tall one said. 'This was a joke, you understand? For a wager we came over the fence, it was just a foolish game.' He was still grinning and the other was nodding. The girl still looked frightened, gripping the wire behind her with hooked fingers.

'You'll be sorry you did it,' McKenna told them. I'll ask you just once more, what are your names?'

'I am Kalim,' the spokesman announced. 'The lady is called Leila, and this is my friend, Shofal.'

Jenkins had lowered his stick to waist level and was pointing it at Kalim. 'You'll be going for a ride in a couple of minutes,' he growled. 'Just stay where you are for the time being.'

Kalim nodded obediently, then his grin vanished and he slapped Shofal's arm. McKenna froze with his thumb over the switch of his radio, wondering at the change, then Shofal moved so fast there was no way to stop him. The torch went up in the air as McKenna's arm was kicked and Jenkins swiped blindly with his stick, hitting nothing. A moment later something metallic and brutally sharp struck McKenna, tearing nose and lips. He fell sideways and Jenkins tripped over him, his face slamming into the wet ground. The girl moved away from the fence and kept walking, her back to her companions as they knelt on the two fallen patrolmen. She had only taken a few steps when she heard the first dull plop, then the second. She hesitated, then carried on, keeping her eyes on the runway lights two hundred yards away. It was not long before Kalim and Shofal caught up with her and fell into step on either side.

They reached the back of the refrigerated storage bay in less than five minutes. In the shadow of two giant freight boxes they removed their combat jackets and buttoned the denim jerkins they wore underneath. Kalim took the components of three American 180 submachine guns from the holdalls and assembled them, while Shofal and Leila strapped a short-range receiver to an oval plastic bomb and placed it gently into a gaudy polythene carrier bag. A sack containing fifty impact detonators was carefully unloaded and the contents distributed among the five pockets of Shofal's jacket. Leila combed her long hair and applied bright lipstick with the aid of an illuminated pocket mirror, then picked up the carrier bag. The two men remained in the shadows as she made her way around to the side of the bay and across the short stretch of darkened roadway to the cover of the next storage area. By keeping to the dark side of three buildings and following a wide route towards the departure complex, she managed to turn up eventually in the brightly-lit doorway of a staff canteen, full of transport and baggage workers. She stepped inside and smiled awkwardly, playing the silly, confused tourist, and asked how she could get back to her friends in the arrivals lounge.

Three men tried to help her at once. Only one of them was stuffy enough to point out that she had wandered further than was permitted. It was a young driver who finally escorted Leila to the milling arena of incoming, outgoing and stranded passengers. She thanked him so profusely that he blushed and hurried back to the hoots and jibes of his mates.

Striding easily and swinging her bag, Leila walked past the baggage check-in bays, returning the smiles of young and not-so-young men who were responding to her presence. She even paused to flip through some magazines in the book stall, and on her way across to the cafeteria she picked up a plastic ball and returned it to its young owner. At the self-service counter she bought a cup of coffee and a cheese sandwich and took them to a table near the entrance to the ladies' room. She ate the sandwich and took her time over the coffee, then rose and went to the cloakroom. As she was pushing open the door, her bag hooked casually on her elbow, an elderly American in a plaid suit winked at her. To his delight, she winked back.

There was a great deal of turbulence in mid-Atlantic and several times the 747 dipped and heaved through low pressure pockets. An economy-class passenger, Mrs Ida Craig, had thrown up most of her dinner in two separate toilets, and swore that this, her first ever flight, would be her last. Her husband, a civil engineer who had crossed the Atlantic many times, tried to console her while Jo Hampton patted her brow with a frosted towel. Elsewhere in the three economy cabins passengers were sleeping, reading or just talking among themselves. A small girl, travelling with her Swedish governess to join her American parents in London, kept running around telling everyone she was called Betsy and she was nearly four and she could say the alphabet backwards, if they wanted. In the crew space behind the door of the flight deck, Dan Bradley and his partner Lou Sherman were trying to rationalise their position.

'Personal prejudices are unavoidable in a set-up like this,' Sherman declared. 'We're on board to maintain security, which is OK as far as it goes. What's bugging me is that bunch upstairs. It's because of them there's any danger in the first place. And they're hostile. So what do we do in a showdown?'

'How come?' Dan Bradley had been in the service for three years, and until now he had only ever heard of Sherman. Stories varied, but most people agreed Sherman was a tough operator who maybe stuck too close to the book. Bradley was twenty-eight, nine years younger than Sherman, and he represented a different breed of agent. His code of procedure was simple and flexible – do the job, and always leave room for some social work along the way. Suppression was not his sole function, or so he felt. Sherman, on the other hand, was a classic hammer man and Dan Bradley did not think he liked him too much. 'What I mean,' he enlarged, seeing a blank look spread across Sherman's features, 'is how come you think we could have a showdown? We're here to safeguard everybody, the Israelis included.'

'They're hostile,' Sherman repeated, folding his arms like a stubborn kid and jamming his shoulders against the panelling. 'Those guards they have with them, they're a straight snub to the department, right? They come on board one of our planes, putting hundreds of American citizens at risk, and they isolate themselves, with their own bodyguards, to underline the situation. I'll tell you . . .' He raised a stubby, warning finger. 'I know how the militant Jewish mind works. In a crunch, it's them and us, they'd jettison everyone else to save their necks.'

'But there's no need to speculate along those lines. It's a straightforward surveillance job now.'

'Yeah?' Sherman was practically sneering. 'I wouldn't bank on that. Those people have just pulled off a stroke that gives their plucky little nation the muscle to start behaving the way they've wanted to for years. The Arabs have been sore before, and you know what happened. Now – well, hell, *think* about it. First off, the Arms Commission will get it in the neck . . .'

'But not here,' Bradley said, shaking his head. 'If there's trouble it'll—'

'It'll land when nobody expects it.' Sherman jabbed his chest. 'Me, I'd let them go. I don't see it's any part of my duty to defend representatives of the most warlike nation on earth, especially when I know they'd blow a hole in my back if it suited them.'

Bradley sighed and shifted his feet. That kind of talk made him uncomfortable. 'For all we know, they're probably four very nice people, doing a job for their government just the same as we do. And they *are* on our side, remember.'

'Nice people?' Sherman squeaked. He reached into his pocket and pulled out a notebook. He flipped the pages and folded it flat. 'Here's your good guys, Bradley. Top man is Avrum Maller, former adviser on anti-personal weaponry and known assassin. He was responsible for wiping out no less than fifteen men when he was with Dayan's hit squad. Nowadays he's a staunch defender of Israel's expansion programme and – get this – he doesn't favour US involvement in strategic planning.' Sherman waved the book under his partner's nose. 'He'll use our missiles, of course. That's different.'

'None of my business,' Bradley said sharply. 'I'm not supposed to get that involved.'

'Experience will teach you different.' Sherman returned his attention to the notebook. 'Maller's aide is Joel Singer, an American-born expert on tactical warfare. He used to be a soldier. Like Maller, he's been quoted as saying he dislikes American interference. Then there's Abraham Glazer and Nathan Danzig. Glazer's strictly a politico, some kind of lapsed pacifist, and Danzig is the real darling of the bunch, American-born like Singer and a government adviser on covert operations.' He looked up ominously. 'We know what that means, don't we?'

'We should,' Bradley mumbled. They were both operatives of the CIA's Covert Action staff, seconded for the time being to the Operational Services Division.

'So we should watch the bastards.'

'I think I'll check out the flight deck,' Bradley said, itchy to be doing something and growing depressed by Sherman's patter. He made to go through the connecting door and Sherman detained him with a hand on his arm.

'When you get a chance, just check out the two Civil Security officers, huh?'

'Why?'

'Because they're top boys and they're here to defend their diplomats, nothing else. Know your enemy.' Sherman winked. 'They sound like a comedy team, Mendel and Mark, but there's nothing very funny about them.'

Dan Bradley muttered something and went through the door to the flight deck, closing it firmly behind him.

In the first-class lounge Kay Morgan was busying herself with arranging the bottle shelves and trying to pretend she didn't notice the squabble that was going on. The two guards were looking embarrassed, trying to lock themselves into a conversation but drying up every few seconds as voices were raised to shout level. Two of the diplomats were saying nothing, but their red faces and taut knuckles were expressive enough. The battle was between Joel Singer and Abraham Glazer, and neither one was giving any ground.

'You're like an old woman,' Singer was growling, 'an old woman with the shakes! You commit yourself to something then when you realise you have to live up to the terms of your commitment, you get qualms.' There was no trace of Israeli in Singer's accent. Like his square face and tight, thin mouth, it was purest uptown New York Yiddish. For thirty of his forty-four years he had lived away from the States, but no other influence showed on the surface.

Glazer was only slightly older, but as different as one man could be from another. He was slight with delicate shoulders and the gaunt, owl-eyed expression of the Jewish archetype. His thinning hair and hooked nose gave him the appearance of a worried, underfed refugee, a man who would go to great lengths for a crust. 'I am not an old woman,' he hissed, craning forward to make his point. 'I am a concerned individual who feels he has been duped. The ink is barely dry on the agreement and you're using phrases like "selective negation" and "tactical encroachment". Do you think I am an idiot? What you are talking about is clear, unvarnished warmongering. I co-signed a defence agreement, not a licence to go marauding.'

Singer glared at the ceiling and slapped his palm on the table. 'I was talking about safeguards, Abraham, the kind that ensure peace, not jeopardise it. What are we supposed to do? Sit behind a wall of missile emplacements and hope their bite will be taken for granted?' He lowered his voice. 'You know my views on Sadat and his so-called initiative. You also know that my views are far from exclusive. All that musical comedy going on, and in the meantime there are breaches of border treaties, dozens of them, committed under the current smokescreen of naïve talk and handshaking. We have the power now to set the picture right. We have the solidity to hold our position without retreating an inch. If we all listened to you, we'd be in the lunatic position of shelling out millions to keep things the way they've been for years.'

'The missiles,' Glazer said, 'are to be used exclusively to ward off aggression, and in the light of anti-Sadat rumblings among the Arab states, they can be justified. Where I made my mistake, I believe, was in overlooking the fact that you and your kind employ only convenient definitions. The mere threat of aggression would now perhaps be construed as an aggressive act, no?' He smiled without humour. 'Perhaps I am an old woman in many ways. For one thing, I am not alert enough to militarist double-talk.'

'You're the same as every other liberal administrator,' Singer replied, letting his voice rise again. 'You sit and scrutinise your own motives until you find yourself over on the other side. You're just plain negative.'

'I'm just plain frightened,' Glazer said quietly.

David Mendel, the guard whose shirt now bore the dried marks of his first encounter with Kay, stood up and wandered across to the bar again. He asked her for a glass of soda water and carefully stood clear as she pressed the handle of the siphon. Kay laughed, relieved by the diversion. She handed over the drink and Mendel accepted it with a small bow.

'You are most kind,' he said, smiling.

'I'm also being most careful,' Kay replied, relaxing. 'I'm accident prone, and it's not just with fruit juice.'

'That was not the first time, then?' He inclined his head when he spoke, and he narrowed his eyes as if he was trying to say more than his mouth could. At the other end of the lounge, Yosef Mark, his partner, recognised the technique and yawned. Mendel was always trying to get around some woman or other.

Kay embarked on an edited account of her mishaps over the past few weeks. She had reached the point about buttering the passenger's dress when she stopped suddenly, frowning and looking towards the stairs. Mendel turned and saw Lou Sherman.

'Hi,' Sherman said, addressing Kay. He came across and ordered another beer. 'Thirsty work, policing a jumbo.' He took the beer when it was poured and slurped it noisily, ignoring Mendel, who continued to stare at him. Halfway down the glass Sherman paused elaborately, looking from Kay to Mendel and back again. 'Did I break up something?'

'Of course not,' Kay said quickly, flushing.

'Nothing that can't be put back together when you've gone,' Mendel added.

Sherman emptied his glass and put it down. In the space of seconds his neck had turned purple. 'You're really cute, aren't you?' He was glaring up at Mendel, making no effort to conceal his dislike.

'I don't follow.'

'Sure you don't.' At the table, Singer was raising his voice again and Sherman turned to watch as the two men bobbed their heads and snarled at each other. 'A nice example of peaceful co-existence.'

'I think you should go,' Mendel said.

'I told you before—'

'I know what you told me before, but I did not happen to agree with you. The security arrangements with regard to the commissioners are the responsibility of myself and my brother officer. Your presence amounts to no more than a nuisance.'

Sherman started to say something, then he swallowed it and stamped off, taking the spiral stairs two at a time without touching the handrail. At the entrance to the first class cabin he bumped into Dan Bradley.

'Where's the fire?'

'Come with me,' Sherman muttered, leading the way aft to the vacant front row of seats in the first economy cabin. He threw himself down and fumbled for a cigarette, which he lit with some difficulty, his hand shaking with anger.

'You look like you had a fright,' Bradley observed, sitting down beside him.

'Fright? I just stopped myself punching that kike Mendel in the mouth.'

'Oh.'

Sherman puffed furiously on the cigarette and snatched it away from his lips. 'What's that supposed to mean? Don't give me the big eyes and the "Oh" like you were some kind of disapproving Aunt Jemima.'

'No offence,' Bradley assured him coldly.

'That bastard!' The cigarette was half gone in five or six puffs. 'He's up there handing the stewardess his line and playing the big shot. Know something? Him and his sidekick are going to spread the word they put us down, just like their boss-men make a habit of doing with anybody that's in their way . . .'

'Steady, Lou.' Bradley was looking alarmed. 'You're coming over all unbalanced about this thing.' He watched Sherman finish the cigarette and stub it out. 'Now what did you want me to come back here for?'

'I want a policy rap. We have to line up and make our authority felt around here. Security is our baby, right? No two ways about that in the briefing. So we assert the fact.'

'But why? So long as there's no risk . . .'

'I'm talking about the image of the department.'

Bradley groaned. 'Lou, only a few more hours, for God's sake. Then we see the last of them. Why get all screwed up like this?'

'I told you, we have a reputation to maintain. No half-assed greasers are going to one-up on me or the organisation I represent.'

'I see.' Bradley shrugged. 'So what do you propose doing?'

'Laying down the law.' Sherman's neck was still an angry

mauve and as he spoke he kept pulling at the collar of his shirt, as if it were suddenly too tight. 'When they make any move outside that lounge up there, they come right under our jurisdiction. We lean a little, just to keep the balance.'

'What about *inside* the lounge?' Bradley delivered the question with just enough irony.

'Let something go wrong,' Sherman rumbled, 'and they'll find out what policing really means.'

Bradley stared balefully at the bulging eyes and twitching mouth of his partner and wished suddenly he was back home, vetting union leaders, shadowing leftist agitators or even just finishing some filing – anything but this. He began to remember something else he had heard about Lou Sherman. Back at Langley, one of the older field operatives had said that he was great under pressure, just so long as his own feelings weren't involved. If the thing got personal, it was a different story. Lou, the man had said, could turn into an animal when the conditions were right. Looking at him now, Dan Bradley could believe every word.

THREE

By 4.14 a.m. Leila had rejoined Kalim and Shofal, minus her carrier bag. They made their way forward into the clutter of commercial vehicles and freight stores, arriving by individual routes at the main entrance to Air Traffic Control. The tower was screened by a security fence, manned by two guards, but at the rear it was open. Kalim went into the shadows of the doorway first, followed a moment later by Leila. Shofal remained at the side, hugging the wall.

Leila strapped on the ammunition belt handed to her by Kalim. After tightening the buckle she took the gun, too, and tucked the stock into her right armpit.

'Check the sight,' Kalim hissed.

She pressed the switch beside the flat circular magazine. A red dot appeared on the floor. Leila waved the gun around, making the spot dance along the walls, then she cut the switch.

Kalim squared himself at the foot of the stairs and waited for Leila to fall in beside him.

'Right!'

They ran up the stairs, breathing deeply as they had been taught, keeping their eyes level to avoid loss of perspective or balance. It took them just over a minute, and when they arrived on the landing outside the main control room Kalim was breathing almost as evenly as when he started. Leila was panting but she was not tired. Kalim waited until she was breathing easily again, then nodded. They both switched on their laser sights. Leila brought the muzzle of her gun up to waist height and watched as Kalim set his higher, the stock resting on his shoulder.

'Now!'

The door flew wide as Kalim twisted the handle and kicked it inwards. A flight control assistant, passing the door as they jumped into the room, froze with a pencil in his mouth. For just an instant he stood, bemused, then Kalim hit him on the shoulder with his gun and knocked him across the front of a console. Leila shut the door and stood with her back against it as Kalim moved forward, pointing the gun menacingly.

'This tower is now under the control of the Zenima Squad.'

Mike Evans spun on his swivel chair and glared at them. The rest of the staff had paused at various angles, blinking at each other.

'You will stop what you are doing and listen to me!'

Somebody knocked over a tea cup and Kalim's gun swung round. A girl tried to say sorry, but the words never came. Kalim gestured behind him to Leila, who came forward and stood in the centre of the room, her gun trained on the door.

'Who is Evans, please?'

Mike stood up and raised his arm. 'That's me. What the hell's this all about?'

'Listen and you will learn, Mr Evans.' At desks and consoles the entire early staff, nine people, watched unblinking as Kalim pointed his gun deliberately at the head of a male assistant on the opposite side of the room. 'You will notice the red spot on your friend's neck. Where that falls, a bullet can follow, just as easily. Or ten bullets. I will not even need to aim. Please remember that when any of you are tempted to be brave, ladies and gentlemen. Now—' Kalim returned his attention to Mike Evans, who had stepped closer. 'I wish you to maintain a normal pattern of flight control. Make no attempt to issue warnings or pleas for help. If you should try, there will be a minor holocaust.'

'You must be crazy.'

Kalim stared calmly at the scowling mouth of the Senior Controller and waited until he settled down again. 'I am probably the sanest person in here, Mr Evans. I see things particularly clearly. My judgment is not fogged by petty allegiances or conditioned mill-treading.'

'You still must be crazy to think you'll get away with anything like this . . .'

'Do you feel obliged to talk like that? As if you were programmed by a B movie screenplay?' Kalim's eyebrows were arched, his look scornful. 'We *are* here, Mr Evans. We *have* taken over. Accept that, and do what I tell you. If you need further proof of the obvious, I'll be glad to furnish it.'

He moved his gun slowly around the room, gliding the spot across heads and shoulders. He stopped it on the protruding bust of a girl standing by Evans's desk. 'One squeeze of the trigger and the young lady dies. Another and she also disappears, a piece at a time.'

Evans was trembling. By degrees it had come through to him, the reality behind a dozen security pamphlets and Home Office circulars. Terrorists, standing right in the middle of the control room. He wondered for a moment what they had done outside, how much damage they had caused to gain this position. 'What do you have in mind?' he asked Kalim.

'You will proceed as normal. I am conversant with control jargon, so please, for your own sake, do not be clever. The people outside will learn, in time, that we are here. That does not matter. What matters is that no incoming or outgoing flight crews will have any idea. Do you understand, so far?'

'No, I bloody well don't.' Red-faced, Mike Evans took an impatient step nearer and found the red spot sitting on his chest. He stopped and placed his hands on his hips. 'What's behind it?'

'I was getting there,' Kalim said patiently. 'You have an incoming flight from Washington, Pan Am 898, scheduled to land here at approximately 8.30 this morning. Correct?'

'You're not seriously . . .'

'Is that correct?'

Mike Evans nodded sharply.

'You will issue new approach co-ordinates to the Washington flight when it comes within range. It will now land on Emergency Runway 16.'

'They'll query that,' Mike said.

'I know they will. When they do, you will simply repeat the instruction.'

Mike shrugged. 'Just as you say. But it won't work.'

'It had better work.' Kalim waited until Evans had returned to his console, then he took a transceiver from his pocket and spoke one word into it. 'Clear.'

Outside, Shofal acknowledged the signal and pocketed his radio. The bag on his shoulder was heavy and he adjusted its bulk carefully before moving off. He would have to take a wide route again, an estimated twenty-five minute walk that would bring him eventually to the western perimeter and Runway 16. There was a talisman in his pocket, a fragment of rock from a small hill close to Mount Sinai. Shofal touched it and turned it in his fingers as he lowered his head against the driving wind.

In the tower Kalim had made four of the staff, two women and two men, lie face-down on the floor. The others could keep the place functioning, he judged, until his purpose was served. After issuing one more clear warning about the consequences of any act of bravery, he crossed the room and leaned on the side of Evans's console, watching closely as flight information was flashed onto the monitors. Each time Mike lifted a telephone or flipped the switch on an intercom, the submachine gun waved gently, like the head of an alert cobra.

After putting through a course correction to a DC-9 coming in from Germany, Mike consulted the radar scope and ordered one of the assistants to signal a height adjustment between two internal freighters that were drifting beyond their beacon co-ordinates. He had no deputy at that time of the morning and his perfectionist's approach to the tidiness of flight patterns was at a peak. Kalim took in every move, smiling sometimes at Mike's robot precision.

'Your masters must be proud of you, Mr Evans. You serve them with blind obedience, don't you?'

Mike scanned his monitors, assuring himself the picture was neat, then swung to face Kalim. 'Don't use the Valentino scripts on me, friend. You're about as much of a hill Arab as I am.'

'I was making a simple observation.'

'You made one earlier, about B movies. Still, I can just believe you see everything in terms of masters and servants.'

Kalim glanced across at Leila, who was still covering the door. She was standing very still, but the tension was evident in her stance.

'Does she serve you well?' Mike asked.

Kalim's soft brown eyes narrowed. 'Are you needling me, Mr Evans?'

'You might just be right about that.' He folded his arms and sat back, staring glumly at the barrel of the gun. 'I can't pretend to admire hooligans, whatever fancy names they give themselves.'

Kalim laughed, a hard, throaty sound. 'Well, well. Michael John Evans, thirty-eight years old, blue eyes, fair hair, Senior Traffic Controller. Former Flight Lieutenant, Royal Air Force. One wife, two children. Cosy suburbanite.' He leaned closer. 'To that specification we can add armchair politician and bland spokesman for the deservedly silent majority. Yes?'

'You're quite good at the needling yourself. Where do you get your information from?'

'An immaculate source,' Kalim drawled. 'So you see me as a hooligan, do you? How very disappointing.'

Mike nodded. 'Whatever you like. Freedom fighter, urban guerrilla, liberationist, all the titles boil down to the same thing. Hooligan. Terrorist. What's your cause, anyway?' The growing edge of confidence in Mike Evans's manner was being encouraged by something he recognised in this young man. Over-confidence, the built-in abort device that brought down anyone over-reaching himself. It was good policy to keep these types on edge, Mike believed. Just so long as his own confidence didn't outstrip its resources. 'A sub-division of the PLO, perhaps?'

'A predictable assumption,' Kalim said, bristling. 'The Zenima Squad is the military arm of a vast movement, Mr Evans. Vast but closely unified. You can't be blamed for thinking of terrorists as wild-eyed, deranged servants of idealism. That is the picture most frequently painted, and in essence it is correct. But we have no place in that picture. Our cause is planned preservation . . .'

'By way of destruction.'

Kalim shook his head, rocking slightly, nursing his patience. 'If a healthy organism is preserved by the removal of a cancer it is hardly an act of destruction.'

'Very few motives are that simple,' Mike said, being careful to keep his face straight and expressionless. 'You managed to avoid telling me about your cause, just by explaining it.'

Kalim sneered. 'Preservation of tradition, custom, natural evolution and territory, that is our cause. We represent interests rather more substantial than those of the hysterical rabble.'

'What interests?'

'The rulers', Mr Evans. The men whose hereditary rights and territories are being stolen and threatened by your *real* hooligans.'

Evans was silent for a few moments, listening to the unnatural hollowness of the voices around him, conscious of the people lying on the floor. 'What do you get out of the deal? Don't you think those self-same rulers might just ditch you when you're no longer useful?'

'Oh, dear,' Kalim laughed, keeping his eyes fixed on Evans, taunting him with his own ignorance. 'Back to the old B movies again. I did say we are unified, Mr Evans. The rulers have no plans for eradicating me, because I am of their kind.'

'That would explain the education,' Evans said.

'The best, my friend. Cambridge, four years.'

'It would explain where you get all your information, too. I'm told the West End Arabs can buy anything.'

Kalim straightened, bringing the gun's muzzle up close to his shoulder. 'I think we can terminate the idle conversation now. You have work to do. Do it.'

Out on the northern perimeter a guard was moving warily towards something dark and bulky beside the fence. He was nervous. The possibility of finding something he couldn't cope with was a spectre he had lived with for eight months.

'Is that you, Loudon?'

The voice made him jump. It was his partner, Lawrie.

'Yes, it's me. I wish to Christ you wouldn't creep up on me like that.'

Lawrie approached and switched on his torch, making Loudon squint. He raised his hand to shield his eyes and in the same movement he jerked his head sideways. 'There's something over there,' he said gravely.

Lawrie smiled. Since Loudon had taken up the job he had been building threats and horrors out of every shadow. A stray cat had once frightened him so badly he had thrown his radio at it. 'Whereabouts?'

Loudon switched on his own torch and directed the beam at the vague, dark mass by the fence. 'Looks like sacks or something.'

The two men walked cautiously towards the spot, Loudon holding his torch high and keeping his fingers wrapped around the radio in his pocket. 'We don't usually get people dumping their rubbish here,' Lawrie murmured, then he stopped.

'What is it?'

Lawrie made no reply. He crouched, angling his torch until its beam was added to that coming from Loudon's.

'What does it look like?'

'Ssh!' Doing a crab-walk, Lawrie moved a few feet closer, then he stood up, his astonished face stark in the torchlight as he turned and beckoned to his partner. When Loudon was close enough to see what it was, he gulped once and shoved his radio to his lips, but he could say nothing. He had never seen a dead man before.

Lawrie whipped out his own set and barked into it. 'Assistance please, quickly. North Sector G. Quickly!' He went on staring for a while, only half-hearing Loudon muttering nervously to himself. One arm was visible beyond the dark blue bundle, and at the centre there was a face, open-mouthed, an eye torn from its socket. 'I think that's McKenna,' Lawrie whispered.

'It can't be . . .'

'It's McKenna. Here, hold the torch, and keep it steady.' Air trapped in the dead man's throat escaped in a grunt as Lawrie moved him gently. Underneath, face down with a gaping hole in the back of his head, Jenkins lay spread-eagled, his fingers knotted in the muddy grass. 'Oh, dear God . . .'

Loudon's stomach was beginning to lurch. He dropped one of the torches and let the other one slip as he bent to retrieve it.

'Give me some bloody light!'

'I'm sorry.' Loudon held up both torches again, spreading their pale light across the sickening tableau. McKenna's mouth was relaxed and partly open, as if he was lost in thought. Only two hours before, he had spoken to Loudon in the canteen. The gap where his eye had been was dark and glistening. Without warning, Loudon's stomach erupted and he vomited down the front of his coat.

'Get a grip!' Lawrie hissed, waiting for the light to be restored.

'I can't help it,' Loudon burbled, wiping his mouth with his sleeve. 'I've never seen anything like that.' He coughed and held one torch out at arm's length, its beam wavering on Lawrie's hands as he eased Jenkins's head upwards. Blood came spilling from the blue lips and Lawrie let go. The head dropped softly into the puddle. 'Oh my God,' Loudon whined. 'What the hell's happened to them?'

Lawrie took a deep breath. 'Shot through the head. Both of them.' He touched Jenkins's coat gently and shook his head. 'There's going to be riots over this.' He shivered and peered out beyond the shaft of torchlight. 'Where's that wagon, for Christ's sake?'

As the fact of the siege dawned, hysteria began to crackle at the edges of tower routine. One girl, lying stock still in the middle of the floor, began to whimper and when Leila crossed and casually kicked her on the shoulder she started screaming.

'Stop her!' Kalim snapped.

Leila stooped and punched the girl once, directly over the kidney. She stopped abruptly to suck in air, her face contorted with pain.

'Next time it will be worse,' Leila told her. The girl pressed her lips shut, willing herself to silence whilst Leila took up her stance again by the door.

Close to where Kalim stood a clerk had knocked over a rotary file. When he tried to pick it up again, the shaking of his fingers made him scatter loose cards on the desk and floor. Kalim watched as the clerk's remaining composure disintegrated and he sank to his chair, burying his face in his hands.

'Stiff upper lips just aren't what they were in the days of Empire,' Kalim said.

Mike Evans ignored him and went on checking his print-out of incoming flights.

Kalim shouldered his gun and walked around the console, touching coloured switches with the tips of his fingers and watching Evans all the time. 'I believe I know what you are thinking,' he observed softly.

'Yes?' Mike looked up, his reading glasses on the point of his nose. 'Is ESP part of your training?'

'Perception is part of my nature. You are of a type I understand very well. You're thinking you'd love to get this little wog alone and smack him in the teeth, am I right? You are boiling inside with suppressed hatred, the kind that bubbles up every time you see an Arab on the street or passing through a terminal building. Oh, I know your kind, Mr Evans.'

'Why don't you keep your insights to yourself?'

Kalim smiled. 'You put on a very brave show. Just make sure you don't do anything stupid.' He looked at his watch. 'What special control arrangements have been made for Pan Am 898?'

'I thought you would know that.' Mike was studying his papers again, a small knot working in his cheek where his teeth were clenched.

Sighing, Kalim propped himself on the end of the console and stared at Mike until he was obliged to look up. 'Do I have to remind you, Mr Evans, that your freedom to swing your arms stops where my nose begins? I asked you a question. Answer it, and tell me the truth, if you value the safety of your people.'

'The plane is on a security corridor.'

Kalim frowned. 'What is that?'

'It's a precautionary arrangement. The radio link is on a narrow frequency, so that we have exclusive contact. It cuts down the danger of jamming or signal interception.'

'What else?'

'We have two-way warning codes.' He indicated a yellow button on the console. 'A touch on that warns them something's wrong on the ground.'

Kalim stared at the button as if it might explode. 'And

what happens if such a warning is transmitted from either end?'

'If we send it, the Captain of the craft will automatically divert to another field. If he sends it, we get heavy ground security going.'

'I see.' He peered at Mike Evans, as if there was something hidden behind his blank features. 'You *are* being truthful?'

Mike nodded. 'I'm bearing the consequences in mind, just as you told me.' He glanced aside at his staff lying on the floor. 'I do value their safety.'

'That's just as well.' Kalim turned to walk away.

'Tell me,' Mike said, stopping him. 'What do you plan to do when that plane lands? There's going to be a very dense security curtain around it.'

'We plan to make a gesture, Mr Evans. An effective gesture. The security arrangements will make no difference.'

'Oh.' Mike resumed his study of the read-outs, but Kalim remained where he was, watching him. The tension between them was growing, building on each man's personal dislike of the other.

'You are content, in your way, aren't you? Content to serve the wheel without ever questioning its direction.'

'You're needling me again,' Mike said.

'I am observing. Comparing, if you like. You are a man of obvious intelligence, yet you seem to have no fire, no drive other than the one dictated to you.'

'Some people call it stability.'

'Some people call warmongering "defence". I was not inviting a discussion on semantics. To be frank, I was wondering how people of your kind can withstand the boredom of their existence. Cradle to grave with nothing but bland conformity in between.'

'I certainly don't have to compensate for some streak of self-loathing by risking my neck playing soldiers.'

'You understand very little, Mr Evans.' Kalim's bunched fist came down on the edge of the console. 'My certainties grew in here by themselves.' He tapped his head. 'I am the emissary of a cause, the cause of strong men, men who can take in their stride what you would call calamities. Men who have waited long enough for politicians to do their appointed jobs. Now the power of born rulers is being unleashed. It starts with a gesture. But it does not stop there.'

'You're certainly confident enough.' In the congestion of Kalim's eyes and the rising tremor of his voice, Mike had detected a need for soft-pedalling.

'Truth provides confidence,' Kalim muttered hoarsely.

Leila's voice cut across Mike's next remark. She sounded nervous.

'Kalim! The door!'

Moving backwards, keeping his eyes on Mike and the staff around him, Kalim crossed to Leila and nudged her with his arm. 'What happened?'

'The door opened,' she said. 'It closed again, very quickly.'

'You should have fired!'

'I know. It was so fast . . .'

'Stay there.' He crossed to the nearest window and looked down through the darkness beyond. A group of men were standing by the security gate, beckoning to another group by a police van. As Kalim watched, three motorcycle policemen drove up into the pool of light by the gate.

'I think your cavalry are arriving, Mr Evans.'

Mike stood up and motioned to the others to keep working. 'If they know you're here, it'll be an all-out alert. I should warn you—'

'You?' Kalim spun, glaring angrily. '*You* warn me? Have you some surprise for me?'

'I was going to say, they'll be here in their dozens. If you try to fight it out you won't stand a chance.'

'Idiot!' Kalim shouted the word so loudly that the girl on the floor began whimpering again. He crossed to Mike and grasped a handful of shirt. 'I find it annoying, the way you choose to underestimate me. I did not come here thinking I would find myself up against a couple of plodding constables if I didn't watch my step. I can handle anything they care to try, Mr Evans. I'll thank you to keep your paltry warnings to yourself.'

'They'll be armed,' Mike insisted.

'We are armed!'

'But if you start shooting . . .'

The girl on the floor was howling. Leila glanced down at her, then at Kalim, who ignored her and went on glaring at Mike.

'If we start shooting, somebody may get hurt. Has it entered your conditioned head that I don't really care, Mr Evans? The men outside have their guns. I have you and your people. Plus my guns. The advantage is with me. Get back to work.'

Mike was back in his chair and trying to make sense of the dancing letters before his eyes when the girl's scream brought him back to his feet, his heart thumping. Kalim was crouched beside her on the floor, his hand clamping her neck against the tiling. A man lying nearby had closed his eyes and was shaking violently.

'What are you doing?' Mike yelled.

'I am reinforcing my warning about obedience.' Kalim looked down reflectively at the girl's quivering back, then his free hand shot forward and grasped the hem of her skirt. She screamed again and he raised her head from the floor for a moment, then slammed it down hard, striking her nose on the tiles. He hoisted her skirt along her thighs and paused with the material bunched in his fingers. 'There are things I can do,' he said slowly, addressing the entire room, 'that would startle you.' His hand dropped and moved sideways, up under the skirt. The girl's scream was different this time, a cry of real pain in a register that was barely human. Her face was smeared with blood from her nostrils, and as she twisted her head against the restraining hand more blood came forward, frothing out over the floor.

Kalim stood up abruptly and turned away from her. 'No heroism, ladies and gentlemen,' he said, as pleasantly as a steward welcoming passengers aboard. 'The young lady will remain on your consciences if one wrong move is made.' He glanced over his shoulder at her, wrinkling his nose with distaste. 'Somebody clean her up, then put her on the floor again.'

Mike sat down, seeing Kalim from the corner of his eye peering out at the darkness again. The firm directives of all his security briefings were there, goading him to cautious action. But fear was there, too. Fear for that girl, and for himself. It was mounting simply because Mike Evans did suffer from conditioning, the kind that insisted he do something, however small. There was no telling how alert Kalim was, or indeed how unobtrusive the warning signal to the Boeing would be. He had told one lie and got away with it. Was there room for another? Mike steadied his hands on the console and checked the clock. Very soon, Pan Am 898 would be within range for the initial contact signal.

FOUR

Nicholas Turnbull was thirty-five and took deep, secret pride in the resemblance women saw between him and George Segal, the actor. His sideburns were shorter than Segal's and his hair receded a little more at the temples, but where it mattered, in the large dark eyes, firm prominent nose and square jaw, Nick was a dead ringer. Sitting by a window to the rear of the forward economy-class cabin, he frequently looked at his reflection in the curved plexiglass and tried to draw comfort from the handsome veneer of self-assurance. For a couple of hours it had worked, but now he was scared. He closed his eyes and pretended to be asleep.

Looking back it was easy to see where he had made the mistakes, but at the time the order of events had had a different slant. The emphasis had been on climbing and making gains, and that had reduced his caution, until it was too late to do anything but run. It was much harder, Nick thought, to abscond from the top of the hill. The sudden loss of everything could produce a terrible despair.

To settle the fluttering unrest in his stomach he thought about Claire. Sweet, soft, with enough occasional aggression to make her delightfully unpredictable. Claire, the Other Man's Wife, a necessary part of the equipment, like his Toyota Celica, Quasar TV, Germain suits, customised Dopp Kit and Onyx aftershave. She had clinched his status and made him the envy of every other man in the business. Now she was behind him, a thing of the past, like all the abandoned hardware in his Virginia Beach apartment. But if he called, *if he ever could call*, she would come running surely. And that made a difference, the difference between total despair and faint, precious hope. Behind his eyelids he could see her, laughing, waving to him, coming out of the automat, grinning with pleasure from the deep folds of his Scandinavian bed. Claire was the thought to hold.

Everything had happened so fast. One minute he was putting through another deal, the next they were on to him, mean-faced feds who knew more about land swindles than he did. Nick could still congratulate himself that he had been smart. He had run at the first sign; he hadn't waited around until they put a net over him. He could even feel a shade indignant, because what he had done was no crime in his book. It was a technique, a means of making a quick turnover and hurting nobody. The law saw it differently, of course. To use land as collateral before it had actually been acquired was in the list of felonies: the bulls took no account of the fact that Nick worked on certainties, or that he always did, eventually, obtain the rights and register them. In his view, the law was geared to protect the faint-hearted and the unambitious as well as the weak. It didn't pay a man to show initiative.

'Can I get you something?'

He opened his eyes too quickly and too wide, he realised. Jo Hampton was smiling at him, a friendly, solicitous approach that wavered only slightly as he jumped to alertness. She must have known he was not asleep. He would have to work at the basic techniques of deception. That kind of slackness, for all he knew, had drawn attention to him in the first place.

'No, nothing. Thank you.'

She went away and he sank lower in the seat, feeling the wads around his waist and thighs pinch at the flesh. He had sixty-two thousand on him, another ten thousand in the lining of his attaché case and a few hundred stashed in various seams and pockets in his baggage. At the airport he had almost panicked when he saw the personal checks going on, but it had not been so bad. They relied a lot on the detectors and only his pockets and armpits had been scrutinised. In London there was maybe another hundred thousand at the Chase Manhattan Bank, and he had taken the small risk of mailing a bearer bond for twenty-five thousand to his hotel in Knightsbridge. All in all he was running with plenty of heel leather.

The curtain at the cabin entrance moved aside and the fear returned, clutching his throat. An old lady came through, yawning, no kind of threat at all. Even so, they were on the plane. Nick hadn't imagined them. Two close-cropped characters with hard eyes and a swagger of authority; government goons if ever he had seen any. At first, when he had watched them roaming the aisles and staring at people, he had told himself they were just going through some routine, a necessary check what with all the hijacks and bombings that had been going on. But afterwards, when they were in the air, away from any possible escape route, Nick had started to wonder. Did they know about him? Were they in fact keeping a watch on him, just waiting to put on the cuffs over London? Twice, he had seen the older one looking in his direction from the doorway. As time passed the possibility had crept towards certainty. Now, slumped there with high denomination bills clutching him at thigh and gut, he began to feel very vulnerable.

Turnbull rose and walked slowly to the nearest toilet. Inside, he bolted the door and sat down on the padded lid of the bowl. Retreat took many forms, he thought bleakly. Back home he had a small room, five by five by ten, carpeted on floor, walls and ceiling, with one hooded spotlamp overhead and a fat cushioned seat against the back wall. Claire was the only other person who knew about it. He had spent hours in there at a stretch, reading, letting the muffling softness support him and quieten his mind. Sometimes he suspected he was mad, but other times he realised it was no more crazy than having worry beads or a security blanket. It was streets ahead of uppers, downers, White Crosses and Black Beauties, the brain-fogging crutches used by so many of his overamped buddies in commerce. He kept his system clean and released the stress in his padded room. But he had been caught, so maybe there was a moral hiding in there somewhere.

He stood up and touched the walls on either side, convincing himself of their solidity. Shielded like that, he could recharge and get back his cool. Only at that moment it did not work so well. He still felt threatened. He knew that when he opened the door he would step right back into trouble. A severe, official face would meet his, and a set of bracelets, too. An old directive came back to Nick as he examined his features in the washstand mirror: think out all the routes ahead of time. He sat down again and sighed.

If he got to London safe and sound, there would be no problem. He would go to his hotel, make arrangements for a cover-up identity, then ease himself across Europe by stages until he could surface in Lausanne with his trail wiped clean. That had been planned ages ago. But if they were on to him, if they were out there even now, about to hem him in, what then?

'I'm not giving myself up.' He said it aloud and startled himself with the firmness of his voice. But he heard determination, which was really no surprise. Nick Turnbull was a determined man, a front runner, and he had taken the trouble to find out all about life inside. He would never survive anything like that. The charge, if they ever brought one, would carry a minimum of ten to fifteen years on conviction. That was out of the question. No way would he even contemplate the horror of it. So, what alternative? He reached into the inside breast pocket of his jacket and took out a stubby, silver-plated matching pen and pencil. By levering up the retaining clips he would put a spring under pressure inside each cap. The springs had a firing pin on their free end, and the ornamental plugs on the caps covered short, .38 calibre barrels, each loaded with a single bullet. Nick had bought them on a whim, but now they looked like his salvation. He could bargain with those trinkets, and if bargaining failed they would still make sure he never saw the inside of a prison.

On the 747 a flight engineer's job was both complex and humdrum. John Mitchell was required to understand his equipment thoroughly, and in the event of an emergency he was qualified to operate intricate switchover mechanisms to run the craft on redundancy and auxiliary systems. He also had to apply the instincts gained from years of experience, little clues provided by eyes and ears to give the warnings no computer was designed to provide until damage or danger was a fact. He could tell from a minute change in hull vibration just when drag was going to cause a problem. He knew, too, that alteration in the dihedral angle of the wings was signalled by a momentary sideways roll, and he knew how to correct that within seconds. There were a hundred checks and procedures where his expertise would come under pressure, but there was also the yawn-provoking certainty that the chances of anything going wrong were minimal.

At 4.35 a.m., UK time, boredom had become almost total. Harry Turner was out doing his PR tour among the passengers while Second Officer Bob Fields was slumped at the controls, reading *Playboy*. The aircraft was taking itself across the Atlantic without anybody's help. John Mitchell, after one more check of his smugly accurate instrument panels, decided to go and get himself some coffee from the galley. He was buttoning his jacket when the flight deck door opened and Lou Sherman stepped in.

'Just thought I'd stop by and learn a thing or two,' he said amiably. 'Things are pretty quiet out there. My partner's gone to sleep on me.'

'Not much livelier in here, I'm afraid,' Mitchell apologised. 'Still, if I can do anything to entertain you, I will.'

Sherman stepped forward, leaning over the engineer's seat until Bob Fields was forced to look up and acknowledge him. They exchanged thin smiles and Sherman began gazing at the bank of dials and shaking his head, like everybody did when they first saw the deck. 'Sure is one hell of a piece of machinery. Are we on automatic pilot?' He nodded pointedly at Bob Fields, who was now examining the centrefold with the concentration of an explorer reading his maps.

'That's right.' Mitchell indicated the appropriate segment on the panel above his desk. 'There you can see our bearing and the degree of correction that's being applied to counteract wind and fluctuating pressure.'

'How does it do that?' Sherman's question was put flatly, as if he had been told to ask it and didn't really want to know.

'Inertial navigation.'

'Sorry?'

'It's an airborne navigation system, automatic and independent of external radio beacons.'

'Sounds like magic. I suppose the working is secret?'

'Not at all.'

Sherman seemed surprised. 'You mean a thing like that is down on paper, where anybody can find out about it?'

'Not everybody could use it,' John pointed out. 'It's the result of design evolution, anyway. There's no dark electronic devilry involved.'

'Well, it sure sounds like some kind of witchcraft. You're saying this plane is flying by itself, with no navigation aids on the outside, yet it knows where it's going and it can make course corrections? Hell, I know enough about guidance systems from the army to tell me that's something special.'

'Sounds like the cue for a guided tour,' Mitchell offered. There was a small edge of vindictive glee in his voice as he crossed to the navigational readout panel. It had been this one's partner, Bradley, who had over-reacted when John dropped his clip board, but Sherman it was who had nudged him into action. The irritating factor was the certainty in the man's approach, his conviction that most people were worth suspecting. John had some worthwhile service experience of his own: heavies like Sherman had a bad time coping with tricky ideas.

'This tells us the system is functioning.' He underlined an oscilloscope and a string of dials with his finger. 'The mechanism is encased, of course. Put simply, it's a system of accelerometers mounted on a platform and kept level by gyroscopes. OK so far?'

'Uhuh.' The first crease of puzzlement appeared on Sherman's brow.

'Now, forces fore and aft, and those in the lateral and vertical planes, are measured by the accelerometers. From these calculations the computer works out the speed, heading and distance travelled. Right?'

'Check,' Sherman mumbled.

'At the start of a flight, we tell the computer our latitude and longitude. After that, the navigational system will give us any required information about the scheduled destination. Hooked up to the auto pilot, the whole thing becomes self-handling. And that's it.'

'Wow. That's really cute.' Sherman cleared his throat noisily and turned to stare at the pilots' bay. 'Yes sir,' he puffed, rocking on his toes, 'mighty sophisticated thinking.'

He spun suddenly, one eyebrow lowered knowingly. 'Of course, when it comes to high-level sophistication, our boys in defence are the real aristocrats.'

Innocent surprise illuminated John Mitchell's face. 'Really? Missile technology, you mean?'

'Sure. Missiles. Rockets. Hot stuff.' He winked.

'It's a hobby of mine,' Mitchell said, 'studying missile systems and satellites. I suppose you guys have to be pretty well clued-up on things like that.'

Uncertainty hovered in Sherman's eyes, then cleared. 'Yup. But I can't talk about it.'

Bob Fields sat up in his chair as the radio light came on. He clamped the headset over his ears and flipped the receiver switch. There was a double bleep, then the Heathrow controller's voice came through.

'Good morning, Speedbird 898. This is Heathrow Control.' The reception was weak, even on the boosted frequency. Delivering his words slowly, Mike Evans asked for a rundown of co-ordinates.

Speaking just as slowly, Bob fed back the information, then turned and gestured towards the door with his thumb. John Mitchell nodded and went off through the door, leaving Sherman blinking after him. A few seconds later he returned with the Captain.

'What's the trouble?' Harry Turner had been chatting to a very attractive lady in the forward cabin and was clearly annoyed at having to return to the flight deck.

'I'll tell you in a minute.' Bob opened the transmission circuit again and asked London about the weather. He received a straightforward report, then London closed down, as they normally did at that point.

Fields pulled off the headset and pursed his lips, gazing at the radio panel as if it might do something.

'So tell me,' Harry Turner said patiently. Sherman was already over beside him, professionally alert.

'Heathrow prefixed with a double bleep.'

'Are you sure?'

The Second Officer looked offended. 'I heard it.'

Turner dropped into his seat, rubbing his leg thoughtfully. 'It could have been a mistake.' He drummed his fingers on his knee. 'No, it couldn't have been a mistake. No other clues?'

'None.'

'Then I suppose we just wait.'

Sherman came forward and stooped between them. 'What's the trouble?'

For a moment it appeared that Harry Turner might tell him to mind his own business.

'If there's any hassle, I have to know about it,' Sherman insisted.

Harry folded his arms. 'We've had a warning from Heathrow ATC. Something's wrong, but we don't know what.'

Sherman stepped back, scowling at the Captain. 'So why don't you ask them?'

'Procedure,' Fields said, getting it in quickly before the skipper lost his temper, which he was prone to do when people got pushy. 'The special prefix indicates an irregularity, one that can't be discussed. We have to hold on and be ready for further information.'

'From where?'

'Heathrow.'

Sherman stared at the darkened window for a moment. 'They'll tell you later, but they can't tell you now? What kind of sense does that make?'

'It makes perfect sense,' Harry Turner snapped. 'We've been alerted. For reasons best known to London ATC nothing can be said at present, but at least we're ready for the word when it comes through.'

'It has to be mighty serious if they can't even talk about it, for God's sake. Get back on the line to them and get this thing cleared up.'

'Look!' Turner was rising from his seat, a warning finger pointed at Sherman's chest. 'I don't question the procedure that's been laid down. I'm the Captain of this craft and if that's good enough for me it's damn well good enough for you. We'll wait.' He turned to Bob Fields. 'Better get the Israeli security boys down here right away.'

'Now just a minute . . .'

'Yes?' Turner turned, squaring up to Sherman and matching his belligerence.

'This has nothing to do with the Israelis.'

'It has a hell of a lot to do with them. My instructions are specific. They have to be informed of any possible problems, here or on the ground.'

Bob Fields stood up and went to the door where John Mitchell stepped aside to let him out, a shadow of a wink passing between them.

Sherman propped himself defensively on the engineer's chair back, his arms stiffened behind him. 'What about us? Do we get any consideration?'

'The same as the Israeli security men. You have the facts, such as they are, already. Now I'll tell them.'

'Then what?'

'We'll see,' Harry Turner said dismissively. He sat down and folded his arms again.

Fields arrived with the Israelis and indicated they should go straight to where the Captain was sitting. Both men were grim-faced, and as they pushed past Sherman the one called Mendel was careful to frown.

Turner explained the situation. The Israelis looked at each other, as if they were communicating by thought wave, then Mendel took out a note book and consulted it.

'I understand that in the event of a warning signal you wait ten minutes before making contact. Is that correct?'

'Right,' Turner said. 'That's considered to be time enough for something to be lined up on the ground.'

Mendel glanced at Sherman, who was fuming silently by the engineer's bay. 'Are you satisfied that the passengers are all clean?'

'Sure. Why do you want to know?'

'Because the electronic signal could mean there is something wrong on board the plane.'

'Yeah?' Sherman tried hard to look pitying. 'And don't you think they would have said so, instead of pissing around with bleeps?'

Mendel's stolid expression didn't change. 'Not necessarily. No risks will be taken with this flight. The chance of someone unauthorised being on board, perhaps actually sitting on the flight deck, will have been considered. Washington could have discovered something suspicious about the passenger list since we took off. There are many possibilities.'

'The passengers are clean,' Sherman grunted. 'If there's a problem, it's on the ground.'

Mendel said something to his partner in Israeli.

'Let's have it so we all know what's being said,' Sherman warned. 'Save the gobbledygook for your friends.'

'It was a private matter,' Mendel told him curtly, then turned and addressed the Captain. 'I presume there is a divert procedure?'

'Of course.' Turner consulted a chart clipped to the side of his console. 'There's an American air base at Mildenhall in Suffolk. They can take us. There's also Gatwick, but that wouldn't be too clever. Planes have diverted there before in a security emergency, and found duplicate trouble waiting. The layout at Mildenhall makes it hard for anybody to try there.'

'And nobody would suspect we'd try to land at Mildenhall,' Bob Fields added. 'Officially, they can't accept jumbos.'

'But in fact they can,' Turner said. 'However, I hope none of that will be necessary.'

'You and me both,' Mendel said, betraying some feeling.

Sherman came forward, displaying his readiness for an argument. 'Doesn't it make sense to divert if there's even a hint of trouble at London? What's a little inconvenience, compared to a probable threat?'

'There would be great embarrassment,' Mendel said, without looking at Sherman.

'My heart bleeds.'

'Our Foreign Minister is in London for talks with the British Prime Minister. He will be waiting to meet the commissioners at Heathrow. A great deal depends on a smooth pattern of activity. If we were to divert, it would be known that there was trouble, and it is not Israeli policy to swerve in the face of a threat.'

'And it sure as hell isn't American Government policy to risk a plane-load of passengers just to back up Israeli arrogance!'

'Please, gentlemen.' Turner waved a placating hand between them. 'Let's not go off at tangents. We still don't know what's up. We'll just wait a few more minutes. If nothing comes through in that time, I'll radio Heathrow and tell them we have engine trouble.'

'What'll that accomplish?' Sherman asked.

'It's a way of acknowledging their signal, and its gives us a legitimate excuse for arriving late. We don't know who's listening, remember. We have to be discreet.'

Sherman's eyes closed for a moment, and although he was simply referring to memory, it looked as if he was in pain. 'I thought the radio link on this flight was on a special no-interference frequency? We were told that at the briefing.'

'Quite correct,' Turner said. 'But no frequency can completely obviate interference. And there could be a dozen other reasons why Heathrow doesn't want anything said openly.' He slapped his hands together. 'But we're not going to start speculating about all that, are we? Let's just go through the drill and do what we have to when we have some solid data.'

In the forward galley Dan Bradley was trying out his charm on Kay Morgan, who did not really appear to be listening. She reacted with little smiles and nods, but her head was elsewhere, he had decided.

'Are the VIPs making you nervous?'

'A little,' Kay admitted. 'But ordinary passengers make me nervous, too. I'm into nervousness full time, now.' She was making coffee and had already scattered the granules across the work top. To the few girls who knew Kay really well, there were signs that she was entering one of her moonstruck phases. There was a long fuse on her susceptibility, but when it was lit nothing would put it out. David Mendel had produced a spark and it was distracting her rather badly. Last time, it had been a golf pro. He had promised to give her a call, but never did. The big Israeli was much more handsome and he looked like a man of integrity, somebody worth pinning a couple of hopes on. It was funny, Kay thought, how passing interest was gelling into fascination.

'I like it white,' Dan Bradley said.

'Sorry?'

'The coffee. White.'

'Oh, sure. Coming up.' She poured him a cup and let him add the milk himself. The CIA man was quite a looker himself, but there was so much about him that was familiar. He was a Johnny-Good-Guy, the kind she had been attracting since school. They were always attentive, generous, and fresh within limits that must have been laid down thirty years ago. A man like Mendel, on the other hand, with his exotic aura and his connection with high-power politics was like a breakthrough, the perfect compromise between respectability and upbeat worldliness. How many times she had been warned about snap attachments, she could not remember. Warnings made no difference, anyway. Mendel was a beautiful man, and Bradley was only a nuisance in the circumstances. A decently behaved nuisance.

She was on the point of concocting something trivial to say when the curtain swung aside and the other one stepped in. Sherman, the ugly one.

'Coffee?' Kay said brightly.

'Not just now. Dan, I have to speak to you.'

'Right.' Bradley smiled politely at the stewardess. 'Thanks for the coffee. I'll bring the cup back later.'

Sherman led the way to the vacant row of seats they had used as a conference area before. He did not sit down, but indicated that Bradley should do so. 'There's trouble,' he said ominously. 'London put through a signal that indicates a hitch.'

'What do we do?'

'I want us to divert, but that prick Mendel wants to press for a landing at Heathrow. Listen, do you have any idea what kind of weaponry they're carrying?'

'Nope. But I suppose they have plenty. They're known for that kind of thing.'

Sherman fumbled with a cigarette and eventually lit it. 'The bastards could get us caught in a full scale bloodbath. My responsibility is to this plane and its passengers. I'm going to lean on the Captain, just as soon as we're clear about what's wrong.'

'Maybe it's nothing,' Dan suggested.

'Trouble is trouble. You know the pitch. One hint of bother

and we back off. The Israelis are acting like they run this show and I'm not taking that.'

Bradley emptied his cup and put it on the floor. 'What do we do in the here and now?'

'Check out the passengers again.'

'But we already cleared them.' Bradley had been hoping to keep up the gentle pressure on the stewardess. 'What do we have to do it again for?'

'Insurance,' Sherman growled. 'I want us to come out of this spotless. There's an outside chance the London signal meant something nasty here. So we check again. Anything the least bit suspicious, you let me know.'

A few minutes late Dan Bradley entered the galley and handed back the plastic cup to Kay Morgan. 'Work to do,' he said glumly. 'I'll see you around.'

'Not trouble, I hope?'

He looked for a long second at her anxious little pucker, wondering what it tasted like. 'No, I don't think so. Just routine. Something to pass the time.' He stepped outside again and sauntered towards the forward tourist-class cabin. Sherman, naturally, was checking in first-class. That was what privilege was all about. As he stepped into the cabin he saw the same uninteresting array of faces he had already scanned and found guiltless. Even the jumpy one who had taken his attention before, the man called Turnbull, looked as if he were asleep. People in the mass, Bradley decided, were just damned dull. If there were one dangerous individual among that drowsy crowd, he would go right back to the galley and eat his plastic cup.

FIVE

Airport Security had gone into a flat spin for fifteen minutes after the bodies were brought in from the fence. Arthur Douglas, Head of Security, sent out an immediate alert to Special Branch, who in turn contacted the Anti-Terrorist Squad. Policemen in various guises began turning up at the airport from all directions, while a confused and over-taxed security staff tried to make sense of the killings. If there were hostile elements present, nobody had a clue where they were, and finding even an obvious villain at Heathrow was a monumentally difficult task.

Armed SPG officers began scanning all three terminals. From the Airport Manager's office a furtive check was made on the various administrative sectors. All appeared to be functioning normally. Working on the principle that panic equals paralysis it was decided to keep the bad news under wraps, and even though a few astute individuals began to suspect something was wrong, there were no open signs of an emergency. Security men, police and a team from CIA Clandestine Services ran a check of bars, restaurants, cafeterias, toilets, baggage bays and car parks. The CIA men, who had been on hand as a matter of routine, began to suspect the worst, as they were trained to do. The Pan Am flight from Washington, which they had been detailed to cover, would have to be diverted. While runways were being checked and double checked, the senior CIA operative went to the control tower, accompanied by a nail-chewing field worker from the Ministry of Defence. The door to main control was only two inches into its inward swing when the CIA man saw the girl with the gun. He shut the door so quickly that it struck him on the chin. The two men descended the stairs at speed and made straight for the co-ordination point, where the news was broken to grey-faced men representing a dozen levels of authority. The tower was under terrorist control.

It took five minutes to work out the bare bones of a plan.

First, everyone would work on the assumption that the incoming plane from Washington was the terrorists' target. A way had to be found of contacting the captain of the jumbo and telling him to divert. Two of the men present knew that was only possible via the tower radio, and when they said so expressions hardened. The tower had to be released. All other arrangements would revolve around that necessity. Terminals had to be controlled and incoming traffic stopped. Riot police would be needed, and perhaps an army artillery unit. Step by rapid step the strategy took shape: a security cordon right around Heathrow, and sharply-focused fire-power directed at the tower. Searches of other parts of the airport would continue, while the people from Terrorist Control devised the finer details of just how to eradicate the threat without triggering a mass slaughter.

On the roof of a warehouse fifty yards from the tower, two men set up tripods and mounted their equipment on them. A Nikon F2SB camera, fitted with a motor drive and a 500-millimetre telephoto lens, was screwed to one tripod, and a prismatic telescope with infra-red filter was attached to the other. Movement inside the tower was monitored through both instruments, and while the man at the telescope radioed his observations to police on the ground, the other fired off rapid sequences of pictures every time there was movement inside the control room. Within ten minutes a canister containing 80 undeveloped exposures was passed to the ground and handed to the man in charge of photographic intelligence. In his mobile darkroom he processed the negatives and printed twenty of them while the film was wet. The resin-coated prints were taken, still damp, to the co-ordination point, where four anxious experts examined them.

The information they gleaned was sparse, but harrowing enough. Only two terrorists, but they had the fire-power of twenty. To those who were not so well informed about weaponry, a ballistics officer from Scotland Yard put the picture across with grim clarity: 'The guns they have are American 180s. A child could become a lethal menace with one of those. They've got laser sights and enough cutting power to mow down a platoon in seconds.'

'Where did they get them?' somebody asked.

'I've no idea. Or I hope I haven't.' To his unstated knowledge, there were only four of the guns officially in Britain, all of them housed at Scotland Yard. They had been impounded when the manufacturers brought them from America with the forlorn hope of selling them to the British police. The weapons had been carefully examined and detailed drawings made. It was not outside the bounds of possibility that somewhere along the line the drawings had been copied. The design was ingenious, but any gunsmith of even average talent could make the weapons, given the plans to work from.

From that point, opinion began to rage out of control. The CIA were in favour of rushing the tower. The police favoured something more subtle, although they were not sure what. The SPG Commander reckoned it would be possible to gun down the terrorists from the spot where the camera was mounted. Airport Security were adamant that gun play would be disastrous, however applied, and the Ministry of Defence agreed.

Finally, the head of the Anti-Terrorist Squad, Commander Dorian Brooke, called for order and pointed out to everyone that the show was his. He made a short speech, and prefaced it with the reminder that an undisciplined assault would get them nowhere. He was a short, florid man with white mutton-chop whiskers, and when he spoke he punctuated his remarks with one chubby fist slamming the open palm of his other hand. 'As yet, we haven't made any attempt to talk to the tower. They are working normally, but we don't know the strength of the threat hanging over them. We have to assume that the terrorists will kill if they are impeded in any obvious way. So, three major points must be observed. One, the lives of the tower staff must be safeguarded, at all costs. Two, we must find out exactly what the terrorists want, and then carry out our counter-plans accordingly. Three, we have to determine the outlook and policy of whatever group these buggers represent. That last point is very important, because there are ways of talking some of them out of their crusades. They look like Arabs and in the circumstances it's safe to assume they are, but the shade of their fanaticism can make a lot of difference to our approach. The pictures are being shown right now to some Eastern Intelligence people who might come up with something. In the meantime, our first move should be to talk to them, now that our forces are being gathered and deployed.'

The CIA spokesman had a question. 'Have you seen a pattern like this before? I mean, there are two people up in the tower, right? We've combed the place and we haven't found any others. What are they doing up there? Their target's the plane. Do they think they can make the pilot do something crazy like crashing or over-shooting?'

Commander Brooke shrugged. 'The pattern is unfamiliar, I'll admit. Now we know the terrorists are here, they've no chance of getting near the plane when it lands, and they certainly can't make the Captain endanger his craft. Unless, of course, they plan to divert the plane all together. I must say the idea of sending a jumbo jet off to some terrorist infested airstrip out in the wilds doesn't strike me as plausible. I'm as much in the dark about their motives as anyone else. As I said, we must talk to them before we can do anything positive.'

A call was put through to the tower on the loudspeaker system. Brooke stated bluntly that he knew the control room was under siege, and he asked for the terrorists' spokesman to pick up the telephone and dial the co-ordination point. The phone rang only seconds after the Commander finished talking.

'Who am I speaking to?'

Three voice-amplifiers were hooked to the telephone and the foreign-accented rumble was startling in the quiet, crowded room. 'I am a representative of the military wing of the Brotherhood of Zenima.'

Brooke indicated to the others, with wide eyes and a shake of his head, that he had never heard of the movement. 'Ah, what exactly is the position in the tower?'

'We are in control.'

'What do you intend to do?'

'That will become clear.' Kalim paused, and when he spoke again his voice was louder, harsher. 'Listen carefully to me. If any attempt is made to interfere with our plans, the people in this tower will die. So will anyone foolish enough to think he can overpower us. We are heavily armed and it will be a simple matter to exterminate opposition. Do you understand that?'

A CIA man waved a big fist ineffectually at the loud-speakers.

'Yes,' Brooke said. 'We understand. We have no wish to imperil the tower staff. Do we have your word that they are in no immediate danger?'

'At present everyone is well. You will make no further attempts to speak to us. All telephones except those used for control work will be disconnected. If you should try to speak to any of the control staff, you will bring about their death. Please understand, we are prepared to shoot anyone in this place who does not conform to our instructions.'

'But what are your demands?' Brooke asked hastily.

'That we be left alone.'

The receiver was put down. Brooke turned and faced the others, not quite meeting the eyes of any of them. 'That taught us a lot.'

'So what do we do?' The senior CIA man was becoming edgy again. 'They've got us over a barrel, haven't they?'

'The procedure is to wait,' Brooke said quietly.

'Until they accomplish whatever it is they're here for. That's terrific.'

'We will wait.' Brooke picked up a clipboard from the table and studied the personnel list attached to it. 'We have a riot squad on hand. If they are posted outside the door of the control room, we'll be as ready as we can be to get in there when a chance arises.'

'Rush the bastards!'

'They could kill everybody in the place within seconds,' said Brooke. 'The staff must be protected. We wait, and we try to find out as much as we can in the meantime.'

As Kalim put down the telephone the priority radio indicator flickered above Mike Evans's console. He reached for his headset, but Kalim snatched it from him and pulled out the jack.

'Put it on the speaker,' he said.

Mike nodded and depressed the switch. The speaker crackled for a few moments, then the Captain of Pan Am 898 spoke. 'Heathrow control, do you read me, over?'

Mike acknowledged.

'We have a touch of trouble with one of the engines. Nothing serious, but I'm cutting back on our speed a little. The delay, as I estimate it now, will be about a half-hour.'

'Noted,' Mike said, watching Kalim. 'We have a revised approach procedure for you, Speedbird 898. Are you ready to receive, over?'

'Fire away, over.'

Mike read out the approach data that had been computed in the last ten minutes, directing the plane to Emergency Runway 16. There was a long silence from the other end, then the Captain cut in again. He read back the data the tower had fed to him, and then asked if anything was wrong.

'Everything's fine,' Mike assured him, and saw Kalim's fingers tighten around the stock of his gun.

'Why the change of runway?' the Captain wanted to know.

'Security precaution. Last minute arrangement, as usual.'

That appeared to satisfy the Captain. He signed off and Mike Evans leaned back in his chair, rubbing his forehead.

'Well done,' Kalim said, but he was not looking particularly pleased. As Mike began tidying the papers before him, Kalim went on staring. Eventually, he leaned very close to him and said, 'You did something, didn't you?'

'What do you mean?'

'You sicken me, Mr Evans. Your tawdry valour is a joke, a pathetic joke. Are you so wrapped up in notions of bravery that you can't understand your position?' He pointed sharply to the girl on the floor. Her face had been washed, but there was still some blood caked around her mouth and nostrils. 'It's her life you're playing with!'

'Damn it, I didn't do anything!'

'Liar! Pathetic, inept liar! That switch.' He pointed to the black radio toggle Evans had used when he talked to the Washington flight. 'When you first made contact with the plane, you pushed the switch up. This time you pushed it down.'

'So what?' The controller felt a trickle of sweat at the margin of his hair, threatening to run down over his face. 'Either way is on. The central position is off.'

'I am fastidiously observant,' Kalim said. 'Anything I see is subjected to a great deal of scrutiny before it is filed in my memory. Inconsistencies stand out clearly. If I pushed that switch upwards now it wouldn't move, would it?'

Mike had no clear idea what he should say, so he remained silent.

'It wouldn't shift because I would first have to twist the shaft to the right. Now is that correct, Mr Evans?'

'I suppose so.' Mike's eyes flicked to the girl on the floor. Her face was quite calm now, but it was the kind of mute blankness that resulted from excessive fear. She would never get over that, he realised. 'What difference does all this make? A switch is a switch.'

'And that one has a warning device built into it,' Kalim grated. 'You passed that warning to the Boeing. Then, lo and behold, ten minutes later they come on the radio and tell you that a plane checked and re-checked for mechanical fault has developed engine trouble.' He backed away from the console. 'I don't think it worked. I think they have accepted the revised landing instructions. But you tried to thwart me, Evans. Against every warning and in the face of odds you should have heeded . . .' Kalin took two steps forward and swung his fist in an arc, striking Mike on the cheek and knocking him halfway out of his chair. Leila turned from the door momentarily, her raised gun quelling any impulses to defend the controller. As Mike pulled himself up Kalim hit him again, a short, vicious blow that contacted with his chin and jarred his teeth. 'Sit there and reflect on your bruises, Mr Evans.'

Mike fumbled for his handkerchief and pressed it to his mouth. He could taste blood and his teeth felt as if they had all been dislodged. The punch on his cheek had done something to his balance, and as he breathed carefully through his nose and tried to decide if he was sitting upright, he remembered one of the prime rules handed out at the anti-terrorist lectures. Never, ever, provoke them to violence. On his own reckoning, he was making a fine mess of the situation so far.

Suddenly Kalim had become busy. He strode around the perimeter of the control room yanking out telephone cables and smashing intercom sets with the butt of his gun. Staff tried to carry on calmly as pieces of plastic flew into the air around them and the crashing of fallen components echoed off panels and windows.

'Kalim!' Leila had put a finger to her lips and was nodding at the door.

He paused with his gun raised over a battery pack. 'What is it?' When she responded by moving closer to the door and tilting her head, Kalim strode past her and pressed his ear to the panelling. There was near-total silence in the room, broken by the distant whine of a jet engine altering pitch. The staff had stopped working and those lying on the floor were raising their heads cautiously. Kalim went on listening for a few seconds longer, then he stood back from the door and faced it, spreading his feet. With his gun resting at chest height, held tightly in line by his arm, he raised a finger towards Leila, like a steward with a starting pistol. The girl stepped to the door and put her back against it, grasping the handle.

From his chair across the room, Mike Evans found himself gazing intently at Leila's face. She was beautiful. He had not noticed that before. A girl like her should have been posing for a *Vogue* spread or gracing the back seat of a Rolls-Royce. Standing there in her denims and holding on to an ugly submachine gun, she looked painfully incongruous. Mike realised he was still suffering from the stunning effects of Kalim's assault. The tension of the situation was taking second place to that lovely girl and the wrongness of her presence. Looking harder, Mike noticed something else. She was scared.

Kalim brought his hand down slowly and placed it by the gun's trigger guard. As his forefinger curled in and around the shiny spur of steel he nodded once. Leila jerked open the door and pulled it wide.

Three men were outside, wearing flak jackets and holding revolvers. Their eyes behind the gas visors were frozen for a moment, startled. Behind them, four other men were turning towards the sudden opening, caught off guard and bumping against each other.

Kalim waited until one revolver came up in his direction, then he squeezed the trigger. The red spots danced across the men as a continuous volley of .22 bullets tore through cloth, flesh and bone, spattering the cream walls with dark blood as three men went down, one of them almost headless before he touched the floor. The sound was no louder than a typewriter as Kalim went on spraying at random. There was a man lying on the stairs, clawing at the side wall as blood ran freely from his neck. Another, caught halfway towards the lower landing, twisted and stood gaping down over his shoulder at the smashed white bone jutting from his trousers. Only two men had made it down the stairs. One of them was unwounded. The other was missing three fingers and most of his other arm.

Kalim released the trigger and stepped back. Leila slammed the door and took up her previous position. Behind them, Mike Evans and his staff were still trying to believe it had happened.

'On your feet!' Kalim was standing over the girl who had become the symbol of his power to punish. Shakily, the girl obeyed, rising too quickly and almost toppling.

'Leave her alone, for God's sake!' Evans yelled. 'She's half demented with fright as it is. She's no danger to you.'

Kalim took her by the arm and led her to the bench by the tall window facing the approach to the airport. 'I am no direct threat to the young lady, either. You are, all of you.' With a short-bladed pocket knife he cut loose several feet of cable from one of the disconnected telephones. Doubling it, he drew up the lower ends and began fashioning them into a noose, with an elaborately coiled knot. 'Stage dressing,' he muttered, dropping the noose over the girl's head. 'Now, stand up on the bench.'

Obeying, she began to cry. Pushed out beyond any

reasonable hope of rescue from her misery, she had acquired a quality of meekness that reminded Mike Evans of old films he had seen, archive prints of Jewish children being herded towards the gas chambers. She was only twenty, a girl with no promise of distinction in her career, a very ordinary young woman with a nice Mum somewhere and a studious boyfriend. In that moment, as she clambered awkwardly on to the bench, the plain little girl called Jessie Malcolm suddenly became very special indeed to him. Some men had just died, he had watched it happen. Yet this was far more overwhelming. Trying to protest again, Mike found he could not speak.

'I want you to do no more than stand there,' Kalim said briskly. 'Move close to the window, where you can be seen. That's it.' He turned and addressed the others. 'Nothing will happen to her if you all behave as you have been told. Carry on with your duties.'

Mike found his bottle of aspirin and swallowed three, washing them down with cold tea from his neglected cup on top of the console. Everything in him was jangling. He had physical pain, gnawing and searing by turns, and the ache in his head was an amalgam of growing despair and frustration. Kalim, he noticed, was moving about calmly, as if he had never murdered those men. Leila, with her back to him, looked as tense as before. Of the two, it was Kalim who was the alien, as foreign in his approach as a Martian. This thing had to end soon, Mike realised, for he was not sure he could carry on without doing something insane on sheer impulse. The outcome did not bear thinking about.

Over in the co-ordination room, Commander Brooke was trying hard to hold up under the deluge of bad news. Five men had now been effectively destroyed.

Three were dead, one was almost certainly going to die, and the fifth had suffered such extensive spinal damage that he was unlikely to be more than a cabbage at the end of the day. Of the two who had escaped, one would have to be pensioned off. From Eastern Intelligence the word was just as bad. The Zenima Brotherhood, if informed speculation was reliable, made the Mafia look like a comedy act. Membership was secret, but rumour listed five oil men with political leverage and a host of Arab notables whose territorial rights were enormous. Until that morning, it had been believed that the Brotherhood was no more than a mutual comfort arrangement, providing members with extra bargaining and negotiating weight whenever they needed such help. The worst news of all had been saved until the end of the hastily compiled report. The tower was in the hands of a known psychopath who, it appeared, cared as little for his own survival as he did for anyone else's.

'His name is Kalim Bakir,' Brooke told the assembly. 'He's twenty-six, and he holds a BA degree from Cambridge. His subject was English Literature, oddly enough, but his instincts seem to lie in the direction of political and social reform. He views it all from the right, apparently.' There was a photocopy of a file card clipped to the report and Brooke detached it. Entries on the card had started in 1974 and covered every line. Brooke scanned them and delivered an impromptu summary. 'He published an article in the American magazine, *Luminary*, discussing his belief in the divine right of kings and setting out a programme for reversing the present trend towards governmental sovereignty in the East. A year later he led a delegation to the American Embassy in London, petitioning for recognition of primogenitive supremacy among sheikhs and emirs. Got himself arrested and finally acquitted on a charge of obstruction when an Israeli trade mission visited London. After that, he went to America for a year, and when he returned he set up an outfit called the Centre for Eastern Reform. Ten months ago, he was committed to a mental institution . . .'

Somebody groaned and Brooke added a sigh of his own. 'The psychiatric picture is messy.' He read the two-page copy of a report made by two doctors, who both appeared to agree that Kalim Bakir was incurably psychotic. He had been committed in the first place for attempting to strangle a student who had argued with his elitist dogma. 'This man is deeply paranoid,' Brooke said, running his gaze across faces which had heard that kind of news before.

'He's the nephew of a sheikh and his father has been a legend to him all his life. He died in a small peasant revolt when Kalim was only two, and that seems to have started the warp in his outlook. There's also evidence that he underwent para-military training in the States. Look, I'll put the papers on the table and you can muddle through them yourselves. There's someone waiting to see me.'

In a small, bare ante-room, a man in Arab robes was standing by the window, watching the moving lights across the runways. He turned as Brooke entered and immediately extended his hand. He did not smile. 'Commander. I am Ahmad Ayyub.' He held the Commander's hand firmly for a moment then released it. 'I was told by an acquaintance at our embassy that I could be of some assistance to you.'

'We need all the help we can get,' Brooke said. 'It's good of you to come out here at this hour . . .'

'It is no problem.' Ayyub had large dark eyes that looked much younger than the rest of his face. 'In matters of this kind, we should do all that is possible to aid the authorities. I understand Kalim Bakir has taken control of your tower.' He sounded as if it was no surprise to him. 'He is a sorely misguided young man.'

'And a multiple murderer,' Brooke added.

'I am sorry. I was not told.'

'It probably happened when you were on your way here. Tell me, what's your connection with this man?'

The lines of Ayyub's face remained placid as he spoke, and his eyes never left Brooke's. He had the disconcerting authority common to men set apart by great wealth. 'I have several business interests in London, and I have lived here for two years. I have met Bakir socially many times. I have also been disturbed by his zealous political obsessions. To be frank, it has been a practice of mine for some time to watch him.'

'Why?'

'He is a threat to the standing of the Arabs in this country. Co-existence can be difficult enough, Commander, without the intrusion of fanatical elements. I have been reporting Bakir's comments and activities to the embassy for many months.' He paused and cleared his throat behind a delicately furled hand. 'The timing of this development is unfortunate. I believe that within a few weeks he would have been forcibly checked.'

'What about this Brotherhood of – what is it?'

'Zenima.' Ayyub permitted himself a thin smile. 'Kalim Bakir has certainly endeared himself to the membership of that organisation. He has led them by their noses, Commander. They are powerful men and they rightly believe in the added power of unity. But Bakir talked urgency into their hearts. They allowed him to form his Zenima Squad on the strength of his clever words and superior command of political strategy.' He shook his head slowly. 'I am sure none of them dreamed he would do this. They valued a loud, defensive voice, but they never envisaged any kind of open aggression, certainly not on British soil.'

'You're not connected with the Brotherhood yourself?'

'Certainly not. They may be powerful, but they are also children. Inherited power and wealth can go a long way towards reducing a man's sense of reality, Commander. I do not oppose the Brotherhood, but like a number of others I keep myself at a distance from them.' He nodded towards the window. 'After this, I can imagine there will be a lot more like me.'

Brooke was drumming his fingers on the nap of his overcoat, betraying an impatience that had no idea where to go. 'This man is well-equipped, and he appears to be tightly organised. Have you any idea who would have helped him? This isn't the kind of job an amateur could carry out.' At the back of his mind there was a vague hope of tracing some vital root and destroying it.

'Information is easy to buy,' Ayyub said flatly, 'and for Bakir money is easy to obtain. Large sums of money. What he did not buy or coax from people, he probably obtained by his own direct effort. He has some stupid young followers and their connections, because of inborn privilege, are wide. I would be tempted to believe that Bakir did all of this himself. Bear in mind that he is mad, Commander. That condition frequently confers a measure of immunity to fear. Without fear, a man can become formidable.'

'So, we can assume he isn't backed by a larger terrorist

group, and he's acting in the name of an organisation that won't want to know him, now. How big is this operation likely to be, do you think?'

For the first time Ayyub's expression shifted towards uncertainty. 'In terms of numbers? Not very large, I would guess. Indeed, probably quite small. There are some who follow his lead with their mouths, but they would never do anything. I'm afraid I cannot be precise, but I would say there is no more than a handful.'

Brooke then put the question he had been withholding, because he could only take so much bad news at a time. 'Have you any idea what his plans are? We know he's here because the Israeli arms commission is flying in this morning, but beyond that we're in the dark.'

'Bakir has been secretive in the past few days,' Ayyub said. 'Even so, he has expressed his views on Israeli aggression every time I have seen him in recent weeks. I can't say what he plans, but I am confident it will be something large and grotesque. He is not capable of moderation.'

Brooke nodded, acknowledging what he had been sure of all along. 'He's certainly determined. Three of my men are dead, a fourth is dying and one is hopelessly mutilated. Is it possible, in your view, to talk him out of this?'

Ayyub stared at the floor for a moment. 'In the light of what you have just said, I would think not. However, there is his cousin . . .'

'Yes?'

'A quiet man, quite the opposite of Bakir, but they are close, nevertheless. I am sure you could rely on his help, but there is no way of saying how effective it would be.'

'Any hole in a hurricane,' Brooke said, suddenly brisk at the prospect of something to try. 'Would you come with me, Mr Ayyub? I want to introduce you to a trusted aide of mine who also has permission to break speed limits.'

SIX

It was Sherman's big opportunity to show his weight, and he was taking it. There were five of them on the flight deck besides him: Captain Turner, Second Officer Fields, Flight Engineer Mitchell, the Israeli security man Mendel, and Dan Bradley. Sherman was talking at them collectively, his eyes locked on Mendel to keep the adrenalin pumping.

'It smells, we all know it smells, and the drill when a stink starts up is to divert. There's no buts or maybes. The bleep signal was grounds enough. Now we get a new landing specification. On a flight with priority, at that.' He jabbed his finger sideways, as if the plane would instantly obey. 'We *don't* land at Heathrow.'

'You are being rash,' Mendel said. 'No decision can be reached on the basis of the existing evidence.'

'When I want your kind of opinion, I'll ask the man at my corner deli. Captain, you've got your orders, just like I have mine.' Sherman dug his fingers into the flesh above his hip bones. 'Or do you prefer to wait until somebody launches a couple of rockets at us?'

Harry Turner put both palms forward, as if he was being pushed, which was precisely what he felt. 'Slow down. Mr Mendel has a point. If anything, the second message cancels the first. I got the impression there was nothing wrong down there.'

'Then why didn't you mention the bleeps?'

'Because I'm not one hundred per cent sure, and I don't want to stride when it's safer to tiptoe. We have to wait.' He checked his watch. 'We've fully three hours to landing. There's plenty of time to find out more before we start throwing everything into chaos by diverting.'

Sherman could see that his partner was lining-up with the rest of them. Treachery came easy to the younger ones. They were filled up with all the liberal crap they read in the papers about every voice being heard and every avenue explored before reaching decisions. A man had to take a stance. If he shifted his bearing the opposition saw it and they used it against him. Bradley was diluting the department's image, and he was doing it because he believed all the patter about cautious progress, the new style directive that would see them all down the drain within a generation. Sherman was about to start laying it on them, the whole truth about their mushy, indecisive pussyfooting, when Mendel spoke.

'I think the commissioners should be told what is happening. They are entitled to a vote in any eventual decision.'

'Vote?' Sherman thought he might choke. 'They're the reason we're having all this upheaval! If the passengers had gotten a chance to vote before we took off, your commissioners would still be cooling their heels at Dulles.'

'You make a habit of overstepping yourself,' Mendel said, and Dan Bradley began examining his fingernails.

'That's for my superiors to tell me.'

'And I have no doubt they will.'

Sherman had organised the way he disliked certain people. They fell into mental categories with big labels, and Mendel was right in the middle of the section marked Instant Recoil.

'Gentlemen,' Harry Turner warned, 'I don't want you carrying on your battles on my flight deck.'

'I am sorry,' Mendel said.

'Look,' Sherman blared, venting his frustration into the air above their heads. 'Are you going to follow the clear directive we have on this job, or does the witless virgin bit go on? I'm keeping notes on everything, and the absence of moral fibre on this deck will go down in black and white.'

'I imagine that's the way you see everything,' Turner said with some force. 'We remain on alert, Mr Sherman. Make sure you put it that way when you're carrying the tale back to your ringmaster.'

'Everything gets told the way it is,' Sherman growled, 'and your attitude won't miss scrutiny, Captain. If you decide to align yourself with aliens in the face of a threat to the security of American citizens, that's your look-out.'

He turned and moved to the door. 'Come on, Bradley. There's things to discuss.'

Later, David Mendel took word of the situation to the commissioners. Two of them, Avrum Maller and Nathan Danzig, had been drowsing. They sat rubbing their eyes and licking dry lips as their faculties strove to handle the information. Joel Singer and Nathan Glazer, who had lapsed into tense silence following their most recent outburst of argument, sat higher in their seats and glared at each other.

Finally, it was Maller who spoke. He was an old soldier, uneasy in the role of diplomat. Giving orders on a field of battle was entirely different from the business of armchair strategy. His voice, conditioned to shouting when he approached subordinates, was uncomfortably controlled.

'There is no problem for the present,' he said, indicating that Mendel should go and sit beside his colleague. To the others at the table, he added, 'We would be foolish to pay any attention to something so inconclusive. It sounds like another administrative error, anyway.'

'I wouldn't be surprised if there was trouble at London,' Singer said. He was still looking at Glazer, even though his remark was addressed to Maller.

'Nor would I,' Maller replied. 'But it would be wrong to presume anything of that sort without proof.' Stating the obvious, Maller had found, was an important part of procedure when a man entered politics. He glanced at the haggard face of Abraham Glazer and tried a small joke. 'Don't let this add to your worries, eh? You have a full plate already.' It was difficult to minimise Glazer's growing hostility. He gave the impression of being enshrouded with guilt for the very fact of his presence at that table.

Danzig, the other American-born member of the commission, had said practically nothing during the flight. Now, he nudged Glazer, who was sitting beside him. 'Ground security's been taken care of, Abraham. Take my word for that. There's nothing to fret about.' Danzig's word on matters of security and espionage could certainly be relied upon. He had served in senior roles with Modi'in, the army intelligence unit, Sherutai Habitahon, the Israeli equivalent of MI5, and Mossad, the research and intelligence service, where he had controlled the movements of agents operating abroad. His current involvement with ISS was unspecified, but most Israeli politicians believed Danzig was very close to the top. He had the look of a shrewd impresario and concealed the expression of his eyes behind tinted spectacles. 'The British have a good record,' he added, as Glazer continued to stare ahead of him. 'One day they could be as good as we are.' His thin laugh tailed off as the tension between Glazer and Singer began to rise again.

'He wouldn't mind a martyr's death,' Singer murmured. 'He could die with an easy conscience then, couldn't you, Glazer? Suitably punished for signing that sinful agreement.'

Nobody had ever taunted Glazer into pointless retaliation. He clasped his hands and stared down Singer's malicious smirk. 'If there are angry people waiting for us in London, it can hardly be a surprise to anyone. From the outside, people can see the beginning of a new spiral. Think how ugly it looks to the ones who know it spells disaster for them.'

'You really are the whimpering Jesus figure, aren't you?' As Singer's voice approached the now familiar cruising pitch, Maller pointedly closed his eyes again and Danzig, who had some privy worries about pacifists in general, pulled some papers from his case and stared at them.

'It is noteworthy,' Glazer said calmly, 'that a man on weak ground will resort to personal abuse of his opponents. I said there is a visible spiral, and I stand by what I say. We have the missiles. In the event of the slightest sign of opposition to our territorial ambitions, a few key positions will be flattened. Just to make a point, of course. It will be tactically viewed as a rap on the knuckles. But history shows that we do not stop there. The spiral goes up, it does not stop until it encloses opposition. How long until we have the nuclear capability to indulge in genocide at the push of a button?'

'You're talking like a cheap rabble rouser!'

'On the contrary,' Glazer retorted. 'I am trying to stay

reasonable with a head full of facts and probabilities that would induce hysteria in anyone brave enough to confront them all at once. The US Joint Committee on Atomic Energy tends to agree with our internal estimates. Within months, perhaps, we will have the technical power of life or death over the whole world. Will that be a straightforward deterrent, just as our new missiles are alleged to be?'

Singer, whose speciality was tactical warfare, had no wish to be drawn on what he knew about Israel's nuclear goal. 'Don't start talking about things you can only make wild guesses at, Glazer. You've already said enough to show me you've no right to be on this commission in the first place.'

'Of course I have,' Glazer said. 'I'm the token minority member. No commission is complete without one. And I am not guessing.' He unclasped his hands and slid them in the opposite directions along the table, clasping his elbows and leaning forward. 'I do have access to classified matter, don't I? And, unlike certain ostriches I could name, I do not pretend it isn't there. I've even taken pains to do some research. I know of your own interest in ERWs, for example. And I know what the enhanced radiation weapons can do.'

'I've no intention of discussing this,' Singer said petulantly.

'Well, I have. I confess myself appalled that ERWs exist, and sickened that supposedly civilised administrators would consider their use. A two kiloton neutron bomb is quite a dream toy, isn't it? It can deliver a body radiation dose of one hundred thousand rads within a five hundred metre radius, and do no damage to property. Just think what you could do to a couple of important cities with a thing like that. All the buildings, all the machinery and communications systems intact, with nobody left alive to stop you taking control. And it won't really matter about the people who are on the perimeter of the burst, will it? They will die, too, but much more slowly.'

Seeking an ally, Singer turned to Maller, but he went on pretending to be asleep. Danzig remained firmly entrenched behind his papers.

'They will be no danger to an invader,' Glazer went on.

'There will be no need to watch them, either, for they won't be going anywhere. The unpleasant details of their dying needn't be monitored. Men, women and children will suffer cerebral bleeding, terrible nausea, vomiting. Then it will become really distressing, but only for the sufferers, for no one else will have to watch. Bone marrow disintegration, dissolving eye tissue and agonising paralysis, all multiplied thousands of times over, until death intervenes. That can take days, of course.' There were drops of perspiration on his face as he moved back in his seat, his lips contorted with disgust.

'You are a dissident alarmist, Glazer! You should be locked up!'

'That's what the Nazis did. It would be fitting.'

'Listen,' Singer lowered his voice, noticing that the two guards were overhearing them. 'Israel has no plans whatever for adoption of devices like that . . .'

'Officially, no. But people like you are interested, when you should be using your considerable powers to bring about a total world ban on such obscenities. A few years ago everyone was decrying the nuclear warhead. Things change, because attitudes are allowed to atrophy while new imperatives spring up all over the place. We have just signed an agreement to receive weapons equipped with nuclear warheads. Will it really not be a couple of ERWs next time?'

'I'm not listening,' Singer told him through a counterfeit yawn. 'You just wait for excuses to get on your hobby horse. Your misinformed bigotry is as irresponsible as anything you criticise.'

'Fine,' Glazer said, waving his hand dismissively. 'Go ahead and sleep. Dream about conquest. It's a long time, anyway, since I believed a concerned voice could make any difference. Just remember, if there *are* people waiting to demonstrate or throw grenades at us, we asked for it.' He sank back and turned his face towards the window. It was dark outside, as black as his foreboding. To his own reasoning, he was as odd a component of the commission as the others thought he was. But at the beginning it had not seemed that way. He had believed that a deterrent was needed, and he had even thought his brand of sanity would ensure a decent outcome to their Washington visit. Pride had done that, Glazer thought. Remnants of stupid pride. He should have realised he was out of date and doomed to be carried along by events. It was too late to preach survival when the world had already learned the joys of flirting with suicide.

'You have a really creepy mind, do you know that?' Sally Judson poked her employer, Paul Brent, in the stomach and giggled in his face. 'Where do you pick up stuff like that?'

'Out of the air,' he said. 'You know how polluted the atmosphere is these days.' He had just told her that the increase in rape was a backlash against the fact that the warfare had gone out of sex. There was too much frivolity and joy surrounding an activity that was basically a contest. He had backed his argument by raising some bogus figures about the shift towards violent sports, now there were so few wars for men to fight in. 'The aggressive component,' his summary ran, 'can never be removed from a human activity without causing an imbalance, and that leads to big trouble.'

'You could make up an argument for anything,' Sally grinned. In the subdued cabin lighting his dark skin looked more like a tan, and she gave way to an impulse to touch his face. He was smooth, far too smooth for a man, yet the ruggedness was there in plenty. It was even in his well-trained voice, a husky tenor that could sink to a baritone whenever he wanted. 'I bet you don't complain about girls being so easy nowadays,' she whispered.

'Yes, I do.' Sometimes he surprised himself, the way he could improvise the meat of a conversation and still be somewhere else inside. Right at that moment he was looking out over the trackless waste between himself and his wife. And there were a number of smaller terrains waiting to be charted. His career, for one, and his leaking bucket of expectations for another. Being a hip black actor was great in lots of ways, but it also highlighted the limitations. Losers in that game saw only a cluster of opportunities up ahead, if they ever got out of the mud. On the high plane of acceptance, Paul saw the cluster from a different angle. The pickings were thinly laid out, even if you did look better than Poitier ever had.

'Honey?'

He realised he had gone quiet. Sally was peering into his eyes and frowning like a bemused kewpie. 'I was just thinking about what you said. I reckon things were better when the girls were hard to get, or played it that way. See, the war's taken out of it now, right? No struggle. No mystery, either.' He put on a tragic, wild-eyed face. 'Ah juss *longs* fo' de days when a fella had to use some o' dat ole skill on a chick.' He brought his head forward a few inches and kissed her on the nose. 'How about fetching us some black coffee, huh? I think I want to read some script.'

'You could call the stewardess.'

'It's not the same as you bringing it.' He saw the disbelieving response and thought how odd it was that the truth often made her suspicious, while she would swallow most of his lies.

'I'll be right back, master,' Sally said, standing and edging out into the aisle.

'It's a cute reversal,' he called after her softly.

'What is?'

'Me having a white slave.'

When she had gone he fished out the script from his attaché case and set it on his knees. It was a fat manuscript, but very little of it concerned him. He would probably have ten minutes on the screen, and a snappy editor could cut it to five. No close-ups. No audience sympathy, either. The days of casting the negro in a good-guy role were over: they were all pimps, pushers and perverts again. In this film Paul would play a masochistic heroin courier, stranded by his masters in a London house after he had made what was to be his final delivery. Paul would never have landed the part if it had not been for the director insisting on an authentic American black. So he had his return plane ticket, maybe two weeks' work and a faint chance of rousing some more interest in his talent. Things could have been worse. Even so, they were bad enough.

He flipped over the script at a marked page and read one of his lines, mumbling it under his breath: 'I'm out here on a limb an' some bastard's takin' a saw to it.' Hardly the ringing metre of Albee. It wasn't Pinter, either, or Bolt or O'Neill or Stoppard or any of the others he had read before mirrors and to the occasional producer. But who put black actors into the majestic stuff? His chances all lay down the other end, where political overtones and heavy symbolism and sometimes farce could make room for one or two coloured characters.

His mind wandered away from the script. He thought about Irma, the woman who loved him so much it was always a pain to be near her. Paul returned her love the way a worn-out mother responded to a clinging child. It was an impatient acknowledgment of duty, a loyal, disheartened gesture of involvement in the trap. He cheated every chance he got because it always seemed, beforehand, that he deserved a reward for his suffering. And afterwards there was just some more suffering, guilty thoughts about Irma's undoubted faithfulness, fears of what it might do to her if she ever found out.

'Your coffee,' Sally said, pulling forward the little folding table before she slid back into her seat beside him.

'You were quick.'

'I'm only slow where it matters.' She giggled again as she poured two cups and handed him one.

Paul sipped and made appreciative lip-smacking noises. 'Beautiful.' He pecked her cheek. 'Mind if I just go on with my reading for a while, honey?'

'Carry on. I'm sleepy, anyway.' She leaned back and put her head on the seat rest, first making sure her blonde bubble cut wasn't going to be ruffled.

He turned the pages without reading anything. The closeness of Sally Judson was such a mixture of things. A warm pleasure. A rebuke. Sometimes he resented the girl terribly. She was living testimony to his weakness and vanity. Who could afford a secretary? Not him. But he had Sally Judson because the status payload was huge. She did some real work, like typing his mail and doing the bookkeeping for his little fancy goods store, but it was all stuff he could do himself. She went the rounds with him so other actors and show people could see the set-up. Paul Brent and his foxy white secretary, making them all envious and mad, sending his stock way up. When he was feeling guilty and taking the score with the recurring cold pain in his gut, he resented her very badly for supporting the charade. At other times, like now, the uneasy guilt withdrew and revealed a firmer truth, which was that he loved her.

He flinched as her hand dropped casually on to his leg. That reaction persisted, there was nothing Paul could do about it. It was definitely OK to be provocative in public, but you provoked them only so far. Even when she took his arm on a street there was an uncomfortable feeling that he was going too far and running the risk of trouble. Early conditioning stuck.

'Paul . . .' Her fingers tightened on his thigh and he realised she had been trying to attract his attention.

'What?' He looked at her, then at the place she was looking. They were in the centre row of seats, and across from them on the right of the cabin there was a man sitting alone by a window. 'Don't tell me,' Paul mouthed, 'he looks like George Segal. What are you trying to do, undermine me?'

'He's doing something,' Sally whispered.

'Sleeping.'

'No. Watch.'

Paul watched. A moment later, like someone plagued by a bad dream, the man started shifting his legs and snatching at the sides of his trousers. It went on for several seconds, then he stopped and slid lower in the seat.

'I didn't see anything too special,' Paul admitted. 'What's bothering you?'

'Look at the shape of his pants,' Sally hissed impatiently. 'He's got something tucked under them.'

Paul started to laugh and she dug her elbow in his side. 'Sorry,' he mumbled and looked harder at the man. Sure enough, the outline of the trousers suggested the presence of something in addition to their wearer. 'Maybe it's a hot water bottle.'

Sally turned hostile eyes to him. 'Will you take me seriously, Just once?'

'But I always do, Miz Sally.'

'Oh, you. Listen, a couple of minutes ago he was pulling something up along his legs. I could see it moving. He had his eyes shut all the time. Then he seemed to be having trouble and he opened his eyes and looked about him, all suspicious.'

'How come he didn't see you watching him?'

'My own eyes were half-shut all the time.'

'Devious,' Paul said, shaking his head.

'Well, he undid his belt and fished inside his pants for a little while and I could see this sort of *mass* shifting up around his waist. Then he fastened the belt and closed his eyes again. Since then, he's been fumbling at it on and off.'

'What's your theory?'

'I don't have one. But it's suspicious, isn't it?'

'Yeah, I suppose it is.' Paul watched a little longer, but nothing else happened. 'Just you keep an eye on him, Officer Judson. If he makes any more funny moves, we'll call in the guys from vice. Strikes me he's some kind of preevert.'

'God, everything's a joke.' Sullenly, she turned her head aside and resumed her half-lidded surveillance of the man across the aisle.

Paul folded open the script at a page where he had three little speeches. He knew them all by heart already, but seeing them printed on the page did something for his objectivity. His performance would take the words full cycle, print them on acetate eventually, metamorphosed into a two-dimensional talking black man.

'He's at it again,' Sally mumbled beside him.

'Good,' Paul said absently, wondering what would happen to him if the day came when Sally decided to leave. No guilt then, he told himself. No self-reproach. No instant dislike from the man and woman in the street, or not so much. And no feeling of being alive in every corner of himself. She was a genuine kook, sitting there spying on some oddball and guessing God-only-knew-what about him, yet she had a spark that was nothing short of precious to

Paul. Maybe everything on top was a joke, the way she complained it was, but he was terribly glad she had made it that way.

SEVEN

For over an hour Shofal had worked steadily across the runway, setting the detonators in a zigzag pattern in accordance with the drawing he had memorised. When his hands became too cold to handle the little pyramids safely, he retreated to the runway light inspection pit and huddled down beside the junction boxes and switches.

He still had fifteen units to plant. As the circulation returned to his fingers he unwrapped one from its plastic cover and loosened the wax strip over the adhesive base. The year before, on a stretch of barren land between Las Vegas and Pasadena, he had watched a team from Buenos Aires demonstrate the unique properties of the detonators. Direct pressure on the top would cause a unit to explode at once, sending its steel shards in every direction. Embedded in rock, one detonator could be fired remotely and produce the devastation of a barrel of TNT. Kalim, one of the ten prospective purchasers at the demonstration, had shown particular interest in what the manufacturers called Remote Concussive Fulmination. If a number of the detonators were set firmly on hard ground, with a space not exceeding ten feet between one unit and the next, they would explode in response to the vibration set up by, say, a heavy truck. The vibration only had to be steady and forceful, for a minimum duration of twenty seconds. Shofal still recalled clearly the amazement on Kalim's face as he watched thirty yards of disused road disappear, taking with it all traces of an old army truck weighted with enough concrete to set up the rumble.

Shofal hefted the palm-size pyramid and wondered at the power locked up in something so small. And the cost. The price asked was two hundred and fifty American dollars each, and that did not include delivery, which in any case was not available outside the American continent. Kalim had bought fifty and spent a further three thousand dollars having them fed to London singly and in pairs, from various source points on the East Coast of America. A day would be coming, he told Shofal, when they would earn every cent paid for them. With that day upon him, Shofal felt the importance of his mission like a divine burden. This was the most important thing he would ever do.

Listening to the wind whip across the mouth of the shallow pit, he wondered briefly about Leila. Her involvement worried him. She was as dedicated as any of them, but Shofal knew other things that gave him doubt. When they first met she had been bathed in theory and partisan fervour, a fierce believer in the rights of those who ruled in the East by hereditary mandate, a hater of the Israelis and anyone who supported their barbaric plundering. But there was softness beneath the hard shell. Shofal and Leila were lovers, and he had been close to so much in her that worried him. She did not favour cruelty or the infliction of prolonged anguish. Terrorism, she had said, was a swift act, a lesson for people to absorb by themselves. To buckle a human spirit by long-term fear was unworthy of any activist. And there was the biggest of several problems: Leila was in the control tower frightening people, perhaps driving them insane with fear and threats, so that a clean and sudden act of protest could take place. If her compassion or pity came under stress, their plans could go dangerously wrong. Shofal prayed for her and was still muttering his prayer when he climbed out of the pit.

Enough light was scattered in the air to show him the surface of the runway, dull grey criss-crossed with threads of black where cracks and margins occurred in the concrete. The detonators already planted would look like no more than tiny lumps of earth, even in daylight, and their distribution could only be seen as a pattern from above. A jumbo landing anywhere on the strip would be a blazing wreck within seconds, either from having its undercarriage blown off or from ploughing into a hail of concrete and toppling into the inevitable crater. Deliberately, two zones of potential explosion were being set, with an unseeded area in the centre of the strip. At the very least a plane would be brought to a sudden halt, creating a shock sufficient to kill every passenger. Shofal moved quickly along the edge of the runway to the point he had marked with a stick, then walked carefully out on to the surface, counting his steps.

He had planted two detonators when he heard a voice calling out from a spot near the place where he had sheltered. He flattened himself on the ground, keeping one hip raised to avoid pressing too hard on a pair of detonators in his pocket. The voice came again, a shout with no form, and when Shofal lifted his head he could see the dim shape of a man, perhaps a couple of hundred yards away. After a moment it became clear that he was a guard, and he was facing away from Shofal. He called out one more time, then began walking away from the runway.

It was not necessarily a good thing that the man was leaving, and for several seconds Shofal sat crouched with a wadded strip of cloth in his hand, wondering about his chances of catching the guard before he made contact with anyone else. Without the detonators on his person he could have done it. He could have rushed up behind the guard and stuffed the cloth into his mouth, and from that point the whole spectrum of violent techniques he had learned in the USA would be at his disposal. Victimology had captured Shofal's imagination, and he was inclined to look for opportunities to use the craft. That guard was a legitimate target, because his going might mean he would be back with reinforcements, to investigate some possible discovery. But he was too far away, and Shofal did not dare run after him.

He resumed the steady work of laying the detonators. All the time, he held a careful picture of himself in his mind: he was bold, talented Shofal, handsome young fighter for right, a terrible threat to any enemy who came near and a lethal arm of a great cause. To sustain himself against the biting cold he would pause and remind himself of the grandeur in this undertaking. One man doing his job carefully in the dark, setting the ground for an event that would reverberate around the world. The idea touched every fine nerve, and there was an added jolt in realising that he would not be sacrificing his own life. He was too valuable to the cause, he would survive to be a threat wherever the Brotherhood needed him.

Kalim's words before setting out on the mission still rang

clearly in Shofal's head: 'We are privileged to show the world that only fools would oppose us or challenge the sovereignty of true rulers. The cause is just, and we will be feared and honoured by millions.'

Millions! Was it such a hardship to be alone in the cold on that bleak strip of concrete, when the end was to be so hugely gratifying? Shofal blew on his hands and continued fixing the detonators to the ground. Nothing worthwhile was achieved without effort. In those circumstances, he hardly felt he was doing enough.

Emanuel Kolpmann was brought to the makeshift office that had been set up for Commander Brooke. He was a small, nervous Israeli whose finicky eye for tidiness had rendered his dress and wavy black hair as spruce as a window dummy's. He approached the Commander's desk at speed and stopped with both hands on the edge.

'Please explain this entire matter to me,' he said.

Brooke looked up from his papers. He had changed his overcoat for a flak jacket with green and brown camouflage splashes. He was still wearing his white shirt and tightly knotted polka dot tie, giving the appearance of a civil servant pressed into emergency military duty. 'And who are you?'

The police inspector at the door coughed discreetly. 'This is Mr Kolpmann, sir. He's from the Israeli Embassy.'

'Ah, yes . . .' Brooke extended his hand without standing up, and when he had pumped the visitor's fist just once he released it and pointed to a chair. 'Sit down, Mr Kolpmann. I had a call to say you were coming. You have the gist of it all, I presume?'

'An outline, yes.' Kolpmann took the chair and sat with his knees pressed together, spreading the extended tips of his fingers across his kneecaps. 'I would like to know a great deal more, however. Some Arabs have taken the control tower, and the incoming Washington flight with our arms commissioners on board is their probable target. That is all I have been told.'

Brooke nodded. 'What else do you want to know?'

'Everything.'

'That would take up a lot of time,' Brooke pointed out. 'I'll be happy to accommodate you if you can be specific.'

Kolpmann narrowed his nose and breathed noisily through the constricted nostrils. To Brooke the effect looked very odd, but the habit had been with Kolpmann for so long that he no longer knew when he was doing it. 'I was being specific,' he snapped. 'I need to know *everything*. But perhaps you could start by telling me who the terrorists are.'

'They call themselves the Zenima Squad.'

The little man took the news as if it was a joke. 'What? Are you telling me they are part of the Brotherhood of Zenima?'

'That's what they say, and we have reason to believe it's correct.'

'Ludicrous! They're nothing more than a band of strutting clowns . . .'

'They've killed men here this morning,' the Commander interrupted, hardening his voice. 'I don't find them funny at all. And they aren't stupid, either. Their planning has been meticulous, and they know a thing or two about strategy.'

The spidery fingers on Kolpmann's knees began to dance agitatedly. 'I don't see how it could have happened,' he said, implying by his tone that he had never come across such lax security. 'They march in and take control of an airport, in full view of hundreds of people . . .'

'As you pointed out a minute ago,' the Commander said, 'you only have an outline of what happened. They infiltrated the complex, and they did it effectively because they're trained for the work. The fact that this is a civilian airport makes it all the easier to get away with something like that. The security staff can't be everywhere at once, and people are free to come and go, within pretty broad limits.' He clasped his hands and adopted a businesslike tilt of the head. 'Anyway, that's neither here nor there. The terrorists are in the tower and we're trying to find a way to get them out.'

'What do they plan to do?'

'We've no idea. I don't think they're naïve enough to think

they can talk the pilot into anything silly. But they definitely mean business, whatever it is.'

'Then they must be cancelled at once.'

'That's what we're working on,' the Commander said patiently.

Kolpmann unbuttoned his jacket and began twiddling absently with a silver watch chain strung between a buttonhole and his waistcoat pocket. He had something important to say, but he was having trouble in arranging the words for delivery. Finally, he pushed an invisible hair back into place and drew himself up in the chair. 'Our Foreign Minister is meeting the commissioners here this morning. The meeting has significance in numerous directions, as you will appreciate. A cancellation is the last thing we want to consider. Prestige is important . . .'

'I understand all that,' Brooke said.

'Well, I think it is imperative that we act now to set matters straight.'

'We are doing all we can, at present.' Brooke's voice was becoming colder by the second.

'Ahem.' Kolpmann found it necessary to stand up. 'We have contingency plans for an emergency such as this, Commander. If you would be agreeable to a liaison with our Strike Squad, I am confident that the whole business could be settled within the hour.'

Brooke pushed his chair back slowly as he rose to his feet, his arms propping him above the desk. In the brief silence his jaw moved from side to side, his snowy whiskers like shocked antennae. 'What exactly are you saying?'

'You heard what I said. If you join forces with our people . . .'

'People? Are you talking about an ISS team, Mr Kolpmann?'

'Exactly. They are men trained for this kind of work. It's in your own interests to co-operate with them. Their experience is wide in matters of terrorist control.'

One round fist banged the table as Brooke came across and stood inches from the Israeli. 'Where are these men?'

'Ready and waiting,' Kolpmann said with a trace of defiance. 'We have to protect our nationals, Commander Brooke. We do that in the most effective way we know.'

'If they come anywhere near this airport I'll have the lot of them arrested!'

'Be reasonable, for goodness' sake . . .'

Brooke stopped one hand from clutching Kolpmann's lapel. 'This isn't Entebbe, do you understand that? We want no cowboys charging around the complex and setting off wholesale murder. And before you tell me how clever your men are, let me tell *you* we can cope without them. My primary aim is to safeguard the tower staff, and I can only do that by trying to inject reason into a potentially hysterical and barbarous situation. Now go and put your war dogs back in the kennel, Mr Kolpmann.'

The Israeli stood his ground as Brooke went to the door and held it open. 'I can always go higher.'

'Try it!' Brooke pulled the door wider.

'You are being unreasonable!'

'Call it what you like. Those bastards up in the tower have got a girl standing in the window with a noose round her neck. One sniff of your crowd and she'll be an instant casualty.' The Commander's expression clouded suddenly and his hand slackened on the door. 'Just where are your people, exactly?'

'Nearby.'

'I asked you where!' The shout brought the police inspector running. He stood in the doorway behind the Commander, not knowing quite what to do.

'Three of them are already on the airport perimeter. On the inside.'

'Christ on a crutch!' Brooke spun towards the inspector. 'Get a Land Rover from security. I want this one's sharp shooters rounded up and ejected from the complex. Take him with you.'

'This is outrageous!' Kolpmann gasped.

'It certainly is,' Brooke hissed. 'I'm going to make the appropriate stink over it, too. I want to know how we come to have an Israeli strike squad knocking about town, and I'll want firm assurances that the same thing doesn't happen again. And by the way,' he stood aside as Kolpmann approached the door, 'my objective, as soon as I can get those people out of the tower, is to divert the Washington plane.

Add that to your pile of complaints and go as high with them as you can reach.' To the policeman, he said, 'Take a couple of SPG men with you. If you get any argument, contact me.'

Ten minutes later the Commander had a telephone call from a man in Whitehall who suggested it might be useful if he collaborated with the Israeli security people on the current problem. Brooke explained what action he had already taken in that direction. There was a silence, followed by some mumbling, then another voice came on the line.

'Hello, Brooke? Whiteside here, I don't believe we've met. Look, don't you think you're being a trifle bolshy over this thing? I mean, the Israelis have a lot of experience and their track record's good. Where's the harm in some professional assistance?'

Brooke put his case carefully. The position was too touchy, he said. Israeli strike squads got results, but in the present set-up people would almost certainly be killed if they made a move. Negotiation was the first thing to try, before there was any talk of military tactics. While he was talking Kalim Bakir's cousin arrived and was asked to take a seat by the desk.

'Well,' the nasal Whiteside said, 'I'm afraid you'll have to put up with a little bit of Israeli reinforcement. It'll be limited to perimeter survey and that kind of thing.'

'I won't stand for any of it,' Brooke told him sternly.

'If you don't, old chap, you'll be pulled out of there forthwith. That's the way it is, sorry to say.'

Brooke slammed down the phone and stared bleakly at the thin young man on the other side of the desk. The silence was broken by a knock at the door. The police inspector popped his head inside, and when the Commander nodded stiffly the door opened wider and an SPG officer, in jeans and a sheepskin jacket, pushed gently past the inspector and crossed to the desk.

'It's no dice,' he murmured, glancing suspiciously at the young Arab.

'So I gather.' Brooke drew the palms of his hands down over his eyes and sighed. 'What happened?'

'Their colonel has a clearance from Whitehall. Blanket

job. He apologised for using it, said he only flashed the thing when everything else failed. I get the impression they were expecting something all along.'

'They always expect trouble,' Brooke said wearily. 'And they're red hot, make no mistake. I just wish to Christ they'd be red hot somewhere else. What's the strength of the arrangement now?'

'Three men on the perimeter,' the officer said. 'Another four over in Terminal 3. An unspecified number backing the other security bods in the VIP lounge.'

'Too many cooks,' Brooke mumbled. 'The terrorists have made that point. This is no way to treat the situation, especially when we've got three mobs with separate interests. I suppose we'd better let the CIA contingent know . . .'

'They already do, sir. And they're not happy.'

'There's no room for happiness in this mess, son. We'll have to put up with the Israelis, I suppose. But if you get wind of them trying anything smart near the tower, blow the whistle quick.'

The officer left. Brooke located his pipe in one of the voluminous pockets of his jacket and lit it. Finally he turned his full attention to the young Arab, who had sat motionless since he arrived. He had thick-lidded eyes and a permanently sad, downturned mouth. Although he could not have been more than twenty-five, most of his hair was already gone. Brooke took in the stained sports jacket and creaseless trousers, knowing without looking there would also be scuffed suede boots. An intellectual was all he wanted at that point in the proceedings.

'My name's Brooke. What's yours?'

'Ehsan Taymur.' His voice was deep, doleful.

'And you've been told what your cousin is up to, have you?'

'Yes. Kalim is a sick person.'

'He'd be a damned sight sicker if I could get a grip of him,' Brooke said candidly. 'Anyway, do you think you can talk some sense into him?'

'I will try. Kalim is very strong willed, however. A lot depends on his mood. There are times when he listens . . .'

'This better be one of them. Short of your managing to do

something, we're up a gum tree.' He moved round the desk and went to the door. 'Come on, I'll take you over to the tower and we'll have a natter with my men there.' He paused as the young man rose to follow him. 'Tell me, what kind of terms were you on the last time you spoke to your cousin?'

Taymur shrugged. 'We spent a long time discussing politics. In the end there was some gap between us. Kalim has rigid views, mine are flexible, although he calls my tolerance something else.' He glanced off over Brooke's shoulder, into the bustling room beyond. 'Just before I left him, he told me I would perish, like everything else soft and corrupt.'

'That's all we need,' the Commander sighed, leading the way across to the outer door.

EIGHT

Leila had begun to experience the creeping fatigue that accompanies any kind of inactivity. Twice, though her nerves should have been taut as wire, she had found her attention wavering. The door was all important, if anyone managed to throw it open and rush past her then they would be finished, the mission would collapse. The enormous responsibility sitting on her was something too powerful to serve with less than all of her attention: she kept telling herself that, but her concentration continued to dissolve.

Behind her, Kalim was haranguing the controller again. She wished he would stop that. There was a line beyond which pressure was unnecessary, and Kalim had crossed it long ago. It was obvious that Evans had been properly chastened and frightened into full compliance, and Leila believed that any further aggravation would merely wear at the man's ability to carry on with his job. She tilted her head and listened carefully to the tone of Kalim's voice. Before, she had suspected that his emotional stability could be checked from his vocal pitch. Now she was sure of it. When he was in control of himself and doing no more than putting a point of view, there was a deep, anchoring note, lending his speech conviction. Adrift, he tended to whine. He was whining now, and he was answering questions no one had asked.

'There is nothing new in the idea of terrorism, Mr Evans. Even your high and mighty Britain has employed it in the past, and to a certain extent she still does. To inculcate the fear of death and mutilation in order to achieve obedience to the dictates of a cause, you may remember, was a primary tactic of the early builders of Empire.' The whine always came at the end of a sentence, and it sounded like the sharp intake of breath in a man who had been running for too long with nothing to drink.

'I'm not interested in the lecture,' Evans said, and Leila

could have shouted at him to shut his mouth. Did he not realise he was making Kalim worse? She could not see the controller's face, but she could imagine him, his lips and cheek swollen, offering his gentle defiance with his eyes and his soft voice. It had been obvious from the start that Kalim disliked Evans. The continuing resistance, small as it was, could fan the dislike into hatred. Kalim was a fine leader and a rigid adherent to a line of action, but only when his pettier prejudices were not being stimulated. Leila wanted him to remain balanced and behaving like the dependable rock she constantly held in her mind: her own courage had started to dip a little, and it didn't help to know that Kalim was edging into a murderous tantrum.

'Your childish sarcasm betrays your shallowness, Evans.'

On the floor to Leila's left and just on the edge of her vision, a man with tousled grey hair was shaking badly and biting on the skin of his wrist. She found it hard to ignore him. That kind of prolonged fear always made her uneasy. It was as if the man's honest terror put an evil pallor on what she stood for. Many times Kalim had pointed out the stupidity of her thinking, but conviction persisted. Killing was a thing apart from the torture of bodies and minds. It was a release for the victim, a push into painless, fearless limbo, and Leila could certainly justify it. But the miseries of the living could be unbearable, with no justification that could convince her.

She swayed her hips and rested her weight on the other side, trying to find something visual to take her attention and arrest the drift into preoccupation. But the door was just a blank, and to look any distance beyond it was to see the poor girl in the window, stooped and motionless, and on the other side the nervous staff, dismantling her resolve with their fear.

Evans had mumbled something Leila could not hear, but Kalim's response was loud enough.

'You still equate me with the hooligans, don't you? There is no mechanism for distinction in that conditioned mass between your ears. Can you not perceive, just by stretching yourself a little, that there are states of being and conditions of loyalty that transcend anything available to you?

Or are you perhaps so well indoctrinated by your press and the soporific box in the corner of your little sitting room . . .'

'Please!' Evans's voice was suddenly high with anger and genuine pleading, a combination Leila found deeply embarrassing. Such a loss of dignity was particularly unpleasant in a man of his sort, a man no doubt with plenty of decency in his heart and some justifiable pride. Kalim had put him into an emotional corner where his natural desire to hit back was being stifled by his concern for his safety and the safety of the girl at the window.

Leila was becoming restless now, it was like an itch in her legs. The gun was light but it weighed on her arm. She longed to put it down for just a minute and to sit, or walk about the place, anything but go on standing there. Instead, she would have to see the interminable waiting through, and listen to Kalim as he responded to his own unrest. Times like these made the ideals withdraw a little, enough to make her wonder what she was doing in such a place.

'The Israelis,' Kalim was saying, ignoring Evans's plea for peace, 'have done a good job of brainwashing with the likes of yourself. The headlines stuck, didn't they? Because they were simple and easily absorbed, they handed you useful sets of opinions without causing you the discomfort of finding out for yourself. Plucky little Israel, that one really sunk in. And all the photographs of beautifully bronzed girls in army uniform, alongside their handsome officers and fighter pilots. That was very digestible stuff, wasn't it? Convenience food. Lies! All of it! A man with his senses about him can see their rapacity and smell their greed . . .'

Leila tried to start an opposing current in her mind. She thought about things close to her, her family, friends, her lover Shofal. With a stronger intellectual grasp of the cause it would have been Shofal leading them, not Kalim. Shofal had the bearing and he did not lack courage. He was stable, too; he could withstand any amount of pressure without weakening or losing his bearings. But he was no theorist, and he could not speak as well as Kalim. He was also a little too vain; he tended to see an enlarged vision of himself. She closed her eyes, picturing Shofal, seeing him smiling at her, seeing him touch her body. A sudden, unbidden image pushed Shofal's aside, an imprint of shame. Another face was smiling, young and handsome and full of an incandescent pleasure in life. He was Samuel, the boy who had captivated her years ago on a holiday in New Mexico. Samuel the comedian, the attentive suitor, the accomplished seducer – Samuel the Israeli, the knife in her conscience that insisted on turning without warning. Afterwards, when her beliefs were fanned to flame and she had gained a notion of destiny, she had systematically punished herself for that episode, but the guilt never diminished.

'You are not here to sleep!' Kalim's forefinger jabbing at her back made her gasp.

'I was resting my eyes . . .'

'They could be at permanent rest if you do it again. One second is all it takes, they could be in here and swarming all over us.' He spoke with his mouth close to her ear, a whisper as piercing as any shout. 'Try to remember what you are doing, and why.'

He moved away from her and Leila felt the alertness come back, the tightening of her arms, the keen sense of contact between her finger and the trigger. That was much better. There was no room for troublesome reflection when she was the guardian of that door. She could even ignore the talk.

Kalim had paused by the window ledge where Jessie Malcolm stood. He craned his neck, examining her face, then glanced fleetingly at Mike Evans, catching his frown.

'What's wrong with you? Aren't you comfortable up there?'

Jessie seemed to be afraid to answer. Kalim repeated his question.

'My legs,' she murmured.

'Yes? What about your legs?'

'They hurt. I – I feel dizzy.' New tears brimmed and her lips lost control of the power to shape words. A short sentence emerged in a garbled moan and her shoulders began to heave.

'Just stay there, you'll be fine.' Kalim flashed his wide

smile at Mike Evans. 'So long as your colleagues behave, of course.' He turned from the window and squatted beside an older woman who had been lying perfectly motionless since she had been ordered on to the floor. 'Any complaints, madam?'

For a moment she looked at him, then ventured a husky negative. Her polished nails were hooked against the tiles, as if they contained a hidden solace.

'Splendid.' Kalim straightened and returned to the side of Mike's console. 'Are you coping with the staff you have?'

'So far.' The largest bruise was on his top lip, and Mike found himself probing it with his tongue between words. 'It'll get tough in an hour or so. The traffic's building.'

Kalim considered that. 'Tell me if it becomes really difficult.'

Mike gestured towards Jessie Malcolm. 'I could do with her help right now.'

'Really?'

Mike nodded. 'It would make a big difference.'

Kalim stared at him and a hard smile slowly spread, exposing first his top teeth, then the lower ones. 'You really are a miserable liar, Evans. I would have thought you could put more ingenuity into your rescue attempt.' He extended his arm, pointing at the girl. 'She stays there, whatever the pressure of work.' The announcement appeared to give him pleasure. 'And one more thing,' he said. 'For no reason other than my chronic submission to whims, I may put another woman up there beside her. A lot will depend on how you behave.'

Mike turned his swivel seat away, facing the controls. The impulse had been almost too strong to resist: he had wanted to bring up his foot and plant his toecap right between the arrogantly spread legs. He had already swallowed enough, and swallowing that one had nearly proved too much. The fear that he might do something crazily impulsive was still there, and it was as if Kalim knew it and wanted to force a showdown. Mustering his concentration, Mike forced his eyes across the flight data flickering on one of his monitors. He could read it and he was still capable of handling it, but steadily his capacity for even routine judgment was disappearing. The aching imperative was filling his head, like a bottled scream. *Something had to be done!*

A panic had broken out in Terminal 1. A young barrister, arriving in the multi-storey car park opposite the terminal, had noticed a man roaming the shadows by the gangwalk to the main building. Walking slowly, he had managed to get a look at the prowler, and what he saw had sent him running straight to the information counter beyond the electric doors. The girl stared at him for a few seconds, trying to make sense of the gasped little sentences and the flying hand signals. Finally, she asked the lawyer to say it all again, clearly this time. It had been a long night, she reminded him, and she should have been home in bed anyway.

'In the car park,' he yelped, waving behind him again. 'There's a man creeping around over there, and he's got a gun!'

'Are you sure?'

'Of course I'm bloody sure! I couldn't mistake a thing like that!'

Three other people heard. One was a ticket clerk from the British Airways counter and the other two were lady passengers, nervously waiting to take their first flight ever, an early charter to Manchester. The ticket clerk crossed to his counter and called out the news to a colleague behind the rear glass partition, thereby spreading the word to five more passengers. The two ladies, one of whom had immediately started to whimper, began telling everybody in sight. Inside five minutes the sleepy interior of the terminal building, upstairs and down, was alive with jostling, anxious, wildly misinformed members of the public.

An SPG officer, wanting to find out just what had gone wrong, broke from the cover of his *What's On* magazine and hared across to the information point by the first flight of stairs. An elderly man in tweeds, noticing the long hair, wild eyes and suspiciously shabby clothing of the officer, grabbed his arm as he shot past. The officer swung in a circle and his gun, a Walther PP9, went flying from his armpit and skidded across the floor. Several women screamed.

The officer tried to retrieve his gun and was jumped by two passengers, one of them an off-duty policeman from Devon. When the SPG man tried to explain he was a policeman, the burly constable took exception to such an assault on his intelligence and swung a punch that missed wildly. An instant later, a well-aimed and more skilful blow came back at him, jamming his reflexes long enough to let his prisoner kick his way free. By that time, as the officer galloped towards the relative safety of the upstairs cafeteria, one CIA man and a second SPG operative had drawn their guns in readiness for whatever was scaring everybody else. They were seen doing this by several people, and the confusion reached the level of panic, veering towards riot.

It took ten minutes and a bland, placatory speech from the security head to bring the place under control. He was obliged to explain that the men bearing arms were there in the public interest, but he explained no more than that. A little later, when word started filtering through that incoming traffic was being stopped, there was a resurgence of unrest, but it dropped to sullen, rumbling complaint when no official statement was made.

Arthur Douglas, the senior security man, took his own anxiety to Commander Brooke, who was with some of his men outside the control tower.

'This is only the start of it,' he warned darkly. 'The man who spotted the officer in the car park is circulating in the terminal building, asking questions and inventing nightmares.'

'Then stop him,' Brooke said.

'He's a barrister,' Douglas replied sadly. 'We don't want to go disturbing that wasp's nest. He's out to make capital on all this. You know what it'll be next.'

'What?'

'The press. We've been clamping the news about the siege, but that character will be on the blower any minute, and that'll be that. God, just think of it. TV crews, cameras, all those nosey perishers . . .'

'It was only a matter of time,' Brooke said in his weary philosophical tone. 'Fend them off the best way you can.' As Douglas was going away again, Brooke detained him and asked if he knew who the lawyer was. 'Maybe we can swing something, if he's the kind that favours enforcement agencies.'

Douglas shook his head. 'Not a chance. He approached me just as I was coming over here. Wanted to know what I was going to do about the situation. When I declined to comment, he introduced himself. He's on some big committee for human rights. He flew in from Belfast on an overnight charter. Belfast! The parallels he'll be drawing . . .'

'Weather it,' Brooke said. 'If you think you've got worries, you should borrow mine for a couple of minutes.' As he watched Douglas walk away, the Commander quietly informed one of his aides that he had been dreading trouble in the terminal buildings all along. 'I don't want to clear them, though. Think of the mess on the approach roads. More sodding panic, and maybe a shut-off when we want to get through.' He nodded towards the young Arab, Ehsan Taymur, who was waiting by the security gate. 'Maybe he's the answer to everything.'

'But what if he's not?' the aide replied.

Kalim had made a check of the other doors leading from the main control room. He was in possession of drawings that showed the layout clearly, and he knew in advance that the only direct door to the ground was the one being guarded by Leila, but nervousness or boredom was goading him to refine his information. When he was satisfied that the auxiliary and connecting doors were as secure as they should be, he knelt up on the bench where Jessie Malcolm was swaying and watched the movements outside for a few minutes.

'Strangely quiet,' he announced eventually. He looked at Mike, as if he might have an explanation. Getting down from the bench, he still kept his eyes on the controller and finally took up his position by the console again, as if his malice drove him there against his will. 'I scent another ploy, Evans. What about you?'

'I'm just doing my job, like you told me.'

'And harbouring your little grudges.' It was clear he was going to start provoking Mike again, but the sudden hiss from the tannoy diverted him. As the microphone at the other end rattled his hand closed tightly around the breech of the gun.

'Kalim Bakir,' the Commander's voice boomed, 'I want you to listen to me.'

'Go away,' Kalim said to the loudspeaker, his voice quiet and troubled.

'We have someone here who wishes to speak to you.'

'I will see no one,' Kalim whispered.

'He is your cousin. He's coming up on his own. There will be no tricks of any kind. He will be entirely alone, and he will knock on the door when he arrives.' There was a pause, then the Commander added: 'I give you my word, no tricks.'

Leila had turned and was communicating her dismay with her eyes.

Angrily, Kalim made a swivelling movement with his hand, indicating that she turn to face the door again. All movement within the room had slowed. 'All of you,' Kalim shouted, 'get on with your duties.' He crossed to Leila and spoke close to her ear, as before. 'Ehsan should not have come here,' he told her. 'It creates a difficulty. Whatever happens, keep your gun fixed on the door until he is safely inside. Do you understand?'

Leila nodded. 'Kalim, don't be harsh with him. I'm sure he believes he's doing the right thing.'

'I am only harsh with my cousin when he tries to pour his honey on my ideals.'

'He is a good man,' Leila said, her voice disclosing some of the courage it had taken to express the opinion.

'Just keep your gun on that door.' He stepped to one side and folded his arms awkwardly around the gun, staring at the door as if he was willing it to turn into brick.

The knock came and Kalim waited for several seconds before going across and turning the handle. Leila trained her gun carefully and the door was pulled open for the space of only a few inches. Taymur squeezed himself inside and stood before his cousin, his face grave.

'What is it you want, Ehsan?'

'I believe you know.'

'What we are doing here is no concern of yours.'

To Mike Evans, seated several feet away on the other side of the room, the change in Kalim was striking. Before, his overbearing pose had been supported by something within, a real or imagined control of his surroundings. Now he was still posing like the man born to be in charge, but strain was showing, both in the way he stood and in the modification of his voice. There were grounds, Mike thought, for tentative hope.

'Of course it is my concern. You are destroying every trace of what you were, Kalim. And you are degrading all of us.'

'Ehsan, I'm warning you . . .'

'My warnings gave you stability, once,' Taymur replied. He turned his head, the sadness of his mouth becoming more profound. 'And you, Leila. Have you any idea what you are doing? A fine young woman, the pride of family and friends . . .'

Leila took an involuntary step back, shaking her head and pressing her lips tightly together.

'Nothing was ever the way you saw it,' Kalim spat. 'Your fluffy democracy and your pretentious courtship of the enemy ideologies . . .'

'And my days and years of guiding you, guidance you once followed and understood, until the brutal mythologies turned your mind.' Taymur closed his eyes slowly and opened them again. 'Nothing you are doing here reflects the cause you proclaim. This is unworthy of you and you know it.'

There was a crash and Kalim turned on his heel, the gun raised. On the ledge, Jessie Malcolm had dropped to her knees, bringing down a rolled chart and two file boxes.

'On your feet!' Kalim screeched, and Mike Evans was beside the girl at once, helping her up. 'Leave her! She must do it alone!'

In the passing of a second Mike saw the tensions that held them: Taymur gripped by pity and revulsion, Leila folding under a sudden guilt, Kalim locked in the coils of his need to prevail. Mike backed away and sat down on his chair, watching with held breath as Jessie struggled to her feet, pushing herself up, her hands spread on the window.

'If she does not remain standing from now on, she will suffer! Do you all hear that?' There was no mistaking the tears of rage in Kalim's eyes or the loss of power in his voice.

'I am ashamed of you,' Taymur said, loud enough for everyone to hear.

Kalim was still looking towards the window, directing his rage at the girl. 'Waste your shame elsewhere,' he said. 'We're not here to act out your flabby compassion or your spineless philosophy of appeasement.'

'Kalim, you must stop this. You are already a murderer.'

'Go away, Ehsan!'

Leila was trying to keep her eyes on the door, while Taymur inched closer to her, forcing her to see the desolate sorrow on his face. He kept looking at her as he spoke again. 'The Brotherhood will not support this action. You are isolating yourself.'

Kalim swung on him. 'What do you know of the Brotherhood? What possible meaning can they have for someone like you? I am here in their name, Ehsan. I rejected your infantile preaching long ago and I *grew*. The cause is my life and you are no part of it. Go.'

Taymur didn't flinch. 'You are still sick. This terrible thing you are doing is an offshoot of your madness. If you will stop it now you will be cared for. No one will harm you, Kalim. Please, I am begging you.'

A large tear coursed along Kalim's cheek as he brought up his hand and slapped his cousin on the face. Taymur reeled but stood his ground. Leila gasped and started to say something but Kalim silenced her with his glare.

'Leave, Ehsan, leave now or I will shoot you!'

'Have you gone so far into your fanaticism that you would do that? Have you lost all feeling?' Taymur fingered the weal on his cheek, deliberately moving closer to Kalim.

'I have warned you!' The muzzle of the gun was levelled at Taymur's chest. 'Turn around and go! You can say nothing that will change me.' The red spot appeared on Taymur's shirt and Leila emitted an alarmed little squeak. Kalim took three paces back, keeping the weapon steady, casting a warning glance over his shoulder at the others. 'You have ten seconds,' he told his cousin.

Taymur reached out and touched Leila's shoulder. 'Even she knows you are doing wrong. Onc of your most loyal champions. For pity's sake, Kalim . . .'

'Five seconds!'

Frightened, Leila moved away, her gun still trained on the door but her eyes on Kalim. 'No,' she whispered.

Taymur spread his arms. 'Please, Kalim. I beg you . . .'

The gun fired twice. Taymur flew back against the door, his face twisted with pain. One bullet had smashed his right elbow, the other was in his left shoulder. The grey-haired man on the floor howled and Kalim moved swiftly to the centre of the room, swinging the gun ominously. 'Leila! Open the door!'

She did not move for a second, shocked at the sight of Taymur sliding to the floor, blood seeping from his jacket and smearing the paint. The catch on Kalim's gun clicked and she darted forward, wrenching the door against Taymur's weight.

'Guard the landing!' Kalim shouldered his gun and crossed to where his cousin was lying half-conscious. Roughly, he bundled the wounded man to the opening and eased him through on his knees. As Taymur shuffled forward, his arms hanging limply, Kalim kicked the door shut and leaned against it, running his frenzied gaze around the entire room.

'You shouldn't have done that,' Leila said in a small, cold voice.

'Close your mouth,' Kalim breathed, fixing his stare on Mike Evans again, daring him to do or say anything. Mike went on working, trying not to show signs of the anger that was blunting his caution. One stroke, he was thinking, one clean, thorough blow would stop all this, and it would remove for good that feeling of inadequacy and dread.

Commander Brooke and his men were still looking up at the control room windows when Ehsan Taymur appeared at the doorway. The observers on the roof had reported a disturbance of some kind in the tower, but it had been out of their range of view and Brooke was not prepared for what he now saw.

He ran to the spot where Taymur was leaning and sensed the man's agony before he saw the wounds. 'Bloody hell, they've shot him. Get a stretcher, quick.' Taymur tried to say something as the Commander supported him by the armpits. Brooke couldn't make it out and simply kept nodding until the ambulance team arrived.

Ten minutes later another casualty report was added to the pile. Taymur had sustained multiple fractures to his right arm and a rupture of the left subclavian artery, associated with a splintering of the caracoid process, which would mean tricky surgery and the likelihood of permanent deformity. Brooke reported the matter to a Home Office official on the telephone, in the course of a conversation that had moved steadily towards a slanging match from the start.

'We're doing all we can,' Brooke said finally, hoping to deafen the caller with his rasping assurance. 'Your own watchdogs will tell you the same. And there's no point in trying to frighten me by dropping the Prime Minister's name, either. If he's got any quick answers, tell him to come over here with them.' He put down the receiver and turned to his aide, who was standing by the door with a hand across his eyes. 'Right, what is it now?'

'Bakir,' the young man said. 'He just spoke to one of the CIA people on the telephone. He said if anybody else was sent up to talk he'd be shot dead. He also says he's going to kill one member of the tower staff every time we make a move of any kind against him.'

'Hmm. So what's the talk among the Yanks and Israelis now?'

'Nasty, sir. If you ask me, I think they're just working up to group panic.'

'Understandable enough,' Brooke said. 'I feel like joining them.'

NINE

David Mendel lived a day at a time. In five years of service to his government he had lost four colleagues, all young men and all killed doing the same job as himself. Fearing for the future was not practical: if a man awoke each day wondering if it would be his last, he was not suited to the work and he would be better employed somewhere else. The trick, Mendel had learned, was to regard life as a series of short-term episodes. Such a view actually sharpened the nerves, and experience was gained from bold strike-raids on opportunity.

Technically, the stewardess, Kay Morgan, was giving him no difficulty at all. David had begun gently, showing her his capacity for charm. Thanks to the blustering interference of the CIA agent, Sherman, he had also been allowed to demonstrate his tact and strength of character. By all the laws of conquest it was now time to consolidate, but there were brakes, automatic and remote from technique.

'I once planned to marry a girl who looked very much like you,' he told her. It was true. Vera had been a darker-haired twin to this girl. Mendel had loved her deeply.

'What happened?'

'She went away.'

It pained him to sense what was happening. With any other girl there would be no problem. Style, technique and charm, coldly applied, would ensure success. But this one was *so* like Vera: her eyes were the same; she had the identical innocence and lack of cunning. Here was a girl who could touch his heart, and for that very reason he could not go on.

'You must have been very sad,' Kay said quietly.

'Yes, terribly.' And it never grew less, the agonising memory. The people who had wanted to injure him, the enemy he had eluded time after time, had finally worked out their hatred on her. No lesson should have been so hard to learn: a man in his profession dared not cherish anything.

'How long ago was that?' They were in the forward galley and the closeness of the walls muffled Kay's voice, heightening the intimacy that was beginning, suddenly, to make him uncomfortable. Kay was obviously enraptured, which only made it worse. He should never have started this.

'Three years.' He had been too confident in those days. Immunity was something he had felt harden around him as one successful mission piled on another. Then they had struck, brutally, and Mendel had begun to realise how solitary his life must be from that moment on. A day at a time was the rule, and no lasting commitments, nothing precious that could be taken away or harmed.

Kay handed him a cup of coffee and stepped closer. 'Will you ever get married, do you think?'

'No.' He drank from the cup, hoping he had not said it too quickly, too harshly. *He should never have come in here.*

'You must have been very much in love.' For several minutes before he had walked into the galley, Kay had been thinking about him. It was like sympathetic magic, the way he appeared. She tried to give him an understanding smile now, marvelling at the shades of feeling betrayed by those big eyes. Simultaneously, she ran an inventory of her appearance. Her uniform was tidy, she was sure, and her make-up was fresh. She had not spilled anything on herself since the last time she saw him. 'Did you never see the girl again?'

He shook his head. 'Never.' Only that one time, the afternoon they had found her body. They had warned him not to go into the room; they had urged him to wait but Mendel had not listened – he had had to see her. The air in the place was thick, foul. One bare bulb lit the grey walls and the small white figure tied to the chair. They had not touched her face, and that made it worse: the fear and pain still showed with absolute clarity. Dropping to his knees Mendel had taken it all in, the nightmare that never diminished. On arms, breasts and legs she had been branded to the bone. A bottle had been pushed into her until only half of it remained in view. Shock had killed Vera, but not before spikes had been cruelly driven through her hands and into the bones of her thighs. She had a small, tidy grave in Haifa, and Mendel went there with fresh flowers whenever he could.

'Your life must be rather lonely.' Kay was sure she did not mean to be forward, but her mouth wasn't quite taking orders. 'Do you get much time to enjoy yourself?'

'Very little.' He was hating himself. Every alert fibre in him wanted the girl. That was warning enough, yet he had approached her and encouraged complication when he should have stayed away. He straightened, framing an excuse to leave. Then Dan Bradley walked in.

'Oh, I wondered if there was some coffee.' He looked from one to the other, fingers frozen on the curtain. The combined jealousy and disappointment of finding another man there obscured his judgment. The Israeli looked mean, taut, and Kay, he reckoned, was apprehensive. It did not take a top line investigator to work out something was wrong. 'Say, is anything the matter here?' He was instantly stern, a civilised caution to the intruder on his territory.

'Nothing,' Mendel sighed.

'You wanted coffee?' Kay reached for the chrome pot and took a cup from the stack on the bench. She filled the cup and handed it to Dan so quickly it almost spilled. He took it and nodded his thanks.

Mendel put his back against the bench and folded his arms, not wanting to leave just yet.

Dan was still not satisfied. It had looked mighty suspicious. If that had not been some kind of fright on Kay's face when he stepped in, he did not know what it was. Sherman had said the Israeli had been handing her a line earlier. Dan tasted the coffee, pursed his lips for a moment, then said: 'Look, miss, it's my job right now to keep an eye on things. You can tell me if there's something wrong . . .'

'For heaven's sake!' Kay banged the coffee pot back on its heater and scowled at him as if there was a smut on his nose. 'I'm just having a quiet conversation with this gentleman. Why should anything be wrong?'

The reversal in Dan was instant. He saw the little crease of apology as she glanced towards Mendel. He was intruding. The jealous bite came back but there was no decent way to act on it. He was rummaging in his head for a get-out line when the curtain was taken from his hand. It was Sherman, pushing his head into the galley.

'We have enough for a party,' Mendel remarked.

'What are you doing here?' Sherman addressed his question to the Israeli and made no attempt to sound courteous.

'Drinking coffee,' Mendel told him.

'And trying to have a conversation,' Kay added, finding it easy to show her annoyance when someone like Mendel was her ally.

'Your territory is upstairs.'

Mendel nodded slowly, staying where he was, obeying his own rules of confrontation. 'My work is upstairs. But I am taking a break from duty at present, and there is no restriction on my movements in this part of the plane.'

Dan Bradley was backing out of the galley. He had made a fool of himself, he realised. He felt bad. Sherman detained him. 'Hang on a minute, Dan. This has to be straightened out.'

'What has?' Kay demanded.

'Just one moment, miss,' Sherman said gruffly. 'This matter is between me and our friend here.'

Mendel unfolded his arms and stood upright. His face showed nothing.

'I have to police this aeroplane.' Sherman said it as if the burden was as great as the honour. 'I have to make decisions that might upset some people, but if those decisions are in the interests of security, *as I see it*, then I'll stand by them and enforce them any way I have to.'

'And?' Mendel said, his expression still a blank.

'I want you out of this galley, out of this part of the plane. Right this minute, if you please.'

Dan Bradley's embarrassment was swamping him. Why did he have to stand there, after putting his foot in it right up to the knee, and listen to Lou Sherman sounding off? He turned side-on to Kay and Mendel, letting only half his discomfort show.

'Very well,' Mendel said, surprising Kay. 'I will go back upstairs. When I have had another cup of coffee.'

'You go now!' Sherman barked.

'I think not.'

Sherman reached forward, his fingers grazing the sleeve of Mendel's jacket. There wasn't enough courage in the move to carry it through and he froze like that, his arm extended in a gesture of warning.

Mendel turned and reached for the coffee pot. 'Put your arm down, Mr Sherman,' he said, looking at Kay.

'And if I don't?'

'I will break it.'

'Right, pal. That damn well does it.' Sherman spread his feet and held both arms out from his sides, like a threatened ape. Dan Bradley groaned very softly and stepped outside. 'You're directly disobeying an order.' Sherman's statement was meant to sound menacing, but in the circumstances it was limp, almost defensive.

'I do not take orders from you. If you wish to take the matter up with my superiors, they are upstairs.'

Dan Bradley was waiting with downcast eyes as Sherman came flouncing through the curtain. He could see the picture, he had no idea why Sherman could not. Each side had the authority to move around the aircraft and make adjustments to security. But there was not enough authority on either side to make this kind of confrontation a success.

'You were some help,' Sherman accused.

'I didn't think it was my quarrel.'

'Huh? Are you making out this is a personal thing between them and me? Is that what you're saying?'

Bradley shifted his feet. 'Lou, that guy is doing no harm in there. Where's the grounds for trying to shove him around? And where's the point? He knows his rights.'

'Rights, my ass.' Sherman dug his hands deep into his pockets, squinting at an invisible adversary somewhere in the air above Bradley's head. 'Everywhere they go, that kind have to make their mark. See how quick he was to threaten me? I'm telling you, this trip will be one more chalk mark for them. They can sit around the bar talking about how they gave the finger to the CIA.'

'And what if that is the case? What can you or I do about it?'

'Plenty . . .'

'Aw, Lou, you've been talking that way since we took off. Maybe you don't like them, but there's nothing you can do about them. They're here, we accept they're here, and for my money the best thing we can do is avoid them. Face it, you're just wasting sweat thinking you can pressure them.'

'Is that so? Well, let me tell you something.' Sherman lowered his voice, as if a dark secret was about to be uncovered. 'At the very first opportunity, I'll nail that Mendel. It's priority number one from here on in. Make it yours, too.'

Bradley shrugged, the only reaction he could muster. It was bad enough to know he did not stand a chance with the girl, and it put some salt in the abrasion to realise the Israeli was the one making time with her. But did the irritations have to be so comprehensive? Lou could think of nothing but his dislike for the Israelis, so he offered no diversion, no idle chat to pass the time. The other stewardesses were pretty uninteresting, the flight crew were taken up with their work and their anxiety about the radio calls, and the passengers were mostly asleep or wrapped up in each other. He felt lonely and far from home and rejected. Maybe his job put some kind of stigma on him, setting him apart like a pariah. Following Sherman along the passage, he remembered what a beautiful coloured girl had said to him at a Washington party. She had just learned he worked for the CIA. Standing off from him as if he might bite her, she had murmured: 'Isn't it bad enough being white?'

In the galley, Kay was apologising for the way Sherman had behaved. 'He's an oaf. I never met a man so rude.'

Mendel was drinking his fresh cup of coffee, smiling at her, his resolve floundering. It would have been so easy to let himself slip with the current. 'Mr Sherman is simply insecure,' he said, forcing himself away from his own treachery. 'His brashness is no fault of yours.' He put the cup down firmly and moved to the curtain.

'Will you be staying in London?' Kay put the question brightly, barely covering her anxiety to detain him.

'I believe so.' Next, he knew, she would suggest they meet somewhere. The girl was doing no more than following a lead *he* had established, and already she was seeing a prospect that could not be fulfilled.

'So will I, for a couple of days . . .'

'Unfortunately, I will have no chance to see much of the city. So much work, so very little free time.' Why did he bruise himself like this? Reminders of his bleak private existence were not necessary. And this girl, this lovely girl, had not asked to be hurt. 'Will you excuse me? I have to go back upstairs.' He moved past her, feeling the uneasy reversal as keenly as she must.

'Hang on.' Kay drew a notepad across the bench and picked up her pen. The hastiness took something from her and made her feel childish, silly. But she had to try. 'I'll put down the address and number of my hotel. If you get some time off, maybe I can show you the sights.' For a blind instant she couldn't remember where she would be staying, then it rushed into her head and she scribbled it down. 'There you are.' She turned to Mendel, smiling, and handed him the slip of paper.

'Thank you.' He bowed towards her slightly and left the galley, pocketing the paper. He would destroy it later.

Nick Turnbull was jolted awake, his dream invaded by a reminder. He had always been dominated by superstition, all the way through school, college and into business. The dictates of a specific code would make him hesitate before doing anything important, and if the omens of blood and soul were bad, he would abandon a scheme even if it looked great on paper. Similarly he had often taken terrible risks simply because the inner vibes were right. How could he have forgotten all that?

He pushed himself higher in the seat, cursing the wads of money as they shifted again. The very strongest of his beliefs centred on numbers. When cash totals were reduced to one digit, it had to be one of the good numbers, and if it wasn't he would re-cost a deal until the numerology was right. The same with acreage, bond numbers, automobile registration and even theatre tickets. Time and again proofs of the system would confront Nick. Claire, the best thing ever to happen to him, had turned up at a party on the 12th of April. The digits, when laid out and added, gave the surest green light of all time: 12.4.1977 – that made 31, which reduced to the single digit 4, his prime number. So in spite of her husband and a dozen other deterrents to laying claim to the girl, he went ahead, and it had been beautiful. Then there were the more unpleasant grounds for belief. The number on the subpoena he had jumped was 121331, a collection of bad units reducing to the worst – 2. It had been some consolation to note the flight number on his ticket the day before. That came out as 7, a number denoting good things if he was prepared to work for them.

Only now, several hours into the flight, had it all come flooding back. Nick supposed it had been the tension and worry that had driven his guidelines out of his mind: he only hoped he hadn't done anything unwise in that rudderless period. Then a gong sounded in him, fanfare to the sudden discovery of a crazy oversight.

'Claire!' He looked round quickly to see if anyone had heard the despairing squeak. Nobody was looking. The girl across the aisle appeared to be asleep, and the spade beside her was reading. Nick shoved his head back against the cushion and set his teeth, bearing down on the despair. Claire. She was a key component in his fortunes, he had actually designated her his one and only lucky charm. Even the bad times were better with her around. Always. He could think of a dozen occasions. *What if she could not follow?* He had skipped the rules, the ones that had always seen him through, and he'd let simple urgency drag him along. *Lunatic!*

He sat forward and began leafing through the in-flight magazine. He could not start cracking up now. The thing was underway, he was into a transition, one that needed nerve and plenty of cool. Words and pictures danced in front of him, making no sense and doing nothing to reduce the sensation of loss.

'You're a winner, Goddammit!' Hearing the words helped a little. His voice was deep, competent. A lot of people had been swayed by it before, because it rang with the talent and energy that made him what he was. If those nosy inspectors had not started sniffing in his direction, he would still be back there, calling the shots . . .

Patches of memory suddenly came together, congealing in a picture that startled him. He almost dropped the magazine, then tightened his fingers on the pages and pulled it nearer his face. The book, the little green notebook with all the deals coded in it – he had intended to burn it, then decided that was too drastic. He left it with Claire instead. At the time that had seemed a good idea, a safe one. But what if she was having time to change her mind? What if she started to see herself as abandoned? The book was a golden tool, well worth preserving, but there was enough in it to put a dozen operators out of business and half of them in prison. If Claire went sour . . .

'My God . . .' His voice came back off the magazine page, weaker now, not so impressive. The federal pigs could start leaning on Claire, even if she did not change her mind about him. They could make her hand over the goods. Squirming at the thought, he shut his eyes tightly and tried to escape it.

Paul Brent nudged Sally Judson. 'Still spying?'

'Uhuh.'

'Has he done anything really spectacular yet?'

'Such as?'

'Pulling out his dong and swatting flies with it?'

'Nope.' She turned and looked at Paul, yawning and delicately scratching her scalp. 'How's the reading going?'

'I've been scanning somebody else's part. Tell me, how come you have to be white to have higher feelings? Nowadays I don't even get the pretentious crap they used to hand Paul Robeson.'

'You're complaining again. Always on the defensive, aren't you?'

'Well of course I am. That's the prerogative of any shiftless step-and-fetch-it.' He held up the script like a chunk of suspect meat. 'There's a guy in here, an average barkeep, who talks about things like his persona and his coda and stuff like that. All I get to talk about is the pains in my head and the rotten old world having it in for me.'

'The audiences won't have any trouble following your part,' Sally said. 'The common touch hits the mark every time.'

'Thank you, James Agee.'

'Who?'

'Forget it.' He stretched his legs and slowly flexed his shoulders. 'Listen,' he grunted, shifting about in his seat until he was comfortable again. 'I've been thinking, while the print in this thing's been skidding past my eyeballs. It's time for an epiphany.' He watched her puzzled frown and grinned. 'You know, a sign, a significant event.'

'A turning point?'

'That, too. I mean, I don't think I'm going to be content for this part to be a maybe. I need some exposure. What say we get hold of a publicist in London and start inflating me?'

'What brought this on?'

'I think it was desperation. It just came by itself, like a menopause. I could go on for years at my present level, couldn't I? It would take one hell of a jolt to work an advancement, right? So I'm saying the time is now, when I'm tuned-in on the idea.'

'But why do it in London?'

'Because I can play the phoney a lot better when I'm off my home ground. Anybody can. And this job would call for a lot of straight-faced lying.'

Sally thought for a minute. 'I suppose you're right,' she said at last. 'How do I fit in? Or do I get suppressed?'

He grabbed her arm and drew her to his chest in a grand opera gesture. 'You're essential, honey. That without which, and suchlike jazz. You're the big area of speculation. What unspoken power does the *macho* stud ebony actor have over the centrefold sweetie with the pneumatic bazooms?' He cackled at the notion of page four headlines, then stopped suddenly and snapped his fingers. 'Hey! You could give interviews, too. For the women's pages.'

'Oh, sure. And what would I tell them?'

He pretended it was necessary to think about that. 'Well, you could say you're having your obligatory affair with a negro. Or tell them I hooked you on chicken and rice and you haven't been able to move from my side every since.'

Sally wasn't finding it too funny. 'I wish you'd stop making that kind of joke, Paul. There's too much hurt in the way things are for me to see the comedy.'

'Oh, you imagine the half of it.' He knew she did not, but where was the sense in adding his pain to hers? Sally had run the usual gauntlet of anonymous phone calls, obscene letters and excrement through the letter box. Paul refused to discuss any of that with her: to acknowledge the foul truth was bad enough, but going over it was worse. It was a wound he feared might deepen until they were split apart, torn in two with no prospect of healing together again. He settled down in his seat, killing the tempo. 'We'll talk about it when we get to London. All I know is, I need a boost.'

'I understand that,' Sally assured him. She closed her hand around his and turned her head aside, watching the man across the aisle again.

Nick Turnbull was sweating. One small possibility had turned into a landscape of near-certain terrors. By leaving that book behind, he had jeopardised some very big people, and their reach could be long, fearfully long, even if they went inside. Haskins in New York stood to lose a career that had spanned the post-war years and earned him maybe millions. Burke, Pollock, O'Hara – they all had sound names in real estate, but one stink would finish them, and they were vindictive men. Milligan, a Pennsylvania court officer with heavy police connections, had re-routed documents lots of times, and delayed others, all for money and the guarantee that he'd be safeguarded. Turnbull had thrown them to the wolves! What the hell would they do to *him*?

Another thought burned him suddenly. On the little job that had first caught the attention of the government men, he had been assisted by a Washington lawyer, Murray Lang. The man had forged one document, a bill of sale for sixty acres in Lynchburg. The forgery had enabled Turnbull to offer the land as collateral in a real-estate auction five hundred miles away, and in the meantime Lang had leeway to talk the real owner of the land into selling, at a much lower price than the one on the fake bill. Turnbull and Lang had made a lot of money on that deal, but before they set out on the swindle Lang had offered a clear warning: 'If I ever get any heat because of this,' he said slowly, 'you'll get fried, Nick.' And that was the one deal the feds had picked on to start their case. Already, Lang would be on his trail.

He was on his feet without knowing how, walking towards Jo Hampton, who was talking to a woman in the front row of seats. He stopped, cleared his throat. 'I'd like a drink, miss, if you don't mind.' Was there something in her look, something sneaky as if she knew, but had to keep it under her hat?

'Of course. What will it be?'

He told her Scotch, a large one, and wondered again what it was, the thing like a pain behind her eyes she did not want to share. He shook himself. She had a headache, for Pete's sake. He was getting paranoid. The stewardess went off to get the drink and he stood there until she came back and put the glass in his hand.

'Did you want ice?'

'Uh, no, no ice.' He turned and walked back to his seat. He paused before he sat down and looked back at the stewardess. She wasn't watching him, she was back into her chat with the other woman. Get a sense of proportion, Turnbull, he urged himself. Remember who you are and what you can do when the going gets tough. He sat down and took a gulp from the glass.

It was high time he looked at the whole mess squarely, instead of fuming over little pieces of it at a time. That was the trouble with narrowing your attention to one area, you immediately got the feeling that everything else was running out of control. He waited until the whisky was warming his stomach, then he turned his head and watched his reflection smile wanly at him from the window. Nick Turnbull, hotshot, running from some people's idea of justice. Young, healthy and loaded with enough money to weather some pretty big storms. A man with a dead life behind him and the planned prospect of a new one ahead. Superstitious, to be sure, and prone to despair in the dark, but all in all a winner, even when the tide moved against him. The smile from the window strengthened, a flicker of a wink crossed the eye. What were all these queasy fears about? Relax, he advised himself; slide through the channel you've made for yourself.

Dan Bradley chose that moment to enter the cabin and whisper something to the stewardess. The glass dropped from Nick's fingers. Whisky splashed across the knees of his trousers. He pushed himself into the corner, bracing his feet on the bottom of the seat in front, his left hand scrabbling in his inside jacket pocket. The influences *were* reversing, he should never have left Claire behind. The bastards were making their move now; he could see it all in advance: the polite excuse me, then the heavy hands as they put a clamp on him that would not be lifted for years, if they got their way.

But they would not have it their way. He was ready for them. The silver pen was in his hand. Nick drew up the clip slowly until it clicked into the ready position. One touch would do it, and there was another one ready and waiting in his pocket. As he undid the ornamental plug and exposed the end of the barrel, a runnel of sweat touched his eye and set it stinging. He did not blink. He did not dare. Nobody was going to take him by surprise.

Paul Brent looked up sharply from his script as Sally's hand tightened fiercely around his own.

'What is it?'

'Him. Look.'

Paul took in the tense appearance of the man and the gaunt expectation in his eyes. The thing in his hand was like a pen, but the way he held it, there was no mistaking what it really was. 'Holy Jesus . . .'

'What'll we do?' Sally's voice was a cracked whisper.

Paul said no more. He was staring at that thing, scared by it, wondering what it might do to change all those neat plans he had been sitting there hatching.

TEN

The implacability of death was something Shofal accepted. As a boy the prospect of the end had terrified him, so he overcame that fear, as he had dominated his terror of scorpions, by studying it and becoming familiar with its dark recesses. The only unpleasant aspect of death, he now believed, would be the dying, the inevitable moments of transition. He had trained himself to accept that time with dignity. Standing on the runway with his work completed, he contemplated the vast silence and knew he had been prepared to die at any time during the operation. There had been elation in that.

He walked to the edge of the strip and unslung the bag from his shoulder. There were two guns inside, his American 180 and a 9-millimetre Steyr pistol, plus some grenades and spare ammunition. Sitting down on the grass he checked both weapons, then slung the submachine gun on his left shoulder and tucked the pistol into the leather belt of his jeans. With a grenade in each side pocket of his jacket and spare bullets in web packs across his chest, he stood up and kicked loose some clods of earth. The bag was half buried, together with the wad of adhesive covers from the detonators. Tamping the small mound with his foot, Shofal took a long, deep breath and prepared himself for the hardest part of the operation, the waiting and watching. He had to do no more now than guard his handiwork.

He thought of death again as he was walking towards the start of the runway. To a Muslim in the modern world there was always the consolation of the ancient faith and the absolutes it proclaimed as antidote to the morass of change and uncertainty. And Islam held out a dignified view of death, one that Shofal believed in strongly. To die as a Muslim was glory enough, but to die in the service of that faith and its traditions – that was most glorious of all. It occurred to him that although he wished to live through this mission, he would not have shunned it if there had been a strong chance of dying, or even a certainty. Life was beautiful, but it could be abandoned if the cause was strong enough. He resolved to bear these thoughts in his memory and relate them to Leila. That would perhaps improve her opinion of his intellect.

Something crackled away to his right and he stopped, turning on his heel with the pistol drawn. Listening, he realised how far from quiet the place was. The sound had been positive, the reaction of one piece of matter under the pressure of another. There was faint light in the sky, and Shofal was sure it would reveal anything that moved. He stared and tightened the muscles of his face to sharpen his eyes and improve the reception of his ears. The only sounds that came were the ones muffled by distance, and the dim landscape remained static. Perhaps a rat, he thought, or a cat.

All at once the thing erupted on him, rushing forward low in the grass, heavy and swift. It reared up as he was still trying to identify it, an Alsatian dog with murder in its throat and breath he could feel at a yard. It seized his gun hand in a bite that sent pain racing to his shoulder, and as he tried to tear loose the animal knocked him over. His head struck the ground at a bad angle, twisting his neck. The creature straddled him and began ripping savagely at the neck of his sweater.

For seconds he could only lie there, hearing the guttural growling and feeling the dog's terrible heat as it tried to mutilate him. Action was imperative but Shofal's arms were locked. Then it made contact with his throat, one searing bite that tore skin from him and brought him up, his arms alive again and wrapping around the coarse hair of the animal's back. It yelped and ducked its head, biting Shofal on the chin and nose. He tightened his arms and, hoping he was not screaming, strained everything to make the dog yield. Its back legs slipped and Shofal rolled sideways, pushing the scrambling mass under him. For three beats of his tortured heart it went motionless, and that was long enough. Shofal's knife was in his hand. When the raging head came up at him he met it with the sweeping edge of the blade and heard the fur rip. The thing began to whine and Shofal slashed again and again, cutting off the sound as his knife severed the gristle of the larynx. He pressed hard on its chest with stiffened arms until all movement ceased, then eased himself down beside the corpse, feeling the pain start up in his wounds.

It was a long time before he could be sure that he was not badly injured. There was a tear on the palm of his right hand, a raw area of flesh at his throat and some small lacerations on his nose and chin. There was no major bleeding, no seepage that could put him out of action. Shofal bound the wound on his hand with the gag he carried and wrapped a strip of his jacket lining around his throat, tying it tightly. When he made to stand up there was a sharp pain in his spine that brought him down again, but it passed and he rose slowly, thankful for his deliverance. He dragged the dog by its tail to the cover of a stunted bush and gave it a parting kick in the ribs. No one would miss the animal before daylight. They patrolled alone like warehouse dogs, identifying invaders by their smell, perhaps by their anxiety.

For a few minutes, feeling the cold add its discomfort to the throbbing in his wounds, Shofal detected self-pity. That was forbidden. No member of the squad could surrender to the weakening emotions, and Kalim always insisted that the worst enemy was within, the creeping sorrow for the self that left a man defenceless. Shofal supposed it was a chink in his training, or an indication that he was tired. He strode forward, ignoring the pain, reminding himself he was a righteous avenger with a deadly talent. He began to feel better at once.

When he reached the end of the runway he turned and looked across at the dark shapes of the airport buildings. In the space between there and where he stood, there were probably many threats, unwitting guards and prowling vicious dogs, random patterns of movement that could expose him and try to suppress him. Shofal had to be ready. Pacing steadily back to the other end of the strip, he ran the list in his head, the key points in the science of victimology as they applied to surprise attack. Soft areas such as cheeks, noses and fingertips had to be bitten. The dog had known that. Kicks were to be applied where they would have the most damaging effect: in the stomach, groin, chest and head. Silent progress was always important, so all sounds had to be quenched at source by stopping mouths and punching throats. Recalling the rules, Shofal also began to remember the training, the times he had almost been suffocated, knifed and booted to death by those murderously proficient instructors in Buenos Aires. During his period there two men had died in training. Another had his eye burned out with a cigarette. Kalim had distinguished himself by breaking the leg of an instructor in bare-hand combat, and Shofal had emerged from the course with an enlarged awareness of his own lethal potential. So far, the fence guard and the dog were the only victims to his credit. Perversely, he almost hoped there would be more before the mission was over. Killing an aircraft-full of people was not the same as eliminating one man at close quarters.

He began to walk faster. To dwell on the personal exhilaration in an operation of this sort was wrong, as wrong as self-pity. It would be best if no one came near the runway, even if an intrusion meant a chance to exercise the full breadth of his talent. The cause was everything. Even so, the thought of someone stumbling on him there sharpened the young Arab and put added vigour in his step.

The emergency was beginning to affect the airport in a widening current of unrest. The runway where the Washington flight had been scheduled to land was under a security cordon, with two army artillery units backing the anti-terrorist and police elements. One of the Israeli Strike Squad men had made the mistake of walking on to the runway with his gun at the ready and a soldier had taken a shot at him. The bullet had missed by yards, but possibilities of crossfire blundering became clear. Meanwhile, as hasty regulations for troop movements on the runway were being drawn up, a customs officer had challenged two young Arabs at the baggage clearance in Terminal 1. At first the youths pretended not to understand, then resisted when the officer insisted on having a strip search made. Two other officers lent their support, and when one youth was pushed gently towards the search cubicles, the other bolted for the doors. He was seen by a patrolling SPG man who instantly took up pursuit. Other security officials observed this and, noting that the youth was an Arab, they set up a major alert. Within two minutes the baggage clearance area was closed off. Several weary passengers found their torpor livening into fear as they were surrounded by gun-bearing men in clothing that ranged in style from Savile Row snug to King's Road gothic. The fleeing Arab was brought down in an ungainly rugby tackle and both he and his companion were taken off, handcuffed, to the co-ordination room. The arresting officers exercised no discretion in the route they took, and over a hundred people in the terminal saw what was happening.

The lawyer who had first sighted the armed security patrol in the car park went running to the telephone again. He dialled the number of a journalist and waited with drumming fingers as the ringing tone sounded out. A man answered eventually. He sounded angry.

'I'm still at Heathrow,' the barrister said.

'And I'm still trying to eat my sodding breakfast. Have you any idea how many times this phone has rung in the last ten frigging minutes?'

'Did you talk to the television people?'

There was a pause, during which it was clear the journalist had turned aside to cough. 'I talked to them. There's some trouble about getting through to the airport, though. Why don't you talk to them yourself? You've got some swing there. Maybe you could suggest a way for them to make contact.'

The barrister tilted his eyes heavenward. 'George, I daren't come out of this looking like a troublemaker . . .'

'Why not? That's just exactly what you are.'

'I didn't hear that.'

'I'd be glad to say it again.'

'Look, George . . .' He bent his knees as he spoke, as if it might improve the connection. 'You've been told what's going on here. It's news. You've got it ahead of anyone else and I'm sure as hell you've capitalised on that already. All I'm asking is that you front for me at this stage. I'll talk to the TV boys, but only when the slant's right, when it looks like I'm one of the bewildered people here who just happens to have an interest in police tactics. What's the snag, anyway?'

'The approaches are blocked.'

'Really? Since when was that a problem to a news crew?'

'They're suspicious, dammit. They're not going to wade into Heathrow with the skeleton manpower they have at this hour, if the story is really someplace else. Talk to them; let them know what you've found out.'

The barrister sighed. 'They don't believe you, is that it, George?'

'They believe something's happening; they believe what they can work out for themselves. Right now, their attention's on the Home Office.'

'Why? Why should they be concentrating on that place?'

'Because,' the journalist replied patiently, 'they've had some very fishy answers, from an official who isn't usually on duty at this time of day. They've been told there's a security exercise in progress, and they've also been informed that the details are necessarily secret. It's considered to be better reportage if a team can come up with some incisive facts, rather than footage of worried people who don't know what's going on.'

'But I want them over here! I want to talk to them myself!'

'Tough. Maybe you should get back into town. There's no chance of them coming over there for the moment. As I said, they're concentrating on Whitehall.'

The barrister looked around him at the frowns and nudges and huddled conversations. 'You're definitely going to press with what I gave you?'

'Definitely. It'll be in the lunchtime editions. Plural, you'll notice. I did capitalise. And don't worry, they'll spell your name right and include the part about you being concerned about the erosion of liberty.'

'There's something else to add. Two kids, Arabs by the

look of them, have just been arrested and dragged through the terminal. The men with them were armed.'

'I'll get that added.' The journalist sounded impatient again. 'Can I get back to my congealing eggs, now?'

'Yes. It's a pity about the news crew. They could have got some good shots.'

'They've already got all they want. Road blocks and tight-mouthed coppers. Go and have a cup of strong tea. If anything at this end makes the TV people think they should be in the airport, they'll be there. See you.'

For several minutes after replacing the phone in its cradle the barrister stood watching the people milling around the baggage checkpoints, measuring their surly ignorance against the hooded reticence on the faces of the staff. Then he picked up the receiver again and dialled directory enquiries. When they answered he told them he wanted the number of a man called Peter Glenn. As he waited, he played with the introductory phrases and reassured himself there was no breach of protocol in calling George's direct rival. The truth had to be spread through as many channels as possible, after all. Dissemination of facts was his primary concern. People had to be told what was what, and from the correct viewpoint. His conscience was clear.

With his buttocks on the front edge of the desk and his feet spread wide, Commander Brooke looked from one prisoner to the other and tried to make them believe he was important enough to cause them harm. He was hampered by the fact that both youths looked completely docile and incapable of engineering more than an accidental obstruction.

'Why did you run away?' he asked the younger one, a vacant-faced boy who kept chewing his nails.

'I did not understand,' the youth said.

'Of course you understood. You understood the game was up and you tried to make a break for it. What are you here for?'

The other one, marginally more assertive, said, 'We are on a visit. Our papers are in order.'

'Lots of criminals' papers are in order,' Brooke said. 'You came here direct from Vienna. What was your business there?'

'We wished to see where Freud practised,' the first one replied.

Brooke blinked at the arresting officers, then switched on his cynical frown. 'Pardon?'

'You have not troubled to check our documentation.' The accusation was put with some respect. 'We are senior medical students, studying at Cairo University. We both wish to enter practice as psychiatrists. We are spending our holidays visiting landmarks in the history of our chosen profession.'

Brooke had not believed the ground was very solid to begin with. Now, listening to the kind of daft story nobody could invent, he felt the sand shifting dangerously under his feet. 'And what landmarks in the glorious history of psychiatry were you expecting to visit in England?'

The younger one looked surprised. 'Ernest Jones was British. A Welshman.'

The Commander cleared his throat and appealed with his eyes for help. The two officers went on looking blank. 'What was the name? I can check, remember.'

The older youth let a faint smile of derision curl his upper lip. 'Ernest Jones was a psychoanalyst. He was also an associate of Freud, and he introduced psychoanalysis into this country.'

'Yes. Well.' With an effort the Commander pulled himself back to the offensive. 'The point is, you bolted.'

The younger man nodded, but offered nothing more.

'Not a rational act, I'm sure you'll agree.'

'Not in retrospect,' the younger one agreed. 'But at the time, it was rational enough.' He looked at the other youth, who stared back, then shrugged resignedly. 'We had been worried for some time before landing, you see. About our baggage.'

'What about it?'

The young man shifted his eyes until he was not quite looking at Brooke. 'Some research material we purchased in Stockholm . . .'

The door opened and a tall man brought in a wire basket with boxes, bottles and magazines in it. He nodded at the goods, then at the prisoners, and left. The Commander fingered the items for a moment then said, 'This is stuff taken from your bags, gentlemen. None of it is ordinarily permitted to be brought through customs.'

'I know,' the older student said. 'We had debated whether to try.'

Brooke picked up one of the small boxes and read the label. 'Pure spirit. You drink this stuff?' His eyes narrowed. 'Aren't you Muslims?'

'We are not entirely in tune with the traditions of our people,' the younger one said. 'Mixed with fruit juice, and taken in moderation, the spirit can be very pleasing.'

'I know,' Brooke admitted. 'It's lovely. But you'd no right to try bringing it in. What's this?' He lifted another box and opened the flap. He looked puzzled for a moment and tried to remove the contents. Then he let the object slip back inside. 'You can buy that sort of thing here, you know. Cheaper, too. Competition in Soho is fierce.'

'It is for a friend,' the older one said apologetically.

'Your sex life is your own business,' Brooke snapped. He had removed a magazine and was flipping through it. 'My God! Is this the research material you mentioned?'

Both students nodded.

'What kind of psychiatry are you planning to practise?'

'Aberrant sexuality is of prime interest to psychology students,' the younger one said primly. 'The magazines will be used as a basis for discussion when we return home. That is, if they are returned to us.'

'We'll see about that.' Brooke returned the magazine and pushed the basket away from him. 'Listen, now. I'm going to have you thoroughly investigated, which will take an hour or two. Co-operate with the officers as much as you can, and if you're clean you've nothing to worry about. You might even get to keep your goodies, by way of compensation for the inconvenience.'

Outside, a minute later, the Commander struggled to keep his voice down to a roar as he went for the customs man who had started it all. 'Have you any idea the trouble you've caused? Is tact an exploded theory with you?'

'Doing my job, sir,' the man said stiffly.

'Triggering an uproar is no part of your job. You were briefed to exercise caution, but in spite of that you've scared the wits out of dozens of people and sent a panic wave across a whole terminal building. Not to mention putting the wind up two harmless kids . . .'

'Harmless,' the man said, hissing with derision.

'Oh, and you think otherwise, do you?'

'You saw what they had in their baggage. All that filth . . .'

'Look.' The Commander leaned forward from the hips, inviting the officer to face him squarely instead of hanging his head like a wayward child. 'Nobody was ever killed by a tit. From our point of view they're harmless, and we now have to go to all the trouble of proving what we already know. If you think you can keep yourself from doing any more harm, I suggest you get back to your post and leave the moral judgments to people paid to do just that.'

'Very well.' The man straightened his black tie and went away. His place was instantly taken by a raddled-looking woman with wiry grey hair and round spectacles that emphasised her nervous, owlish eyes.

'Can I help you?' Brooke asked.

'I hope somebody can. I'm Miss Harper from Public Relations. We're finding it difficult to cope.'

'How so?'

'We're being bombarded by calls from people who were turned back at the approach tunnel. There are also calls from passengers already inside the airport. The television people have been on, and so have the radio and press men. We don't have an answer to give any of them, and until we have they won't let up.'

Brooke looked at his watch. 'I suppose we've held back long enough. Has a lawyer been on to you? I understand he's in Terminal 1, playing the professional humanitarian and whipping up a bit of rebellion.'

'He's been on, all right. He makes demands, he doesn't ask questions. He wants to know why the place is thick with armed men, and he wants to know who they are. I think he's the one who put the press and TV on to this business.'

'Probably. If he's saying things and we're not, the position can only get worse. I'll give you the outline, Miss Harper, and perhaps you can make a palatable statement from it. The main control room in the tower has been taken over by an Arab terrorist group. You probably know that much already. A situation like this is never straightforward, but this one is more complicated than usual, because we've no real idea what they plan to do. It could be a hijack operation, but that's not likely. We can't find any other terrorists about the place. You see the picture? We're walking about bumping into each other. Whatever the scheme is, it's in deadly earnest. There are a large number of anti-terrorist and auxiliary types on the spot, ready to act when and if they get a chance.'

Miss Harper was nodding. 'You've clearly got big problems of your own. We've all seen that girl standing at the window with the cord round her neck. It looks very ugly. And of course it's just a matter of time before some passengers see her, too.'

Again Brooke checked his watch. 'We'll be making a statement of our own. For the time being, try to get the facts across without inducing hysteria.'

She said she would try. As she was leaving Brooke's aide approached and passed on a request from the CIA contingent. They wanted to have the airport cleared of civilians.

'Not yet,' Brooke said firmly.

'They're very insistent, sir.'

'So am I. An operation that size could get us caught with our strides at our ankles. Have you any idea what it would entail? Besides, there are flights coming in all the time. We can't turn them back or divert them. If we try, that nutcase up in the tower is going to start bumping more people off. We have to function within the normal tide of traffic. At least we've been able to stop flights from leaving. That's something, and in my view it's as much as we dare do with safety. Offer the CIA gents my compliments and tell them what I've said.'

'Right, sir. Is anything happening, anything fresh, I mean?'

'Scotland Yard have traced somebody who's prepared to admit he's a member of the Zenima whatsit. A millionaire, no less. He's on his way out here to try where Bakir's cousin failed. We won't be risking his neck this time. He'll use the speaker system.'

'Do you think it'll work?'

'It's something to try,' the Commander said. 'I'm still convinced we can't rush the tower. It would be a massacre.'

For the next few minutes Brooke sat in conference with a team of technical experts who proceeded to erect a wall where he had hoped there might be a way out. It appeared that the special radio frequency being used for the Washington plane was impregnable. No one had thought, at the planning stage, that there could be much disadvantage in that. As a security precaution it was highly attractive, since only the Heathrow controller would be able to make contact. Spurious instructions could not be sent along the narrow beam, however well they might be boosted, and jamming was practically out of the question. A warning signal, in the event of any kind of danger that could not be transmitted by mouth, was built in. It could be that the controller had used it, in which case the plane would divert, but that could not be relied upon.

Brooke tackled them on the chance of setting up an emergency link to the Boeing, perhaps via one of the beacons along the flight path. Again, they were doubtful. The special frequency was so designed that any attempt at sophisticated tampering would simply mean a reduction in signal strength.

'It sounds depressingly impregnable,' Brooke said finally.

'Well,' one of the technicians informed him prissily, 'it was designed to withstand most threats.'

'So was the *Titanic*,' Brooke replied, dismissing them with a tired wave.

Sue Lawson had become Sue Bishop the day before. Unconsummated, her marriage to Donald was nevertheless a fact with enough force to make her feel wonderfully different.

They had deliberately stayed at the airport all night to ensure two important things: Sue's family would not know where to find them, and they would run no risk of missing their early flight to Tunisia.

When delays were announced, and when it began to look as if there was something seriously wrong out on the runways, Sue had taken it as an omen. They should never have done it this way, she complained to Donald. She would have preferred to have her mother and father and brothers attend the wedding, instead of celebrating something so important on their own in a posh, lonely restaurant. But Donald brought her out of the gloom. He always could. He convinced her she was simply tired and anxious, and reminded her that her mother and father were opposed to her marrying anyone before she completed her nursing training. After having some breakfast in Terminal 3 restaurant, they returned to the waiting area, where Donald again told his twenty-year-old bride there was nothing to worry about. They would have their honeymoon, giving her parents time to get used to the idea of the marriage, then they would come back and face the music, united in their happiness and impervious to disapproval.

While Donald was buying cigarettes, Sue went to the ladies room to freshen up. There was another girl there, about Sue's age, with her face close to a mirror as she applied mascara from a bottle. Her friendly nod was an invitation to talk. A woman, Sue believed, always needed another woman at times of stress. She set down her handbag by a washbasin and took out a box of cleansing pads.

'Something seems to be badly wrong out there,' she said brightly.

'I never knew this place when there wasn't something wrong,' the other girl said. 'I go to the States from here three times a year, and three times a year I run up against some snag or other.'

'I hope we don't have to hang about much longer,' Sue mumbled, drawing a pad down her cheek. Then, with muted glee, she said: 'I'm going on honeymoon.'

'Oh! Congratulations!' The other girl looked genuinely

pleased. It was nice to see a happy reaction. 'Where are you going?'

'Tunisia. It's my first time abroad.'

'You'll love it. I went there with a boyfriend once. Expensive, but a terrific place.' With the mascara effectively coated on the lashes of one eye, the girl moved the brush carefully to the other. 'What does your old man do?'

Sue giggled at that. Old man. She actually had one, a husband. The little shock was there every time she thought about it. 'He's a physiotherapist. We work in the same hospital.'

'That's handy,' the girl said. 'Him being a physio, I mean. He'll keep you in shape as part of the contract.' She returned the brush to its bottle and straightened up, blinking at the mirror. 'There. I can face the world again. Thank God for paint.' She closed her little sponge bag and dropped it into her holdall. Pausing by Sue on her way out, she touched her shoulder and said, 'Best of luck. And remember – have the kids one after another. It's better for the figure that way.'

She had not quite reached the door when the bomb exploded. The blast flung her against the wall and for an instant she saw her hands shoot up before her as if she were being hoisted by invisible threads. Then there was roaring darkness, pain, and abrupt silence. Where Sue had been standing there was nothing but blackened plaster and brick.

People outside were running in every direction, some silent and determined as they clawed their way to the exits, others screaming and holding on to each other. Two SPG officers pushed Donald aside as he stood by the kiosk with his cigarettes in one hand and chocolates for Sue in the other. They clambered over the toilet door, angled on a heap of debris, and edged their way inside. One man had a torch and he shone it around the scarred interior. Thick smoke was hanging in the air and there was a small fire in one of the cubicles. Near the door, the body of a young woman was crushed against the wall. One side of her face had gone, exposing her jawbone and teeth in a bizarre grin.

By the fractured washbasins, the torch beam picked out a solitary human leg.

As pandemonium mounted outside, Donald went on standing where he was, trying to make sense of the explosion. The fear would not rise in him; he could not entertain any possibility so grotesque. The place where they had sat and drowsed all night was several yards away. He would turn and go there, just as soon as his legs would move, and he would find Sue waiting, as they had arranged. No other idea was acceptable. His fingers tightened on the box of chocolates as he saw the two men stumble coughing from the charred doorway, shaking their heads. The chocolates were for Sue: he would find her and he would give them to her.

ELEVEN

On the telephone, Kalim spoke to Commander Brooke slowly and clearly, for he knew the message would be recorded and he wished its content to be thoroughly understood.

'The small explosion in the terminal building is only a warning. We are aware that you have been taking measures to oppose us, and it has been necessary to show you that we are in a position to do anything we find necessary to keep you in check. As far as possible you will see that the airport works normally. We observe from flight control data that outgoing flights have been curtailed. Rectify this, please. Make no attempts to interfere with standard procedures, and abandon your stupid attempts to bring our siege to an end. There will be large scale reprisals if anything I have said is ignored.'

Brooke threw down the receiver and looked at the others who had been listening on the amplifiers. 'Right, you're making your resentment felt, gentleman. I'm anxious not to be your scapegoat, so let's hear your suggestions. What you've said so far confirms me in my position, so you'd better come up with something better.'

The CIA spokesman stepped forward as several others opened their mouths. 'A planned assault on the tower is the only way to stop them,' he said. 'Your waiting game is directly in line with their wishes. You're aiding and abetting them.'

'*New* suggestions, I said.'

'We could do it, if you'd listen,' the man said angrily. 'It's been done before. We need a timed strike at the windows and door. Synchronised. Drop them before they can move a muscle. Christ, there's only two of them up there.'

'And a lot of innocent people with them.'

The man shook his head. 'You don't want to listen, do you?'

Brooke tapped out his pipe thoughtfully, ringing a knell

on the metal ashtray. 'Two of them in the tower, capable of killing everyone else up there in seconds if your proposed synchronisation goes wrong. And how many of them not in the tower?'

'That bomb was probably planted a while ago.'

'Probably,' Brooke agreed softly. 'But who planted it? So far, the only idea that makes sense is that there's more of the swine knocking about in the open. Or on the runway area, to be specific.'

'The patrols have found nobody,' the man countered. 'Let's concentrate on the ones we *do* know are here. Blow the bastards away.'

'Any other suggestions?'

The Colonel in charge of the Israeli strike team took the floor, which was grudgingly relinquished by the American. 'It is possible to enter the control room from the roof,' he said. 'We have examined the plans. A marksman could strike without warning from such a position . . .'

'And if he made one sound?'

The Colonel was not used to entering prolonged arguments. 'Something has to be tried!'

Brooke nodded courteously. 'Something nobody's come up with yet.' He looked questioningly at his aide, who raised his thumb. 'I'm now in a position to try something myself. A prominent member of the Brotherhood of Zenima is here. He has come to tell the terrorists that their action is wrong, and he further plans to tell them it's all over.'

The Israeli spat. 'That barbarian shot his own cousin! Maimed him! What good do you think more talk is going to do?'

'Well, if it fails,' Brooke replied, 'the chances of a resulting disaster are smaller than with your tactics.' Becoming businesslike, he read out a status report prepared by the SPG leader in conjunction with other group heads. The change of tone and topic effectively signalled his decision to argue no further. The report indicated that available personnel were containing the outbreak of panic in Terminal 3, and that the ripples spreading to other areas were being carefully monitored. Internal Security officers were policing toilets, kiosks, bars and restaurants, and a thorough search for further bombs was in progress.

'What about the Arab's instructions concerning outgoing flights?' the CIA spokesman asked.

'They'll be resumed immediately,' Brooke told him. 'Passengers will be warned about the position, though. They can make up their own minds whether to fly or go back home.'

'And the incoming traffic?'

'I think we can keep a block on that for the time being. If some planes are leaving empty, I doubt if the terrorists will notice.' Brooke put up his hand to arrest any further questions. 'I have to go now. The sooner this man talks to Bakir, the sooner we'll know what's what.'

The Arab was brought to the Commander's temporary office a few minutes later.

'Mr Adwan?' Brooke shook his hand and noted, for the second time that morning, how wealth rarefied a man's presence. The portly build, immaculate beard and well-cut suit formed a monolithic authority that could probably be copied, but never duplicated. 'I'm grateful you've come.'

Adwan sat down and removed a cigar from a leather case. He waited while Brooke lit it, then blew smoke in a deliberately slow stream towards the ceiling. 'My presence is not entirely voluntary. In fact it would be no exaggeration to say I was bullied. The people at Scotland Yard have refined the business of coercion. However, I am here, and I understand I am expected to address Kalim Bakir on the error of his actions here.'

'We think he might succumb to reason,' the Commander said, 'if it was pointed out he's unsupported by your, ah, group.'

'What do I do?'

'Come with me to one of the rooms nearby and talk to him over the tannoy system. You'll be in no danger.'

'How reassuring,' Adwan breathed, heaving himself to his feet. 'Lead the way, Commander.'

Before he would say anything, he insisted that only himself and Brooke be in the room. 'I am nervous of public speaking,' he explained, 'especially when I have the feeling

I am doing it at gunpoint.' It was clear that he took particular exception to the presence of the Israeli, who proved to be the most reluctant to leave. When the room was cleared, Adwan picked up the microphone and pressed the switch.

'You won't hear any response,' Brooke warned him hastily. 'Just keep talking. You can rest assured he's listening to you.'

It was several seconds before Adwan spoke, and when he did he intoned his words gravely. 'Kalim, I hope you are hearing me. This is your friend, Abd Al-Adwan. They have told me I must talk to you and tell you that you are making a grave error in doing these things.' He paused and turned for a moment to look at Brooke, who was relieved that English was being used. He nodded his encouragement, and Adwan continued. 'You know that I have loaned my name to the Brotherhood, and as a member I must tell you that your actions do not accord with our wishes. We protect ourselves by our unity, we do not use it as a weapon. That is my feeling as one of the Brotherhood. As your friend, and as one who deplores the vicious theft of our lands and the rape of our culture, I salute your action.'

'Now wait a minute—' Brooke came across the room with his hand outstretched. Adwan curved his arm around the hand gripping the microphone and went on talking.

'It may be said you are sundering the principles of the Brotherhood, Kalim, but even those brothers who condemn you most loudly must feel pride in their hearts. You have my blessing in all you do—' The microphone was snatched from his hand as the Israeli burst into the room.

'You pig!' he screamed.

'Outside!' Brooke shouted. 'And close the door!'

'He should be shot!'

'I said get out. Now!'

The Colonel withdrew, slamming the door. Brooke kicked a chair in front of Adwan. 'Sit down.' The gracious bulk dropped gently on to the curved plastic and Brooke moved in close, letting his anger show. 'Have you any idea what you just did? You encouraged a deranged murderer to carry on. You stood there and boosted his diseased ego, and now you're looking proud.'

'We have our separate views of murder and insanity, Commander. Kalim Bakir, whatever the alleged state of his mind, is pursuing a profoundly sane objective, if my assumptions are correct. You would perhaps do the same, if your country and traditions were as imperilled as ours.'

'He's killed people! Innocent people! He doesn't care about reality, he's up there following shadows, dreams!'

Adwan drew slowly on his cigar and let the smoke drift up around his head like a wreath. 'Shadows and dreams.' He smiled. 'King and Country, the flag . . .'

'Terrorism serves no good end. It degrades whatever it purports to enshrine—' Brooke caught himself and pushed his rage back on to the track. 'Did you do this to get back at the police? Is this your little act of spite for being held answerable to the authorities?'

'Not at all. But if they had respected my legitimate wish to stay away from here, none of this would have happened. I said what they asked – told – me to. It was my right to add some heartfelt words of my own.'

'Really. Well, you talked yourself into an incitement charge. At the very least.'

Adwan smiled again. 'I expected nothing less. My lawyers must be informed, of course. I intend to say nothing else without their advice.'

'The Yard can take care of that.' Brooke buzzed for his aide, and instructed him to keep an eye on Adwan until the police came for him. In the outer room, where a dozen people had heard what was said to Kalim, the Israeli was holding court. Brooke stood back for a time, listening.

'While we are wondering what they plan, we are forgetting what they are likely to do when their unknown mission is accomplished.' He was a tall, muscular man, and his bronzed face was capable of gliding from one expression of alarm to another, like an actor carrying all the parts by himself. 'They will crush all resistance in their immediate vicinity before even trying to escape. Standard procedure, in my experience. The people we are worried about saving at the present will be sacrificed for sure when this is over.

We must engineer a strike attack *now*, while there is a chance of saving *some* lives.'

'Thus ensuring, of course,' Brooke drawled, 'that the commissioners winging here from Washington will run no risk at all of being harmed. Your patriotism is laudable, Colonel . . .'

'You are twisting my words!'

'Straightening them,' Brooke said, stepping into the middle of the floor. 'While we're speculating, let's just imagine what happens when you make your strike. There's not a cat in hell's chance of your getting them right off. Some innocent souls will cop it. Those are very special guns they have. So, at best I'd say you might put the terrorists down after they get five or six of the tower personnel—'

'They are more likely to shoot at the soldiers!' the Colonel shouted.

'Ah, ah,' Brooke cautioned, wagging his unlit pipe. 'Think back to that standard procedure you were talking about a minute ago. They gun the hostages first. Terrorism has its rules. So, as I say, maybe you get them at that point. Or maybe you don't. *Probably* you don't, in these circumstances. But having struck, you go on striking, don't you? A running battle ensues, with bullets flying like lead confetti. All of you know as well as I do that the worst cock-ups in anti-terrorist work are kept quiet. There have been slaughters to equal Arnhem, especially where Eastern terrorists have been involved. I'm not giving the go-ahead to even the faint possibility of anything like that.'

'You are skilled in rejecting plans, Commander.' The note of challenge in the Colonel's voice was the harshest yet. 'For a leader, you have noticeably few ideas of your own.'

Brooke stuffed his pipe back in his pocket and jerked his head downwards once, as if he was responding to an internal voice. 'I'll say this only once more, gentlemen. We are doing all we can. The tower is being kept under close watch. The runway where the Washington plane will land is being heavily guarded. Other runways and adjacent facilities are being meticulously searched. Public panic is being kept to a minimum and services are moving as smoothly as possible. Until something happens to change our priorities, that's all that can be done. I'm particularly keen to avoid creating martyrs here.' He glanced pointedly at the Colonel. 'There'll be no medals for heroism, either, if I can help it.'

From the time of the extraordinary statement over the speakers, Kalim's behaviour had become so unpredictable that Mike Evans decided it was best, for the time being, to shrink inside the margins of his job and suspend thoughts of rebellion. The atmosphere in the control room was charged with the Arab's fluttering hysteria as he went round picking at details. He seemed to be obsessed with possible treachery in meaningless actions, and staff were thinking twice before they even blew their noses. True paranoia, Mike recalled reading, left no stone unturned in the search for reasons to feel cheated.

At one point a youth called Alan had made an error in transcribing computer data to the appropriate slip of paper, and when he tore it up Kalim pounced on him.

'Explain what you just did!'

Alan explained. He had jumbled a coding, and he was now in the process of doing it properly.

'Or perhaps you were preparing some form of coded message? A plan of attack that you wanted to pass to the brilliant and audacious Mr Evans? But you were too frightened to go through with it, weren't you?'

'It was nothing like that,' Alan assured him. 'Honestly, I just made a mistake. I was nervous.'

'Nervous about being caught.' The slyness of Kalim's expression would have been comical if he had not already proved there was nothing funny about him. 'Where is the paper you tore up?'

Alan pointed to the waste bucket.

'Find it!'

On his knees, Alan fished through the fragments until he found the balled pieces. He handed them to Kalim, who made an immediate comparison with the half-written revision. He had no choice, eventually, but to accept the story.

'Just be careful in future,' he warned the boy.

By Mike's reckoning, that made four unreasonable accusations in five minutes. Poor Jessie Malcolm, standing limp by the window, had even been warned about signalling to the people on the ground. If there was any value in drawing information from the signs, Mike had the rapid research notes ready stacked in his head. They all added up to Kalim being quite as mad as his cousin had said. They also indicated he had been unduly elated, and instantly overbalanced, by the support from his compatriot on the blower. Mike had been furtively watching Leila, and a reading of her face revealed echoes of his own misgivings.

Inevitably, Kalim homed in on Mike while he was repeating landing clearance for a KLM flight. He stood by, watching and listening, and as soon as Mike closed the radio switch, he pounced.

'Still planning to overthrow me, Evans?'

Mike strove to look innocent. 'I'm just doing the job, you know that.'

'I'm talking about what I can see in your face. And what you transmit to your staff with your small head movements and significant hand signals. You don't fool me for a minute.'

'I swear to you, I've been doing nothing.' Every time a sharp retort or reaction came into his head, Mike was reminded of Jessie Malcolm. Now, he swallowed and returned his attention to the work before him. Kalim did not go away.

'I have studied the culture of the English middle classes, you know.' He paused, watching the back of Mike's head. 'Did you hear me, Mr Controller?'

'I heard.'

'One of your minor chroniclers, a man with a positive passion for mediocrity, observed that the English white collar worker was the perfect patriot. Honest, industrious, proud of his station and infinitely respectful of his betters. That was sixty years ago, and nothing has changed. You sit there, mortgaged up to your ears, and your burning desire to oust me and my kind would make your race relations people blush. We're not only foreigners, Mr Evans, are we? We're inferior. Tinted, therefore tainted, that's how the saying goes, doesn't it?'

Wide-eyed and hoping he looked bewildered, Mike said, 'I assure you, nothing of the sort entered my head.'

'Of course not,' Kalim crooned. 'You'll tell me next you're not one of the lads who stand round the bar before lunch on Sundays, in checked shirts and cravats, sipping half pints of lager and spouting all the stout British talk that gives your race such a warm sense of comradeship.' He moved closer, breathing on Mike's ear. 'It's hard to imagine a man like you saying you've nothing against the wogs, but you do think it's time they were kept under control, do you not?' He exhaled slowly. 'You're one of them. A soft, declining Englishman still managing to delude yourself into believing you embody greatness. Deluded enough to try opposing me. I do wish you would try.'

Mike emitted his sigh of relief quietly when he realised Kalim had moved away. The goading was getting worse, and now he decided to examine a proposition that had been forming for several minutes. Kalim's paranoia showed signs of spilling over, and nothing seemed surer than the likelihood of him using that gun again. He handled the weapon as if he was desperate to start firing. So, was it not pointless to keep the peace and wait to be shot, when something could be done, something worthwhile, before the inevitable occurred?

To accept the notion was to act at once. Mike ran it again. It was sound. Kalim was on the edge of a hellish drop, and he might go over any minute. Even his girlfriend was looking worried. Then, edging to the brink of acceptance, Mike felt caution braking him again. There were so many shades to certainty, some of them perhaps too pale to hold up.

He turned his head a fraction and looked to Jessie. She was stooping even more now, a child hurled into terrors she had never known of before. She was a dear soul, one without an ounce of harm in her. Mike dwelt on her face, ravaged with unbelief. He could never put her deliberately at risk, slim as her chances were. He returned his gaze to the console. In an instant, he modified his proposition.

There were gaps in Kalim's alertness. Why not simply use one such gap to signal the Pan Am flight again? The worthwhile act would be committed, *without bringing on the inevitable*. When Kalim's craziness prevailed – and it still looked certain it would – Mike Evans would go under with a tidier conscience than he had right now.

The chance came a few minutes later. Kalim was at the window again, peering down at the ground with one hand shielding his eyes from the room lights. Mike twisted the toggle and pushed it up swiftly, then brought it down again. He did it a second time, so there would be no doubt, and as he returned it to the normal position Leila's voice cut across the air like a knife.

'Kalim! He touched the switch!'

Mike bit down on his lip and heard the vermilion split without feeling it. To think he could have been so idiotic! To forget her standing there and focus all his attention on the other one.

'So!' Kalim's flattened hand came down on the top of Mike's head, blanking his vision with winking lights and pain. Then he could see again, suddenly and too clearly. Everything was ugly, high-contrast. He was half out of his chair and being pushed back down. Kalim's face came close, raging, murderously vindictive. 'I warned you! You heard every single warning I gave!' His hand caught Mike's throat, clamping it. 'Leila! Shoot the girl!'

'Dear God, no . . .' Mike wrenched his head round, seeing Jessie take a step away from the window, her face imploring. Down on the floor someone moaned.

Leila brought up the gun, setting the dot on Jessie's quivering chest.

'Don't do it!' Mike roared. 'Please, I beg you!'

Leila froze, vacillating between obedience and persisting sympathy.

'I said shoot her!'

Leila's neck stiffened, the ingrained imperative taking control of her. Jessie opened her mouth and Leila's finger drew back tightly on the trigger. A burst of ten bullets spattered Jessie's neck and shoulders, hurling her back through the window. Splintered glass and metal continued to fall on the ledge for a long time after the girl had disappeared through the jagged hole and crashed to the ground below.

'There!' Kalim screeched triumphantly. 'See what you have done now, Mr Evans. Look and remember.' He forced Mike's head forward, making him see the empty ledge and the ugly splashes of blood. 'A high price for your schoolboy heroics.'

Nausea clawed at Mike's stomach. He could still hear the crash as the glass gave way and broke, a harsh inhuman sound that matched the ghastly image of Jessie Malcolm flying backwards, mutilated and dead before she vanished from sight. His remorse was gathering already, despite the shock.

Still holding Mike by the throat, Kalim ordered Leila to put the middle-aged woman on the ledge. It took over a minute to get her up from the floor, and when she stood she was shaking so badly she could not climb on to the stool. Snarling like a tormented dog Kalim released Mike and rushed to the woman himself. He caught her by the hair and dragged her to the bench, then slapped her sharply on the side of the head. 'Climb up, or I will push you out now!'

Faster than she had moved since childhood, the woman set her knee on the stool and swung the other leg on to the bench. Kneeling there she suddenly buried her face in her hands.

'Stand up! Stand!'

She obeyed, putting the actions together as if they were alien to her, finally managing to plant her feet where Jessie Malcolm had stood. Her face was turned upwards, as if she was beseeching a sign from heaven.

Kalim returned to Mike and propped himself beside the console. 'You look ill, Mr Evans.' His frenzy had gone and he was speaking in a soft, cajoling tone again. 'Were you not so important to me, you would be beyond illness by now. I want you to tell me truthfully, did you pass a signal to the plane? Remember, if I even think you are lying from now on, that one will be shot, too.'

'I signalled them, yes.'

'How will they react?'

'They'll divert immediately.'

'I see. The young lady's death may be on your conscience, but she will not have died in vain. Is that how you see it, Mr Evans?'

'I wouldn't have deliberately put her in danger.'

'No, you're far too much of a gentleman for that.' Kalim rubbed his hands together slowly, the gun bobbing on his shoulder. 'What you have done, in fact, is cause one needless death and possibly three others in the next few minutes.'

Mike tried to make sense of the remark. His head was still full of what had happened. Warily, he looked up at Kalim. 'I don't understand you.'

'No? Well, suppose I mention an address. A very upright suburban address. Willow Bank, Hammond Drive, Hounslow.' He watched Mike's dawning disbelief, savouring it. 'Are bells ringing now?'

'You bastard!'

Kalim slapped the feeble punch aside and knocked Mike back into the chair. 'If I were you, I would sit very still and behave myself.' He waited until Mike's hand dropped in his lap, then smiled. 'Mary, little Jennifer and the boy Michael, your namesake and heir.'

'What have you done?'

'Nothing, so far. But there is one external telephone over there, still functioning. If I pick it up and dial a number, you couldn't imagine what will happen.'

The threat, landing on a mind so badly bludgeoned, made Mike sag. His hands began to tremble violently.

'There is a way out, of course. You simply get on the radio to that aircraft and give the Captain a story that will convince him there was an error.' For an instant, the strain operating on Kalim showed through, the anxiety at the edges of his willed composure making his movements too neat, his voice faintly hollow. He had as much to lose as Mike Evans, and Mike would have known that if his mind had been clear. But he would also have known that Kalim held most of the cards.

'I'll try,' Mike said.

'Oh, you must take a more positive approach than that. You must tell yourself it will work; you have to remember what hangs in the balance.'

Mike nodded and began massaging his bruised throat. Through the jumble of despair and fear he caught a vision of Mary getting breakfast, calling the kids to hurry up. Now or soon, that would be happening. The innocence of it nearly overthrew him. He inhaled sharply, feeling cold air from the broken window revive him a little. He had to prepare himself carefully; he had to force everything from his mind but the task in hand. Wiping the sweat from his palms on the legs of his trousers, he looked up at Kalim and said, 'I'll need a minute or two.'

'Of course,' Kalim agreed. 'Take all the time you need, Mr Evans.'

TWELVE

'There's no doubt about what happened,' Harry Turner told Sherman and Mendel as they stood frowning at him on the flight deck. 'The double bleep, and we got it twice.' He looked to his Second Officer for confirmation.

'Quite right. They didn't say a word, just sent out the warning.'

'What happens now?' Sherman asked.

'We have to divert. No question about it.'

'Like I said you should have done a while ago,' Sherman said.

'I must speak to the commissioners,' Mendel snapped. 'There can be no such decision without first consulting them.'

For once, Harry Turner was content to let Sherman have his say.

'The ruling is positive here, Mendel. We get a clear warning, in this case a handful of them, so we land someplace else. End of discussion.'

'No. I must insist that the commissioners be brought into the matter.'

Sherman's jaw was thrusting forward, preparatory to an underlining of his remarks, when the Captain intervened.

'I'd be quite happy to talk to the commissioners, Mr Mendel, and explain the position we're in. There's no doubt that our instructions in these circumstances are clear, but I don't want your people to feel they're being bulldozed.'

Mendel listened guardedly, then excused himself. 'I will go and speak to them at once.'

When he had gone Sherman turned on the Captain with a look that suggested he had uncovered a major subversion plot. 'Just why in hell do you keep doing backflips to please those jokers? Your duty couldn't be clearer. Why get fouled-up in diplomatic double talk?'

'Simple courtesy, Mr Sherman. They are important passengers, and the diversion is going to put a sizeable crimp in their programme.'

'Oh, sure.' Sherman switched his attention to Bob Fields. 'Any notion why Heathrow didn't say anything this time?'

'Your guess is as good as mine. We have to work on the assumption that if they didn't say anything, they couldn't. No further data, so speculation has to stop there.'

'Boy,' Sherman breathed, 'these Easterners. Trouble follows them the way flies chase their grandmothers.' Receiving no response to his quip, he became surly again. 'If you ask me, it's scandalous they should be travelling on a scheduled commercial flight. What's that all about?'

'It's part of their style,' Bob Fields offered, drawing on his fund of lightweight general knowledge. 'A big private jet is a statement, but this way is an understatement. They do it all the time. Remember the Six-Day War? As long as it takes, that's what they said. Half the world was making bets on it being two, three years. The other half thought they'd lose.'

'Very stylish,' Sherman grunted.

'And effective,' Bob went on. 'It's easy to get laughed at when you're over-reaching, power or display-wise. Nobody ever laughs at the powerful ones who play it modest. In fact, it enhances their impact. When you . . .'

'Yeah, yeah, yeah.' Sherman clapped his hands impatiently and spoke to the Captain again. 'We're doing our jobs, right? I mean, if we have to do certain special things because the plane's carrying bigwigs, then we have to. The bit that stings me is how the Israelis deliberately use private citizens and a commercial aircraft for their display material. We can only provide so much protection, and most of that's being split in half because they brought along their own muscle.'

'I'm sure you'll have plenty to talk about in your report,' Harry Turner said coolly. He had the impression that Sherman made threats so often and so readily that he forgot most of them. Turner, on the other hand, forgot nothing.

For a time Sherman went quiet, examining dials and readouts as if he understood them intimately. He started whistling, then humming. As the minutes ticked by and the expected Israeli assault did not occur, he began tapping his foot to a tune only he could hear.

'Listen,' he said suddenly, 'can I take it that you'll only be soothing the men from upstairs? I mean, we'll definitely be diverting?'

'On the strength of what's happened so far, we certainly will,' Harry assured him.

'Fine. I like to know how things stand.' He paused, then added, 'Nothing's worse than having the carpet taken out from under you just when you're getting into your stride.' He watched the Captain, half expecting a retort, but none came.

The door opened and Avrum Maller, tall and sombre, entered ahead of David Mendel. He introduced himself to the Captain, even though they had already met, and asked if he might be told exactly what had occurred. Sherman stood by, ignoring Mendel's stare, listening to everything.

Maller rubbed his chin and sighed his dissatisfaction. Harry Turner had put it simply, because it was simple, but the Israeli was reacting like a man faced with a complex bundle of information. 'We should not divert,' he said, fulfilling Sherman's expectation. 'I know the ruling is rigid, but its very rigidity, Captain, should not be taken as a barrier to discussion.' He smiled persuasively . 'I am in possession of certain information which you should now share with me, I think.' He turned and looked at Sherman, the way he might study an unpleasant bug on a houseplant, then switched his attention to Mendel, who appeared to understand.

'I think you should wait outside,' Mendel told Sherman, who reddened on the instant.

'Who says?' The challenge was put forcefully, but in a near-whisper.

'A private matter is being discussed,' Mendel said.

Sherman glared at the Captain, the Second Officer, and for a split second at Avrum Maller. They were all waiting for him to leave. Not one sign of support in the place. He moved slowly to the door and opened it. 'Five minutes,' he said gruffly, 'then I want to be put back in the picture.' He banged the door shut behind him.

Maller looked around him and spotted the vacant engineer's seat. He sat down and crossed his legs casually, maintaining a neat cordiality of expression all the time. 'As you may be aware, Captain, it is the practice of our intelligence services to provide heavy protection for our diplomats travelling abroad. Some time ago we anticipated problems if the current mission proved successful. We made contingency plans. One such plan was to keep a low profile in our travel arrangements. Another was to ensure that our arrival in London would be a smooth, uneventful occurrence.'

'It looks like that part might have gone wrong,' Harry said carefully.

'Oh no, not necessarily. From the point of view of the Heathrow authorities it may well have become necessary to issue a strong warning, but, to be frank, they are not in full possession of the facts. There will be a strike squad, trained by the ISS, waiting to cancel any difficulties that may arise.' His smile hardened, signalling firm conviction. 'I have long experience of situations of this sort. Our security people have never let us down. Not when it has mattered badly.'

Harry Turner tried hard to look like someone who would be glad to go along with the argument, but could not. 'If I'd been granted any flexibility . . .'

'You have. I have just told you. The British Government agreed some time ago to accommodate us. You see—' he moved his hands around in front of him, framing a concept, 'I have a directive, from no less a person than our Prime Minister, to pursue every important line of activity to its conclusion. It is terribly important that we step off this plane at Heathrow. It is consonant with policy. We must be seen to carry through our objectives with undeviating confidence. Our Foreign Minister will be waiting at Heathrow, and it is vital we do not keep him waiting. Consider that, and consider our standing with your own government, before you make any decision.'

Turner could not disobey his instructions, but he could look very sad at being in such a position. 'Believe me, I'd be glad to accommodate you, just like the English have, but my inclinations don't count. When the emergency signal comes through, as it has, I have to divert. There are no ifs or buts in my briefing.'

Maller raised his eyebrows, deepening the lines of authority on his forehead. 'Is my personal guarantee not enough for you? We are safe from terrorist onslaught. You know the reputation of our security forces. I have no hesitation in saying it would be safer to land at Heathrow than anywhere else.'

'Sorry,' the Captain said, bringing in the thin edge of his own authority. 'Like you, I have my directives.'

Maller stood up, not bothering any longer to look friendly. 'You disappoint me, Captain. Your decision will result in considerable embarrassment to our government.'

'I assure you, I regret that deeply.'

David Mendel moved swiftly to open the door as Maller strode away from the Captain's bay. Sherman was pushing his way in before the door could be closed again. He stared hard at Mendel, then approached the Captain.

'Did everything go according to plan?' He was smirking, having seen the expression on Maller's face.

'I'm sure you know it did,' Harry said, without looking at him.

'That's just fine.' Widening his thin lips into a smile, Sherman turned to Mendel, who had chosen to stay. 'We've still got some say on our own aircraft, you see.'

Mendel moved to the door. As he did, the radio light came on. Harry Turner reached for his headset. Sherman was beside him in the time it took to untangle the connecting lead.

'Heathrow?'

Harry nodded, adjusting the phones on his ears. 'Do you want to listen?'

'Of course.'

Harry plugged in a spare set of cans and Bob Fields

waved to Mendel, holding out his own set. The Israeli took it, scowling back at Sherman, and slipped it over his head.

'Heathrow Control here.' The voice was the same one as before, relaxed and apologetic now. 'We're in a bit of a flummox here. Did you receive an emergency signal from us a few minutes ago? Over.'

Harry confirmed the signal had been received.

'We thought as much. I'll cut the transmission now. Call us back, to establish the authenticity of this call. Over and out.'

The background hiss was cut and Harry waited a few seconds before altering the radio to transmission mode. His call was answered at once.

'Heathrow Control. Hello again, Speedbird 898. You must be wondering what's going on. It's blunders again, I'm afraid. Are you reading me, over?'

Harry confirmed they were hearing loud and clear, and asked how the top emergency signal could have been transmitted by accident.

'Down here it's been christened gremlin happenstance. We only realised a few minutes ago that it was happening. The output meters showed an emergency-level surge when we talked to a Dutch freighter. The technicians have traced it to crosstalk on this circuit and one of the others. It's a fluctuant condition, I'm afraid. No way of doing anything about it, short of cutting our link. I'm confirming that everything's fine here. I presume it's the same with you? Over.'

'A-OK, Heathrow,' Harry said. 'But you had us hopping for a time. We were visualising a reception committee of missiles and mortars. Can you enlarge on the revised runway co-ordinates? Won't that take the polish off the reception for our VIPs? Over.'

'It's a security whim. I suppose they'll have arrangements to smooth your people's path to the reception area. You know how these things go. I'm just a mouthpiece for footling turnabout tactics – you know, the round peg in a hole full of squares. Over.'

Harry expressed his relief and asked what measures

would be taken if a genuine emergency signal had to be sent.

There was a pause, then the Heathrow controller said, 'I'll whistle Dixie. Seriously, there's an embarrasing hole in our armoury of stunts at the moment. All I can tell you is to ignore the bleeps, if they should happen to come up at your end again.' Another pause, then he added, 'Everything's fine here. We don't anticipate any trouble.'

'Thank you, Heathrow Control. Over and out.'

Harry pulled off his headset and turned a beaming face to his Second Officer.

Sherman was not so pleased. 'What means have you got of checking the credibility of that call?'

Bob Fields worked hard at looking amazed. 'Are you serious?'

'You're right I am. We've had emergency signals, and now we've got a voice telling us they're a mistake. Where's the checking facility?'

'Well,' Bob said, 'we have this really smart device called common sense. It usually gets to the heart of matters.' He noticed the Captain's cautionary frown and turned away from Sherman.'

'I will tell the commissioners,' Mendel said, passing the headset back to Harry Turner, who flipped it into Bob Fields' lap.

'I think I'll come with you,' Harry Turner said, standing and reaching for his cap. 'I'll explain it myself. It's the least I can do.'

'Thank you,' Mendel smiled.

As they were leaving, Sherman put his hand on the Captain's sleeve. 'I'm not satisfied,' he said.

'About what? The radio message, or the fact that you're not getting a chance to inconvenience the Israelis?' Without waiting for an answer, Turner swept out through the door, followed by Mendel.

Sherman stood where he was for a while, feeling amputated from events, then sauntered the short distance from the Captain's bay to the empty engineer's seat. He sat down, rubbing the ache from his shoulders against the padding. Bob Fields was reading something, his nose close to the page, making it clear he did not want to talk. There were times, Sherman felt, when the whole world turned its back, times when even people needing favours would shun him. It had to be something in his chemistry; the job he did and the approach he brought to it couldn't explain everything away. If only they knew what he went through every day of his life, maybe they would see him differently. But then again, he didn't want anybody's sympathy.

From his pocket he took the slim calf leather billfold where he kept his money, his ID, and the photograph of his wife. He slid the snapshot out carefully, smoothing the cracked corners. It was a fuzzy shot and the colours were bad, but it was still his favourite. Carol was kneeling among the flowers in her small garden, the Carol of five years ago with sunlight fuzzing her gold hair and her eyes clear with health. The thing must have been there even at that time, making its slow entry. Motor Neurone Disease, that was the label they stuck on the effect the thing had, but nobody knew what it was or how to make it go away. Sherman had absorbed all the lesser names too, the spreading tendrils with their special categories of misery: Progressive Muscular Atrophy, Bulbar Palsy, Primary Lateral Sclerosis. Collectively they had reduced Carol to a wrinkled, crippled husk, with only the occasional wink of the old sparkle at its centre to remind him of what he had lost. Lately, she had even been denied the power to speak. That was a great sadness to him, even though she had talked about little more than her wretchedness and her pain for almost four years. He stared at the picture for a minute, wondering what new evil the thing would have settled on her by the time he got back.

Returning the picture to the billfold, he had a sudden recollection of a golden moment in his life, a solitary occasion when an eavesdropper did hear good of himself. He had come into the house through the kitchen and was standing with his hand on the door handle. A moment later he would have been in the living room, but her voice from within had made him hesitate. She was chattering in that high, melodic voice she had once had, talking to a neighbour who had grown into a friend. 'I sometimes think it's a shame,' she was saying, 'the way Lou has to put up with being called a bear all the time. That's his approach to the job, it's not *him*. He's really the warmest person in the world.' A simple, tidy opinion, put forward without the need to please him. Deeply touched, he had marched into the room a minute later and proceeded to act like a bear.

He swung the seat round and watched the dancing dials, the components of an aggregate intelligence that could fly a giant aircraft. Normally, the magic of advanced technology could distract him from anything, but now he was only seeing objects that touched nothing in him. Before boarding the plane, he had sat in a briefing room and wondered what would happen to him when they pulled in the chain and stuck him behind a desk. He was wondering about that again. Out in the field he could move, talk, run and jump, do all the things that distracted a man from the inner spectres of what he was, what he was becoming. That would not be so easy behind one of those grey metal oblongs back at HQ in Langley, Virginia. Sherman had watched the rows of desk men quite a few times. They were just sitting there shuffling secrets and waiting to be sent down the chute to pasture. The desk eased the process of ageing for them; it gradually numbed their spirit and took away the immediacy from life. The prospect terrified Lou Sherman.

He stood up, anxious to shake off the gloom. There was no point living something before it happened, he warned himself. Here and now there was a job to do. Or try to do. Most of the time he just seemed to get shouldered out of the mainstream. Was that because of what he was, or who he was? Or a mixture of both? It was fashionable to stick pins in the CIA. He could ride that. What rankled was the steady impression he got of people disliking *him*, his face, his manner, everything about him. He could not change, he was held together by too many strong beliefs and opinions to want to be different. There had been a time when people took to him, bear tactics and all. So what was wrong?'

'You OK back there?'

He turned and saw Bob Fields looking at him. 'Yeah, sure. Just taking five.'

'There's some magazines under the desk, I think. Help yourself.' The young officer returned his attention to his book, and the big bird went on flying without his help.

Sherman picked up a copy of *Time* and riffled the pages. He had heard something said about another agent, words to the effect that the man had become fossilised, alien to the world in which he tried to function. Sherman was used to swallowing hard truths, and if that one applied to him he would gulp it down just as soon as he was convinced.

'HAVE YOU PLANNED FOR THE MIDDLE YEARS?' an advertisement asked him, leaping up off the page with the insistence of a door-to-door salesman. 'IF NOT, WE CAN HELP YOU, AND THE TIME TO CALL US IS NOW!'

That was the big heartbreak, Sherman thought. From about the time he was three years married, clawing his way up the promotion grease pole and getting nothing but tough opposition day in and day out, he had pictured a retirement in Vermont. Just him and his Carol, settled, grey, with some Federal honours framed on the walls and maybe a stream beyond the kitchen window. The serenity of that picture had kept him ploughing on for years. It was all gone, a dream that never had a chance. He could never afford anything like that, and by the time he retired there would be no Carol or anybody else to sit beside him in the twilight. Of the two available reactions to the truth, despair or snarling defiance of fate, he was dedicated to the latter, most of the time. If nobody would ever know him as a suntanned old buff in a plaid shirt and fishing boots, there would be plenty who remembered him as an unmitigated bastard.

Dan Bradley came in, nodding to the Second Officer and flashing a wary smile at Sherman. 'All quiet out there,' he said, knuckling his eyes and propping himself awkwardly by the engineer's desk. 'Anything happening up this end?'

Sherman filled him in on the details of the calls from Heathrow. Dan took it all with a nod. His interest in this particular job had been weak from the beginning, but now he had gone apathetic.

'The boys from Tel Aviv are having it their way,' Sherman observed bleakly. 'They've even got the Captain upstairs playing footsie with them now.'

'That's the way it goes,' Dan said. 'Just so long as there's no hassle, I don't mind who scores points off who.'

'You'll wise up some day. You get on in this business strictly on a points basis. And while we're on the subject of hassle, don't be too sure there won't be any. I think there's something wrong in London, in spite of what anybody says.'

Dan was becoming good at looking interested when he was really bored rigid. 'How come?'

'Nothing I can draw a circle round. There was just a shade of phoney coming off the English controller's story. Maybe it was too pat. I'm not sure.'

'The straightforward truth usually sounds pat.'

'*Too* pat, I said. Anyway, I'm keeping my guard up.'

Harry Turner came back, smiling amiably, and dropped into his seat beside Bob Fields. Sherman watched him, shaking his head sadly.

'Lou,' Dan Bradley said confidentially, 'I think you need a holiday. Everybody's getting in your hair.'

On the point of making a retort, Sherman paused with his mouth open as Kay Morgan opened the door and leaned inside.

'Ah, excuse me . . .' She was addressing Bradley, but Sherman stood up, blocking her view of the younger man.

'What is it?'

'I'm not sure. Could I talk to you out here for a minute?'

Both men went outside. They leaned against the walls with folded arms as the stewardess fitted her facts together.

'There's this passenger, a Mr Paul Brent. He's an actor, a coloured man—'

Dan snapped his fingers. 'I knew I'd seen him before!'

Sherman glowered at him, then nodded for the girl to go on.

'Well, Mr Brent and his companion have been sitting opposite a man who's down on the passenger list as Nicholas Turnbull. They've been watching him for a while . . .'

'Why?' Sherman demanded. 'Why were they watching him?'

'He's been acting kind of funny. Mr Brent says it looks like he's carrying something very bulky under his clothes. Anyway, a few minutes ago, according to Mr Brent, the passenger Turnbull took out something that looked like a gun. He said he was sort of pointing it in your direction.'

Dan blinked. 'Mine?'

'Yes. You came into the forward tourist cabin, apparently, and talked with one of the stewardesses. All the time you were there, the man had the gun on you, or so Mr Brent says.'

'I think we better have a chat with Mr Brent,' Sherman said. 'Where is he?'

'Back in his seat. He didn't know who to tell, you see. I listened to him and thought I'd speak to you first before I did anything else.'

'Do you think you can get him to come up here and talk to us,' Sherman asked her, 'without making the other man suspicious?'

'I could try.'

'Make it good. Take Brent a drink or something. Then tell him to come forward a couple of minutes after you've gone.'

She nodded smartly. 'I'll do that.'

'It sounds messy,' Dan said as soon as the girl was out of earshot.

'Very messy. A gun. Something bulky under his clothes. He could be a hijacker, a kamikaze trying to settle some insurance money on his wife, a plain nut . . . Christ, we didn't need this one.'

'What do we do, assuming Brent isn't imagining things?'

'We start by assuming he's imagined nothing,' Sherman said. 'He could be housing a few pounds of explosive under his shirt. And he might just be holding on to the ripcord. How in God's name did he get on the plane?'

'How do any of them get on? It's happened before, it happens all the time. Look at those guys at Kennedy last year. Searched, put through the detector, and they turned up on the flight deck half an hour later with revolvers and a grenade. Human error, I suppose.'

'If any humans get blamed for this error, we'll be the ones, Bradley. Make no mistake about that.'

'I guess so,' Dan nodded. 'Let's just hope the reprimand isn't posthumous.'

They waited in silence after that. Sherman was remembering the times he had been in fright situations like this, times too numerous to leave him with much trust for strangers. A Puerto Rican had once blown himself to fruit salad ten feet from the point of Sherman's gun. Another time, near a stake-out in Boston, a Yugoslav student, suspected of ferrying photostat documents from a government office to a visiting Soviet attaché, had stuck a gun in his mouth when he saw one of the agents watching him. The bullet had lifted the top clean off his head, Sherman remembered, and actually wounded another man several yards away. In reports made by fellow operatives he had seen pictures of what happened when lunatics set off grenades and bombs in aircraft. On one occasion he still dreamed about, Sherman himself had to disarm two men on a train, and minutes after unloading their weaponry at an emergency stop, one of the boxes exploded, blinding a railway guard. Of all the detestable set-ups the job dropped him into, this kind was the worst. For just a moment he thought about Carol and wondered what she would do if something went wrong and she lost him. He cut the thought by telling himself she probably wouldn't notice he'd gone.

Paul Brent came along the passage on his toes, as if he was trying not to disturb anybody.

'Are you Mr Sherman?'

'I am.' Sherman flashed his ID, which he had been holding at the ready. 'This is my associate, Mr Bradley. Tell us about this man you've been watching.'

Paul clasped his hands nervously in front of him. 'He's a well-dressed guy, about my age. My friend, Miss Judson, was the first to notice he was acting odd. At first I thought he was just some eccentric. The woods are full of them, right? He kept snatching at the legs of his pants, and tugging at the waist, and we could both see something moving, something lumpy, you know? That went on for quite a time. Then Mr Bradley here came into the cabin and started to talk to the stewardess. That's when he pulled the gun.'

'You're sure it was a gun?' Sherman asked.

'That's just it. It wasn't made like a gun. It was a pen. He had the pocket clip sticking straight out, though, and he was holding it like it was a pistol. And the look on his face . . .'

Sherman and Bradley were staring at each other.

'One of those,' Bradley sighed.

'Yeah. I always knew, one day . . .'

There had been a fuss about the marketing of the ornamental weapons, and their sale was eventually banned in most cities in the USA. A principal objection raised by security organisations had been that the guns could be carried openly even when firearms checks were being made.

'Sorry, Mr Brent,' Sherman said. 'You were saying, about the look on his face . . .'

'Yes, well, he looked scared, I mean really terrified. Like he thought he was going to be attacked. He stayed like that for maybe a couple of minutes, then Mr Bradley turned and walked out of the cabin and he relaxed, but not much. He slid the gun into his pocket again.'

Sherman stared at the floor for a moment. 'Is the man still in his seat?'

'Yes, he is. He looked like he was sleeping just now, but I think he's faking.'

'Right. Thanks for putting us in the picture. You can go back to your seat now. We'll take care of things from here on.'

Paul nodded. 'Is he somebody you're chasing?'

'He is now,' Dan Bradley said, trying to smile reassuringly. 'Don't worry, Mr Brent. We'll cope.'

For minutes afterwards, Lou Sherman stood in the corner by the door to the flight deck, sliding a fingernail in and out of the spaces between his lower teeth, his eyes distant.

'What's the drill?' Bradley asked him finally.

'I'm working on it.' As he spoke, his gaze wandered to the stairs leading up to First Class, and stayed there.

THIRTEEN

Suddenly there seemed to be people everywhere. Shofal had seen no more than an occasional fleeting shape, but there were hushed voices and tramping feet on all sides, and none of them were very far off.

Lying between two small bushes with his face and body pressed to the ground, he tried several times to count the voices, but it was impossible. There could be ten men, or only five, or perhaps there were twenty, moving carefully in step to reduce their noise. The submachine gun was on the ground beside him at the ready, and he had the pistol in his left hand. No torches were being used, which was a blessing, but if there were any more dogs he would be in deep trouble. As it was, Shofal was beginning to regret not having taken the dead Alsatian farther off before dumping it.

As the wind blew the voices in a scramble over his head, he heard something familiar and lifted himself a fraction, trying harder to identify it. The sound drifted towards him again, a curt whisper, and for a moment Shofal wondered if he were imagining things. Again it came, and he was sure. It was no dream: the voice was Israeli.

He rolled sideways from his cover, remaining within reach of the submachine gun. Out there, beyond the screen of the twigs and branches, everything was clearer. Distance and direction could be judged. It appeared that some men, perhaps only two, were coming in Shofal's direction from the far end of the runway. Others were on the opposite side of the strip, by the fence, which was three hundred yards away. Another group was at the head of the runway and moving off. He slid back to his cover and tightened the bandage on his right hand. The combined effects of wind, cold and soggy earth were making his facial wounds ache, but he was sure there was no new bleeding. If anything the pain made him alert, so he could almost be thankful for whatever damage the dog had done to him.

He pondered the mystery of the Israelis. In all the planning they had done, no allowance had been made for the presence of the real enemy. Soldiers, including the much overrated SAS and anti-terrorist groups, could be coped with. Their tactics and training were known, and Shofal's skill was greater. But Israelis. Every one of their strike squads was made up from hand-picked men, experts, individuals with wide experience of war and hand-to-hand combat. They were always to be avoided. He would never have dreamed there would be any here. Ruefully, Shofal thought of the constant tendency people had to underestimate those men. Now he had done it, and so had Kalim.

Hearing the voices draw closer from the far end, he realised there definitely were two men, no more, and they were both Israelis. Apprehension gave way to shock: if they were there, out on the runways, where else were they? Was it conceivable that Kalim and Leila had been overpowered and these men were conducting a rounding-up operation? He confronted his thoughts with sudden fierceness, rejecting them for what they were – gutless theorising, inventing a defeat when there was evidence of none. In the same bout of censure he scathed himself for faintheartedness in the presence of his enemy. His mission was to prevail. Failure had only to be considered when it was a fact.

The sky was growing light. The shapes of distant trees and houses could be seen clearly, and details on the ground were becoming visible. Shofal could not leave that spot while his work was in danger of being discovered, but soon he would be too easily seen. He kept his head down and waited for the men to pass, praying neither of them would decide to walk on the concrete.

No farther than ten yards from him, the men stopped. They exchanged a few words, then one carried on walking. The other remained. Inch by inch Shofal turned his head, trailing his nose and chin in the wet earth and grass until he could see the man. Silhouetted dimly against the sky, motionless, with his gun slung on his shoulder, he looked like a war memorial. *Why did he stay there?* The others had all gone, even the voices by the fence were faint now, moving towards the west. Shofal became conscious of his own breathing, sure that it was too loud. The Israeli went on standing there with his face to the dawn.

As Shofal tried to draw the submachine gun closer, the man moved. He turned sideways, looking towards the start of the runway. It could have been a sound made by the gun sliding on the grass, the kind of sound that was difficult to pinpoint. Shofal released the weapon and tried to breathe silently through his mouth. *Why wouldn't he go away?*

After a time the man resumed his former stance, gaunt against the growing light. To Shofal, struggling to render himself silent, it was like a challenge, an ugly taunt aimed at him not by the Israeli but by some beast overseeing the situation, intent on making mischief. Sweat, growing cold at the instant it emerged from his pores, bathed Shofal's armpits and back. He strained to remain in his role as avenging warrior while his suppressed instincts and his inbred fear of superiority tried to offer him up as a victim. Not knowing why or how it happened, he suddenly coughed.

The Israeli spun on his heel, dragging the gun down off his shoulder as he turned. Lacking any alternative Shofal leapt to his feet and darted to one side, then made straight for the man, his head at waist height. The Israeli saw him at two feet and ducked, jerking his buttocks backward and deflecting the impact of Shofal's head on his solar plexus. The movement was a fraction of a second too late and both men landed side by side on the ground. Shofal reared up on his knees and tensed himself instantly for a terminal struggle. He dropped on the Israeli before he could sit up. Before any movement could turn to violent resistance, the Israeli was choking and trying to howl against the pressure of Shofal's teeth on his throat. Shofal was at one with himself. The teeth only had to close for the problem to be solved. Steadfastly, even as the man on his back tried to injure him with jabbing fingers to the groin, Shofal fixed the idea of supremacy in his head and brought his jaws steadily together. He tasted blood, heard a terrible retching sound somewhere beyond his head, then found his teeth meeting with sudden ease.

He knelt back on his heels, one hand wound in the other

man's hair. All noise had ceased and there was no movement beyond a tremor in the limbs. He leaned forward cautiously. There was a tiny gurgle of air escaping from the Israeli's lungs. After a few seconds it stopped. Seized by an overwhelming, bone-deep rejoicing, Shofal fumbled for his knife, found it, and began slashing wildly at the silent face, sundering skin and cartilage. The fever passed and left him cool, marvellously confident.

Concealing the body was difficult. Shofal dragged it to the spot where he had been hiding. He folded the legs close to the chest and pushed the head between the knees, but still it showed. Making sure there was no one nearby, he stood up on the spine and started to jump. Steadily the torso sank into the boggy ground, and after a minute of insistent pounding it had dropped below the level of the mounds supporting the bushes. Content that discovery would be unlikely, Shofal stepped clear of the spot. With his head thrown back, he anointed himself with water from the flask he carried, washing the dead man's blood and mucus from his lips and face. Two dogs killed, he thought, feeling the water turn colder as it ran down his cheeks. Two worthless carcases were all that remained of the resistance he had been offered. And he had done it alone!

Later, caution returned and he sank to the ground again. They could come at him now and he would fear none of them. The myth of Israeli strike power had perished, and Shofal's sense of his own power had increased. He had been granted victory over an enemy he had feared in the depths of his heart, and he saw it as a sign. This mission would succeed, gloriously.

The Colonel in charge of the Israeli strike squad was aware that his movements were being watched. Brooke had insisted that his reach be severely limited. Every time the man went beyond the crescent of army vehicles set around the base of the tower, someone followed him. Three times in fifteen minutes he had tried, without success, to make his way, unmonitored, to the rear of the administration building that stood near the tower. On the fourth attempt he made it, and his deputy was still there, waiting for him.

'How do we get up there?' the Colonel demanded.

The other soldier pointed to a half-open door. 'The stairs go directly to the roof. I could have been there already.'

'I want to handle this personally. Where is the weapon?'

'Behind the door, in a dustbin.'

'Very well. Let's go, before the ferrets come looking for me again.'

Between them they carried the heavy tarpaulin-covered bundle up the four flights of stairs. At the top they had to force the door, eventually kicking it clear of its hinges. The Colonel dragged the bundle to the three-foot ledge and leaned it there. Directly opposite, one hundred and fifty yards away, was the main control room of the tower. 'An excellent spot,' the Colonel said. To their right was a brick ventilation enclosure, neatly shielding them from the sight of the men on the adjacent roof with their telescope and camera. From below, their presence was covered by the ledge.

They set to unwrapping the gun and erecting its tripod. The three Israelis patrolling the fence had brought the weapon across to the building, from the spot on the perimeter road where a van had dumped it. The bundle had lain waiting for an hour before the Colonel could go near the hiding place, and now, uncovering its dull black barrel, he smiled, pleased that the frustrating wait had put him in touch with his objective.

'We must mount it securely. The slightest vibration will ruin its aim.'

The gun was a Heckler and Kock high velocity rifle, specially developed for long range work, delivering a bullet with enough impact to penetrate walls at distances up to a hundred yards. At the present range from their target, the shell would pass clean through a human being. The Colonel and his deputy set the solid rubber blocks on the tarmac of the roof and eased the heavy tripod on to them, taking a sight line to the tower from the vee notch on the top. The rifle, too large and heavy for one man to carry, was hoisted carefully to the circular platform and clamped in position. Through the zoom sight, the Colonel fixed his aim on the centre of the tower window facing them. There was no allowance for sideways movement at that range and the position was tightly locked.

'Go down now,' the Colonel told his deputy. 'Remain close to the co-ordination room. If anyone asks about me, make excuses, and if anything significant happens, try to let me know.' As the man moved off, the Colonel hissed to him. 'Remember, if it looks as if anyone is going to come up here, stop them.'

In the tower, Kalim was standing entranced, watching the clock. The plane was approximately an hour away. The exhausting events of the night had drawn deep shadows under his eyes, making him look older and much more dangerous. The woman on the ledge stood shivering in the cold breeze that entered through the broken glass. She never took her frightened eyes from Kalim, except when a fluctuating tremor of nervousness twitched her head aside. By the door, Leila now stood half-facing the centre of the room. She was very tired. It showed in the glaze of her eyes and the unwitting, hypnotic sway of her gun as she continued to point it at the door. Something else had left her face, besides the vigour. From the time she had shot the girl her confidence had looked false, a flimsy replica of something she had once possessed.

By the console, coping with the building streams of traffic, Mike Evans still found time to drone the litany of his failure through his mind. A girl was dead because he had tried to be smart, and in the end he had been even smarter in ensuring Jessie had died for nothing. He had a wife and two children in jeopardy, and a Pan Am jumbo was coming in to a reception that would probably be ghastly. As a night's work it ranked with the worst nightmares, and God help me, he thought, it was still going on.

The remaining people on the floor had been allowed to get up and assist with the work load. Downstairs, data was being passed steadily forward from the computer, and over the few remaining internal telephone lines correction information, delay lists and runway status confirmations were being sent up steadily. Since the time Jessie had been blown through the window, nobody had dared to pause, for fear of drawing Kalim's attention. The sounds of jets out on the runways were mingling to produce the routine symphony for that time of the day, and delayed flights were being loaded with uncommon speed. For just one instant Mike Evans closed his eyes, noticing how normal everything seemed, if only he did not look round or think.

Kalim's voice grated through the momentary peace. 'You are really quite a gifted actor, Evans.' Since the call to Pan Am 898, Kalim's mood had become buoyant. 'A vocation was missed there, I think. But then, you had a lot of incentive behind that performance.'

Mike went on working. A late flight from Shannon had repeated landing instructions wrongly, and he sent them out again. A weather query from a business charter over the Channel was switched to one of the assistants to handle. An Iranian captain bade Mike good morning on a crackling line and Mike asked him to switch frequencies. It would all have been so straightforward without this senseless, hideous intrusion.

'You will be rid of us soon, Mr Evans. I'm sure that will compensate for a lot. We will be gone a minute after the Washington flight lands.'

Mike turned and looked at him. 'What are you planning to do with the Israelis?'

'I told you before. We will make a gesture. Depending on how you view it, that may land on your conscience, too.' Kalim grinned. 'How does it feel to have your complacency replaced with mountains of guilt?'

Mike did not answer. He was not expected to. Kalim was off on a monologue again, peppering it with his questions as if they were essential punctuation.

'Leila and myself will walk out of this tower, and although I cannot guarantee there will be no more bloodshed, I can tell you none of it will be ours. There will be such fearful confusion in the airport, I doubt if too many people will try to stop us. If they do try, however, they will die. Now isn't that neat, Mr Evans? Have you noted the precision we bring to our planning?' He looked up at the clock again, as if it might have tried something while he wasn't watching. 'We knew practically all there is to know before we came here. We have plans of this airport that even the authorities don't possess. We even have recordings of your voice, Evans, and detailed analyses of the various control procedures. Planning. The basis of success.'

There was something crazily persistent in Mike's need to put Kalim down. Against all the terrible cautions of memory and instinct, he still wanted desperately to beat the Arab, to cancel him and his dominance of events. Even with the evidence of his own lousy mismanagement – it had to be faced, his *failure* – he could feel the urge persisting in his bones.

'I hope our style has taught you something, Mr Evans. No doubt you'll be asked to lecture about your experiences. To the Lions, perhaps, or the Rotarians.'

Mike heard the snigger and steeled himself for more taunting. He thought about the family to stabilise himself, to inject some caution. Pictures brightened and dimmed through one another. Smiling kids, fireside unity, Mary in the kitchen: the scenario was mawkish, discoloured by his fear, and his down-to-earth brood became soft-focus treasures with big eyes and wistful smiles. On the memory of a sick child something jarred. He had just accepted Kalim's threat; he had not really measured the credibility. A terrorist breathing down a man's neck could tilt his sense of truth, after all, and he might just lose his instinct for what was likely. Would Arabs really take the trouble to invade Hammond Drive – would they spread themselves that thin, run all those extra risks? Mike had to know.

He began tensing himself for another star performance. Enough chances had been taken and fluffed. This would need timing and it would have to fit the scene, and he was glad the motive force was stronger this time. Mike stopped what he was doing suddenly and clutched his head.

'What is wrong?' Kalim was beside him, watching closely.

Looking up, his eyes wrinkling, Mike said, 'My family. I was just wondering . . .'

'I can understand that. Your concern gives the exercise its point, of course. So long as you behave yourself, no harm will come to them.'

'My boy – he has measles. He's very poorly. What if he's

needing a doctor?' The distress and the hint of unravelling were not so much an act as a conversion: tiredness always made him look terrible, and weariness looked much the same as grief.

'Oh, I see.' The signs on Kalim's face were more genuine. His pleasure in taunting Mike had to be tempered with a sense of reality. There was no sense in having the controller crack up. 'I am sure the boy is fine.'

'Is there any way you can find out?'

'Yes, yes, leave it to me.' Kalim walked to the phone and lifted the receiver. He shielded the instrument as he dialled, then stood waiting. After a pause he mumbled something into the mouthpiece, then put the receiver down again. 'The boy is sleeping comfortably,' he said. Then he added the refinement that underlined his deception: 'His fever is much better.'

'Thank you,' Mike said huskily, turning back to his work. *Lying little Arab bastard!* That was it, the whole scene was changed. He would be ready now; he would be alert to any decent chance. And it would be no chicken-livered attempt at sabotage: it would be an assault. The lady on the ledge was a cautionary reminder, but she was no obstacle. By Mike's left foot was a heavy steel punch. He had borrowed it a week before and forgotten to return it to the manager's office. Its potential as a weapon had attracted him before, but then he was too low and too scared to do anything. He glanced at it now and swore he would endanger nobody but himself and Kalim when the time came.

'Feeling better now, Mr Evans?' There was no solicitude in Kalim's tone, merely cold interest.

'Yes, much better.' And getting better by the minute, he thought. He was gliding on the relief, knowing they were all safe. There was a sharp lesson, too: acts of bravery could only be realities when the mood was right. Mike knew he was entering the ideal mood now.

Then his heart jolted. A colleague, who had lain terrified on the floor for so long, was suddenly moving towards Kalin, schedules flying from his grasp as his terror gunned him forward.

'Don't!' Mike yelled. 'Dyson! Stop!'

Kalim alerted an instant too late and fell over as the man leapt on him, arms encircling his neck. They both landed badly, separated by the impact with the floor. Dyson rolled over on hands and knees, bewildered suddenly, not knowing what to do next and appealing to Mike with his eyes.

'You bloody fool!'

Dyson gasped as Kalim rose and drove his fist in hard behind his ear. He fell forward and was dragged upright before his face could touch the floor.

'Your valour is infectious, Evans!' Kalim twisted the man by his shirt collar and slammed his face against the corner of a desk. 'Is the death-wish part of the national character? Hah?'

Leila was staring at the woman on the ledge. She was screeching for mercy as the others moved back against walls and benches, silently begging each other to come up with an answer to this. Only Mike Evans, motionless in his chair, could see that if Leila was ordered to shoot the woman, she would not be able to.

Kalim was concentrating on Dyson. He hoisted the man, blue-faced and gasping, and dumped him in the nearest chair. 'I think you need a lesson in obedience, my friend.' He took a fine-bladed craft knife from his pocket and flipped off the plastic cover. 'You all need clarification on the subject.' Some people were trying to resume work, others were watching. Leila, Mike noticed, had looked away.

'Please don't,' Dyson was whining. 'Jesus, God, please don't do anything to me . . .'

Kalim smiled and grasped Dyson's right wrist, forcing his hand flat on the desk in front of them. 'A brief outline of policy, first.' He held the knife on a level with Dyson's eyes. 'Terrorism lacks credibility until its power is demonstrated by example. Do you understand that? I can put it another way.' He waved the knife. 'Persuasion rarely works for minorities. Terror can. Our aim here is to gain your subservience, in pursuit of a larger goal. It seems that despite what has already happened, there is still a current of resistance. Perhaps I am too soft. I will correct that, simply to ensure that our aim is met.' The knife came down a few inches, glinting as it moved. The deep blue around Dyson's lips darkened as he tried to complain, to beg. Kalim said, 'Leila. Listen to me.'

For just a moment there was sharp rebellion on her face.

'Leila!'

She straightened up and nodded. 'I am listening.'

'You will point your gun at the lady by the window.' That brought a choked squeak from the woman. 'If this man makes any move to resist what I do, you will shoot her as you shot the other one.' He brought his face close to Dyson's. 'Is that clear? You will accept what I do, totally. If you show one sign of resistance I will go no further, but she . . .' He jerked his thumb at the window. 'You follow?'

'Please, I can't . . .'

'Well, you know the rules, my friend. What you do is entirely up to yourself.'

For a tortured instant Dyson looked over his shoulder at the woman shuddering by the fractured window. He returned his gaze to his trapped, vulnerable hand, saying nothing.

Kalim gave Leila one stern glance, then began lowering the knife, an inch at a time. Dyson had his tongue between his teeth. The vicious point made contact, softly at first. Kalim paused, looked up at his victim and smiled. Sudden pressure behind the knife brought a roar gurgling up from Dyson's throat and his teeth almost severed his tongue. He did not move his hand. By the window the woman moaned and almost sank to her knees. A girl near Mike Evans turned away, clutching her mouth.

'Kalim . . .'

He paused and looked across at Leila. Her lip was trembling. 'What is it?'

She narrowed her eyes, like someone in dire pain, and shook her head.

'Keep your gun on that woman!'

'This is not necessary,' she complained.

Fury snapped Kalim's head round again and he shouted at her. 'You have received my order and you will obey! There is no other thing for you to do! Simply obey!'

Leila's mouth tightened and she raised the gun again, training it on the woman.

For the next minute Kalim worked methodically. Throughout the torture his face showed nothing but dedication to the task, a grim concentration that fixed every muscle. Dyson was not looking any longer. With his head turned aside he grunted, gasped, cried out several times and finally reached a point where the pain drove him silent, into a deepening shock. At no point did he try to resist.

Kalim finally released his grip on the man's wrist and moved back. 'There,' he grunted. He put the knife back in his pocket without troubling to cover it or remove the blood. 'End of lesson, ladies and gentlemen.' He turned and nodded to the woman on the ledge. 'Your friend must think a great deal of you, madam.'

Mike Evans kicked the metal punch a little nearer the leg of his chair. The enforced lull in activity among the staff had caused a build-up of work. 'Let's start getting these planes sorted out,' he said loudly. The punch was where he could reach it by simply bending down. It had a handle with a good positive grip. He could almost feel the weight of it in his hand already, but he would wait. His caution had climbed a few notches as he watched Kalim working on Dyson's hand, but his determination had not shifted. Sure beyond doubt that there would always be a risk, no matter how he made his approach, he had just recalled something he read in Chesterton. Sometimes, the line ran, a man had to be a little careless of his life, even in order to keep it. So be it. He would go on waiting, but not past the point where a careful surge might save more lives than his own.

Kalim was beside Leila, whispering harshly at her as she continued to stare at the woman on the ledge, her gun no longer pointing in that direction.

'I can see the quality of your dedication now,' he hissed. 'On paper and in debate you are made of iron. You are one of the most sincerely dedicated women I have met, but the limits of your zeal are too narrow. They do not encompass action! I will remember that. I will remember to place women where my instincts have told me to place them all along. In the second rank, Leila.'

'I have already killed for you!'

'Is that such a big thing? You squeeze a trigger and the gun does the work. That needs no special valour. You have no stomach for the practical details, the physical involvement. Shooting is a detached procedure; you are doing no more than issuing an order, a sentence of death that requires nothing but the strength or courage of a baby to implement. A soldier, Leila, a good soldier, is much more than a person who pulls triggers. Perhaps you will see that one day. You may gain the understanding that fiery commitment is not enough.'

'I have tried,' she breathed, still looking across the room. 'There are some things I do not think necessary; it is not a matter of inadequacy . . .'

'It is a matter of imperfection, in your case.' His breathing was shaky suddenly, as if he was facing things he would rather not know. 'The best intentions are depleted if their host is tainted.'

For the first time she looked at him. 'What do you mean?'

'Do you think I am ignorant, Leila? Do you believe I can be deluded? I am the most thorough person you have ever met. Your history is known to me, all of it. I know of your predilection for Jews . . .'

'That is a lie!'

He grasped the shoulder of her jacket and twisted it, drawing her off-balance. 'It is no lie! It was a long time ago, but it happened: you defiled yourself with an Israeli. Do you want me to go on? Shall I name him, give you times and dates?'

'You had no right—'

'Every right,' he snarled, shaking her, 'every right in the world! Your family are prominent, and there is little about such people and their movements that is not recorded somewhere. I was fair, though. I set that information beside what I knew of your dedication to the cause. A momentary lapse, I told myself. An aberration. But not so, Leila . . .' He released her and glanced at his hand, as if it was soiled. 'It was a mark of your fundamental corruption. You are not a fit vessel for your beliefs. I have watched you crumble in the past few hours, and it has made me wish we had never agreed to your involvement here. But you are here and you will do as I tell you until the mission is over.'

'And afterwards?'

'That will be decided when there is time for such matters.' Abruptly he walked away, leaving her staring after him.

Passing the chair where Dyson still sat, his face blank and sallow with shock, Kalim paused and nodded, a craftsman examining a satisfactory piece of work. 'I trust we have no doubts left, ladies and gentlemen? The order of the day is strict obedience. It is all very simple.'

Everyone carried on working. Some had more difficulty than others. The woman by the window stared out at the growing dawn while Mike Evans shifted his papers and issued instructions in a clear, steady voice. At the desk Dyson sat hunched, staring at his hand where it rested on the top, a few inches from the neat pile of his fingernails.

FOURTEEN

The Captain had spoken to David Mendel, telling him exactly what Kay Morgan had said. Mendel returned to the lounge where the commissioners were sitting and made a casual approach to his partner, Yosef Mark.

'We have to talk,' he said quietly. 'There is an emergency on board.'

As casually as he had come, he led the way past the commissioners' table and went back down the stairs with Mark a few paces behind.

Joel Singer watched them and remarked on the quiet way they conducted themselves. 'Is this something new in security arrangements?' he asked Nathan Danzig, who remained enigmatic behind his tinted glasses. 'Do they have their tongues lopped on graduation day? Or do they get penalised for using too many words in any twenty-four-hour period?'

'They are two very good men,' Danzig said, and committed himself to no more than that.

'They certainly fit our new national image,' Abraham Glazer remarked. 'Surly. Glowering. Quietly menacing.'

Singer nodded. 'A lot better than your ideal, though. Snivelling. Conciliatory . . .'

'Please, gentlemen, this is becoming a habit.' Avrum Maller rapped the table, being careful to direct his frown at Glazer only.

'Schisms create noise,' Glazer apologised. 'Ignore me. Most of the things I say now are intended for the air.' Colouring a little, he propped his chin on one hand and stared out at the lightening sky.

'Like seeks like,' Singer murmured, ever intent on having the last word.

Glazer altered immediately. Stilling the automatic warning in Avrum Maller's eyes with an unusually hostile glance, he leaned across to Singer. 'If you imply that hot air belongs in its own element, let me steam your ears with this—' He raised one finger, a bony obelisk to dignify his words. 'I have been sitting here thinking, and I have arrived at the conclusion that my life in politics has been a waste. A total waste, Singer. That is a dreadful truth to confront. Instead of being able to accept it with due sorrow, I have found myself growing impatient to do something, one single thing that might help to slow the journey of my beliefs into oblivion.'

'You talk like a rabbi,' Singer said.

'Better that than a warlord. As I was saying, I was restless to do something, and a few minutes ago I made a decision. In London, I will publicly resign from this commission, and from the government.'

'You will do nothing of the kind!' Avrum Maller was towering out of his seat and leaning across the table.

'Oh, but I shall. I have given it proper thought.'

'Then unthink it!' Singer shouted. 'We're not going to have you undoing the whole show . . .'

'This piece of arrogant showmanship deserves to be undone. There will be no rival show of distasteful Hebrew emotion, gentlemen. In my statement to the press I will say that I am resigning as a protest against policies which are insupportable to a genuine man of peace . . .'

'I forbid it!' Maller growled.

'You can't.'

'You're insane!'

'And you will probably take steps to prove that,' Glazer said quietly. 'In the meantime, I will make my stand. And by the time I am carted off to whatever genteel prison you find for me, there will be even more substance to my protest.'

'I should have known,' Singer howled. 'It should have stood out a mile! You got on the commission just to do this very thing, didn't you?' He reached forward and grabbed the other man by the lapel. 'Didn't you? You creeping, seditious—'

Maller was regaining his control and gently urged Singer to do the same. 'Sit down, please. Let us discuss this . . .'

'There is nothing to discuss,' Glazer assured them.

'You clearly don't comprehend the enormity of what you

are planning,' Maller said, controlling his voice with difficulty. 'Surely you can see the degree of embarrassment it would cause? And apart from that, I am convinced your motive is based on a complete misunderstanding of certain things we have said.'

'Don't reason with him,' Singer said. '*Tell* him. Hit him with the facts. He doesn't get off this plane without a close personal escort unless he gets in line.'

Maller cleared his throat, giving him time to throw a querying glance at the passive Danzig. He received a nod in return. 'Look, Glazer, I would not put it as strongly as that, but I have to tell you that the commission's viability has to be defended. We cannot simply allow you to make us look like another disorganised Eastern nation with civil war in the ranks of government.'

'What would you do to stop me?' Glazer looked interested rather than apprehensive.

Danzig broke his silence. 'There are measures, Abraham. Why force us to take unpleasant action? Have you no respect at all for your country, for its standing in the eyes of the world? Make your protest, by all means, but don't do it in a way that can damage the stature of our nation.'

Glazer was appalled. 'You can talk to me like that? You see me as a senile idiot who can be knocked over by cheap emotional appeals?'

'I was trying to reason with you.'

'Reason is for reasonable men to use! You'll use coercion, but first you try something gentler, more dishonest. That's your concept of civilised persuasion, isn't it?' He folded his arms and sank back in his seat. 'Do what you think you have to do, but rely on this – I'll make my protest heard.'

Several times in the next few minutes Avrum Maller tried to muster an argument that would at least make Glazer consider revising his plan. He said nothing, however, for he disliked campaigns where the chances of victory were so slim. Eventually they all sat in silence. Maller, Singer and Danzig worked at drawing a sense of prevailing unity from each other, while Abraham Glazer watched the sky, feeling more calm than he had for a long time.

At the rear of the first-class seating area, David Mendel

and Yosef Mark were piecing together an approach that would, hopefully, reduce the chances of a dangerous confrontation.

'We have to assume the man is here to harm the commissioners,' Mendel said. 'If we are wrong it does not really matter, but I think we have to convince ourselves that he *is* directly opposed to our interests.' It was a piece of advice handed out early in training but often forgotten, especially by men like Yosef Mark: never entertain doubts about the intentions of a suspect, and always believe the worst.

'I keep seeing three problems,' Mark said.

'Name them.'

'The suspect and the two CIA men. They might as well be the enemy, the way they go on. And they won't be pleased at the idea of us trying to take their glory away.'

'But there is a clear imperative to do so. They are simply watching the man for the moment. I think we have to walk in and take him.'

'He may know who we are.'

'If the commissioners are his target,' Mendel said, 'then he almost certainly knows us. No element of surprise. I think a heavy subterfuge is needed.'

'I'm no good at things like that.'

Yosef Mark was not good at much at all, Mendel thought, apart from close-quarter combat and straightforward, dogged pursuit. He was also good with a gun, which was why he had been chosen to partner Mendel on this mission. 'It is simple enough to devise a technique, Yosef. Think first of the man. What is he watching for? Security personnel. Little else. Anyone lacking the earmarks of security will virtually be cancelled by his observation. So, we have to become our opposites.'

'What would that be?'

Mendel realised he would never be an instructor. Already, he was losing patience. 'It would be the opposite of two alert, tidy, sober security men. In short, a pair of sluggish, dishevelled drunks.'

Mark did not warm to the idea. 'Drunks? On a plane?'

'There's as much to drink on a plane as you'll find anywhere else. And the psychology of such a subterfuge is good. To a man waiting to commit a crime, there is nothing more upsetting than disorder. Chaos, however mild, tends to confuse his drive. The likeliest way for him to react, I would say, is by pretending to sleep, or to look away. He can't afford involvement with friendly drunks, can he?'

Mark clearly wanted to argue with that, but his misgivings did not form themselves readily into words. Mendel, on the other hand, knew the flaw was in the tidiness. Hardly anybody reacted by the book. Just the same, he was keen to use the tactic.

'What if there definitely is a bomb on his person? I mean, can we be sure of disarming it?'

Mendel swallowed his impatience again. 'Which is worse? That he is loose with a bomb, or in custody with one? Your negative thinking will cause you harm, one day.' It would also, without a doubt, ensure that he never partnered David Mendel on any more important jobs. 'We have to grab him and take him bodily to the vacant supplies locker at the rear of the plane. Once we are there, we can start worrying about the hypothetical explosives.'

For a few more minutes they discussed the method of immobilising their man. They settled for a simple neck and arm lock, coupled with the agent's friend, carotid pressure, in the event of a violent struggle.

'What about the CIA? Do we just walk past them?'

Mendel nodded. 'It will be the best way. They will only argue if we try to make them see we take automatic control in this kind of situation.'

Five minutes later, with one brief rehearsal of the drunk act behind them, they began moving along the passage to the forward tourist class cabin. Kay Morgan was standing near the door, flushed and smiling nervously.

'Hello,' she said to Mendel, ignoring his partner. 'You going in there?'

'I'm afraid we have to.' Mendel had a sudden idea. There was nothing like refining the act whenever it was possible. 'Would you do something for us?'

'Oh, sure.' Nothing, her eager face said, would give her more pleasure.

'First, tell us exactly where this suspicious person is

sitting.' He already had the location from the Captain, but it never hurt to double-check. When Kay had confirmed the seat position and number, Mendel drew her aside. 'We are going to pretend we've had too much to drink. It would help if you walked ahead of us, as if you were showing us back to our seats. You will mask our faces a little, and that would be a big help.'

Kay thought about it. Her enthusiasm had dipped a little. 'I wouldn't want to mess it up for you . . .'

'Oh, you won't. I'm sure you'll do it perfectly.' He gave her the widening of the eyes that had drawn her on to his beam earlier. 'Simply walk two or three steps in front of us. When you pass the man's seat, run to the far end of the cabin and open the door for us. Straightforward.' He smiled, passing on his confidence. 'I will make sure you are commended. Officially.'

'Well, OK, I guess. But listen, those other two are in there, sitting just past the door. They're watching the man.'

'We are aware of that,' Mendel told her.

'And it does not trouble us,' Yosef Mark added, collecting a visual rebuke for his pains.

They were lining up for the start of their act, Mendel with his right arm around Mark's neck and both with their heads down and touching, when the door slid open and Lou Sherman walked out of the cabin. He looked at the stewardess, then at the two agents in their awkward embrace.

'What the hell is this?'

Mendel disentangled himself and stepped forward, easing Kay firmly aside. 'We are going to take that man.'

Sherman reacted instantly. He put his hand on Mendel's chest and pushed, keeping up the pressure until the Israeli was against the wall. Mark put a hand on Sherman's arm, then stopped. Mendel was eye-signalling for calm.

'You keep your goddamn schnozz out, hear?' Sherman's jaw was trembling and his eyes were wild. 'This is our affair. We can handle it. Now push off!' He stepped back, waiting for Mendel to move.

'The man could be planning an attack on the commissioners,' Mendel said, remaining where he was. 'In such a case, we are empowered to take action. I advise you to leave it to us.'

'Shove the advice up your keester!' Sherman jabbed a finger against the Israeli's breastbone. 'This is one piece of territory you don't grab!'

'There is a clear ruling—'

'That we police the aircraft, which is just what we're doing, and you're in the way.'

'I don't intend to argue.'

Yosef Mark was looking from Kay, flustered and wringing her hands, to Sherman with his spread-footed stance. This kind of squabble was nowhere in his understanding of the job. He was trained to do things, not to negotiate or argue. He was avoiding Mendel's eyes now, nervous of receiving a message he would not comprehend.

'I'm not arguing, either,' Sherman was saying. 'I'm telling you straight. You're obstructing agents of the CIA engaged on government business. You're out of line, big man . . .'

'You are the one who is obstructing, Mr Sherman. I will say it just one more time, leave this to us.'

Dan Bradley came out of the cabin and stared at them all. Sherman went on gaping at Mendel. Then Mendel brought up his right hand slowly. He was holding a Beretta pistol. Sherman took an astonished step backwards and walked into the point of Mark's gun, which had appeared an instant after Mendel's.

'For Christ's sake . . .' Sherman moved away from the cabin door, prompted by the jerking of Mendel's firearm. Mark, on home territory at last, covered Bradley.

'I regret doing this,' Mendel said gravely, 'but there is no alternative.'

'You'll suffer, boy, put money on it, you'll go down . . .'

'Perhaps, Mr Sherman. But I have to consider priorities. For the moment, the suspect in that cabin is my principal concern.'

Dan Bradley allowed himself to be ushered alongside his partner. All the time he was watching Mendel's gun, wondering where it came from. He had spotted the one under his arm a long time ago, but that was not it. How much hardware did these guys carry?

'Nobody pulls a gun on one of us and gets away with his feathers intact,' Sherman growled. 'What do you plan to do with us now, Superjew? Get your girlfriend to keep us covered while you go and grab some glory?'

'No. I am going to talk to you.'

'We're not listening,' Sherman said petulantly.

'You should. The only reason I am holding a gun is because without it you would not be under control long enough to listen to sense. Make no mistake: if I am attacked I will use my gun, and whatever risk you think I might take by doing so, I will do it nevertheless. My partner will do the same.'

Kay Morgan had pressed her back to the cabin door, watching Mendel with childish wonderment. She had never been involved in anything so dramatic, and it was staggering to see just how calm and superior the Israeli could be under pressure. Compared to him, Dan Bradley looked like a boy scout, all nervy and fidgeting. Sherman was just a bull, and not a very powerful one. In a taut kind of way, she was enjoying it all.

'It is clear,' Mendel went on, 'that you will not agree with us on the matter of precedence here. But has it occurred to you what might be entailed in arresting that man? If he is a guerrilla worker of any kind, he will have come equipped to defend himself properly. We are trained to deal with such people. I know you are not.'

'Who says?' Sherman asked. 'I've personally disarmed bombers and terrorists—'

'Not the kind who are sent on missions of high risk and political assassination. Not the international variety, Mr Sherman. They are murderers by reflex; they are not like ordinary criminals or revolutionaries. Even their own masters treat them with great care.'

'Very interesting,' Sherman sighed, 'but who says this guy is a high-power assassin, anyway? He doesn't look too special to me.'

'Seems quite ordinary,' Bradley agreed.

'And so he should, if he is any good at his job.' Mendel smiled faintly. 'The point is, we cannot take the risk of his being ordinary. That is why I insist we deal with him.'

Before Sherman could say anything else, Mendel came close and lowered his voice confidentially. 'I promise you, as soon as we have the man properly under control, responsibility for his formal arrest and custody will be passed to you.'

That silenced Sherman for almost a minute. He looked at his partner a couple of times, drawing nothing but vacant dependence from him, and finally threw up his hands, letting them fall again and slap his legs. 'If you do it just like you say . . .'

'I have promised.'

'Right. Go ahead.'

Mendel hesitated. 'You will promise, in return, not to interfere until he is taken?'

'We promise. There's some integrity on this side, too, you know.'

In a short time they were ready again. Mendel and Mark leaned close together with their heads lowered, and Kay stood in front of them, ready to open the door.

Dan Bradley, standing several feet away, turned to his partner. 'You surprised me, giving in like that.'

Sherman looked mystified. 'Give in? What did I give in to?'

'Well . . .'

'I gave in to letting those clowns do the dangerous bit and leave the official kudos to us. You call that some kind of surrender?'

Kay opened the door and they began moving forward. Two steps inside the cabin she stopped abruptly. Mark bumped into her before he could catch himself.

'What's wrong?' Mendel whispered harshly, keeping his head low.

'He's not there,' Kay whispered back. 'I don't see him anywhere.'

Sally Judson had chewed the rounded tips off both thumb nails and was starting to work on her index fingers. Beside her Paul Brent was tensely riffling his script with no intention of reading it any more.

'Say what you like,' Sally mumbled. 'Things just aren't under control.'

'You don't know that. You can't know. Those guys out there are CIA, and we all know there's some kind of VIP group on board. Add it all together, you've got a situation that has to be contained. They're not going to do anything too obvious.'

'I don't expect an OK Corral shootout. What I'm saying is, the good guys have stepped outside, and so has the villain. In opposite directions. And what was all that up at the door a minute ago? That stewardess looked like she was going to wet herself.'

'Please, honey, leave it to the troops.'

She squirmed closer to him, putting her head on his arm. 'I don't like being in the firing line. Why can't we move?'

'That would be suspicious. We don't want to do anything that might get the guy's back up.'

'I'm nervous.' Her fingers tightened on his elbow. 'Talk to me, Paul. Distract me. Make me forget there's a noodle running around loose with a gun and maybe bombs and we're up in the air and can't run away from him . . .'

'I'm impressed with your cool.' He put the script on the floor and took her hand. 'Let Daddy tell you what's going to happen when we get to London—'

'*If* we get to London.'

'Whatever. We're going to check into our hotel, and Daddy's going to shower all this mediocrity off him and go right out and find a publicist. We're going to spend money we don't have on photo calls, interviews, flashy restaurants where people get seen, seats for premières and modest bribes to anybody with enough push to get me noticed.' He ruffled her hair and hoped his own nervousness was hidden. Closeness to danger, especially at times when his life was feeling precious to him, was just like living out the childhood fear of the bogey-man coming before the party started. The way things were stacked, Paul could never see himself being really secure inside. Right now it was the uncertainty about the character with the gun. Later, even when he made it to the top, he would sit around his penthouse waiting for a phone call to say he had to give it all back.

That was showbiz, the half-world where everybody smiled to cover their anxiety, twenty-four hours a day.

'Nice try,' Sally said.

'If that didn't work, try sucking your thumb,' Paul suggested.

'Look, that guy isn't here, is he? I mean, we can move to another seat without running the risk of upsetting him.'

'If you insist.' Paul disentangled himself from her and made to stand up. 'Come on, we'll get near a window, so we can jump out if things get really hot.'

As they stepped into the aisle the forward door opened and David Mendel came in again, alone this time and making for Paul. He was only two yards away when the rear cabin door was opened and Nick Turnbull entered, dabbing at his freshly-washed face, like a man testing a recent shave.

'Are you Mr Brent?' Mendel asked, then caught sight of Turnbull skidding to a halt, gaping in their direction. Paul suddenly found himself being thrust to one side as Mendel darted past him. Sally turned too quickly and toppled into an empty seat.

'Don't come near me!' Turnbull took three quick paces back and brought out the silver pen, holding it at arms length.

Mendel kept moving, doubled over with his hands out in front. 'Drop it!' he yelled. 'Drop it!'

Turnbull raised the pen, aiming it straight at Paul, who was pushing himself upright against the arm of a seat. 'I'll shoot him!' Turnbull warned. 'I will. I'll do it!'

Mendel stopped, braking himself with heels and hands. Crouching a few feet from Turnbull he turned his head swiftly and saw the target, standing awkwardly in mid-aisle, his mouth hanging open. 'Don't try it,' he growled.

'Get back then, get clear away from me!' Turnbull's head bobbed wildly as he took a brave, threatening step forward. 'The spade gets a hole in him if you don't shift!'

Most of the passengers were in the forward rows of seats and it took a moment for the situation to impress itself on them. One young woman, looking over her headrest and seeing Sally hunched near the floor behind, began asking what was wrong, then saw it all and converted her words to a shrill scream. Instantly the others began moving, turning to see, understanding there was trouble. Eight people rushed the forward door, colliding with Yosef Mark. Behind him Kay Morgan pushed her way through, her face frightened as she tried to locate Mendel. Lou Sherman appeared, too, waving his gun and shoving Kay as if she were a riot shield. Seeing the pistol a girl began screaming and waving her arms, hitting an old lady in the mouth with her elbow.

Kay stumbled up beside Paul Brent as Mendel started inching back from his target. In her fear she wanted to reach out to him, pull him right away from harm. Paul grasped her elbow, forced her to remain still. Turnbull's distress was climbing as the people at the door clawed and screamed and kicked each other.

'Be sensible,' Mendel warned, still moving back.

Turnbull blinked at him, then jerked, seeing the gun waving by the door. His lips tightened in a rictus of terror and he fired the bullet into Kay's chest.

A woman by the door fainted and Sherman leapt over her, sprinting along the aisle as Turnbull went backwards through the far door. 'You stupid bungling kike!' He pushed past the crouching Mendel and went after Turnbull, his gun in a fixed line ahead of him.

Paul Brent was holding Kay's head up off the floor, yelling at Sally to find a doctor or something. Mendel, frozen by what had happened, kept staring at the growing patch of red on Kay's blouse. She was conscious but did not appear to know what was going on around her.

Dan Bradley appeared behind Mendel. 'Can I help?'

Mendel looked up, becoming alert again. 'Tell the Captain.' He reached down and tore open Kay's blouse, then pressed his folded handkerchief against the wound. 'And you could control the panic, perhaps.'

'Right. Where's my partner?'

Yosef Mark came forward. 'He is chasing our gunman.'

'Maybe I'd better get after him—'

'No, please,' Mendel insisted. 'You can be of more help here. These people must be brought under control. Yosef, try to find a doctor or someone with medical training. Then go to the commissioners, tell them what has happened, and stay near them.' He raised one corner of the handkerchief, trying not to believe the wound was as bad as it looked.

'Try talking to her,' Paul Brent whispered. 'She looks so pale. Maybe a voice would help her . . .'

'She needs her strength,' Mendel said. Kay was looking at the strong hand pressing her chest. Mendel nodded reassuringly at her, and she smiled weakly. 'You will be fine,' Mendel said softly, hoping it might be true.

The woman who had fainted was trying to drag herself to her feet by the door. Dan Bradley ignored her as he went into the passage and confronted the groups of people huddled around the galley area. Strangers were comforting strangers, families were locked in embraces of fright.

As Dan began to tell them everything was all right, there was another shot, further back in the plane. The hubbub started again and fresh screams broke out somewhere behind Bradley. He dropped the idea of talking, there was too much disorder anyway. He headed for the door to the flight deck, pushing past a cluster of old ladies and a man who was trying not to be sick.

Jo Hampton caught his sleeve as he went past.

'Is it bad?'

Dan Bradley shrugged, noticing how her face was ready to collapse if he said yes. 'We'll see, honey.' He took her hand gently from his arm. 'You'll have to excuse me. I need to talk to the Captain.'

A third shot sounded through the plane, harsh and without echo. Jo's lip started trembling and Dan moved off before she began to cry. His mind was closed suddenly, accepting only the summary. There was bad trouble, getting worse. That was the essence, and he held it in his head as he stepped on to the flight deck. No sense getting emotional before he had to – after all, the worst that could happen was the worst that could happen.

FIFTEEN

The temporary mortuary was a vacant supply room, the ground floor of a small building two hundred yards from the control tower. The place had not been in use for over a year, and the fusty odours of dust and mouldering damp hung in the air like a dispiriting fog.

When Commander Brooke walked in the place was busy. Men from the Home Office forensic team were collecting fragments of cloth, fingernail clippings and blood smears from the six bodies laid out on trestle tables. Two photographers were systematically recording the wounds while a third took frontal and profile pictures of the faces. One body, the last to be brought down by the riot squad officers, had no discernible features, but the young man photographed it anyway.

Dr Hemsley, the pathologist who had been brought in to supervise the official cataloguing, looked up from the body of the fence guard, McKenna, a fragment of soft-nosed bullet in his forceps. 'Dorian,' he cried, putting down the forceps and wiping his hands on a towel. 'I thought you'd be here.' He came across to where Brooke was standing, surveying the carnage.

'We've met up in better circumstances, John.'

'There'll be worse times yet, the way things are going these days.' The pathologist was the same height as the Commander, stockier, with a more pallid complexion. He blinked around him through thick lenses and sighed. 'It's like the war all over again.'

'Very one-sided, this conflict. We can't lift a finger, John. It's bloody terrifying.' He walked over to the nearest table and nodded towards the body. 'I've come about this one. Her father's here.'

'Oh dear.'

'I know,' Brooke groaned. 'We should have fobbed him off and slipped him a sedative until we got her back to town, but he's a very determined man, and I haven't the heart to argue with him.'

'How did he find out so soon?'

'Apparently he quite often comes in to pick her up when she's been on nights. He works over in Hounslow. He saw the road blocks and started asking difficult questions. Then he got to a phone box and called up PR. When he heard the trouble was in the tower there was no stopping him.'

'Well, it'll take care of one formal identification, anyway. But he can't see her like this.' An attendant in a red rubber apron responded to Hemsley's wave and came towards them. 'Make the body presentable, will you?' Hemsley said. 'Then get it on to a trolley and put it in the ante-room.'

Brooke watched for a moment as the man began sponging the dark red blood from the strangely peaceful face. The eyes were still open and the attendant gently drew down the lids, holding them there for a moment before taking his hand away. The splintered bones of her chest and shoulders were covered with wads of cotton wool and a sheet was placed over the padding. The result was not particularly attractive, but it reduced the impression of suspended violence in the girl's appearance.

'She was dead before she hit the ground,' Hemsley remarked. 'Landed on her back, so at least there's something left for the relatives to look at.'

'I'd rather face that gunman than go through the next few minutes,' Brooke said. 'How the hell do you explain?'

'You don't. Explanations don't soothe anyone when it comes to this kind of sudden loss. They usually want one of two things: release from their grief or revenge. Explaining doesn't pave the way for either.'

'He sounds vengeful, in a stunned kind of way.'

'In that case, Dorian, just you concentrate on keeping him from doing anything silly. That'll get you through the bad part.'

When the body had been put on a trolley and placed in the small ante-room, Brooke went outside and waved to his aide, who came in a minute later with Mr Malcolm. He was tall and stooped, a man with the kind of eyes suited to mourning. He clumped towards Brooke in his heavy brogues and stared at him.

'This way please, Mr Malcolm.'

All three walked over to the corner where the trolley was standing. Brooke went to the end and grasped the sheet covering her face. He watched the father, seeing the tension build in him, the tightening around the mouth as the man put up one last desperate prayer that it was all a dreadful mistake, that this was not his girl. Brooke lowered the sheet, exposing the sleeping face, and the father's groan was like a knife in him.

'Oh, dear God . . .' Tears slid forward as he bent down, putting his face close to hers. This had been his Jessie, the daughter he had read stories to, taken for walks, controlled and cared for as she grew. A howl escaped the man and he reached forward to embrace her.

'No, don't,' Brooke warned, restraining the shaking hands. 'Please, Mr Malcolm. Don't touch her.'

For an instant there was anger on the sorrowing face, then he sagged and put forward one gentle hand, stroking a curl of hair. 'My poor darling.' His fingers trailed down along the cold cheek, then withdrew and closed, retaining the touch forever. He straightened and looked at the Commander. 'Have they been taken yet?'

'No,' Brooke said. 'Not yet. But we'll get them.'

'Yes.' Mr Malcolm nodded slowly, his eyes wandering back to Jessie's face. 'I'll wait until you do.'

Brooke carefully replaced the cover over the face. He led Malcolm by the arm as far as the door and stopped. 'You must go home,' he said firmly. 'Your wife will have to be told. She needs you. There's nothing you can do here.'

'I don't want to go.' The man's voice was growing harder. 'I have a right to stay, and I will stay.'

Brooke put some edge into his own voice. 'What good will that do? If you've thoughts of going anywhere near those terrorists I must tell you it's impossible.' He was wasting his breath. Malcolm was staring past him, resolved, immovable. The Commander decided to drop the argument. 'If you must wait, you'll have to remain in one of the terminal buildings. And please, Mr Malcolm, don't try to do anything. There's no chance of it working, whatever you may have in mind.'

The man glanced back at the shape on the trolley, then allowed the aide to lead him away.

Brooke spent the next thirty minutes taking progress reports from his people in the terminals. His memories of the war were like this, chaos and fear on every side, with only a trace of civilised order to prevent rioting. The worst scenes were in Terminal 3. By the wide entry two girls were standing with their arms around each other, sobbing quietly. An older woman was talking to them steadily, bringing down their hysteria.

'A near thing, that.'

Brooke turned and saw Jamieson, one of the SPG officers, falling into step beside him.

'What happened to them?'

'Nothing. But they were on their way across to the ladies' room when the bomb went off. The shocks have been piling up for them since then. The little redhead, she'd stopped for a couple of seconds to tighten the straps on her sandals. Her mate stopped, too, when she thought she saw a film star. They added it all up, of course. Without the delays they'd have been inside before anything happened.'

'There must be a few others in the same boat.'

Jamieson nodded. 'Plenty. There's three I know of. One changed her mind about going, the other two were trying to find the place when it blew up. It's bloody terrible the way it's getting to some people. Look.' He was pointing at a man on his knees by an information bay. He was rocking back and forward, hugging a crumpled box of chocolates to his chest. Tears were streaming down his face. 'God knows what's going on in his head.'

Brooke stopped by an empty baggage trolley and leaned his elbows on the handle. 'What's the score in here, then?'

'We're containing things. Every cupboard, corner and water bucket's been checked, the toilets have been double-checked, and we've roped-off everything that isn't necessary to smooth running. Not that anything's running smoothly. All we can do is cope.'

'No suspicious characters?'

Jamieson smiled grimly. 'Dozens of them. I mean, where to you start? We can't evacuate the building without creating havoc somewhere else, so we just watch, ask questions, shadow the ones that look dodgy and try to give the impression we've got everything in hand.'

'Are the anti-bomb people still working?'

'Yes. We've had to put up screens. Some of the debris coming out of there is very messy.'

'Right,' the Commander sighed. 'I won't detain you. Keep me posted if anything flares up.'

For a few more minutes he remained there, leaning, watching. Whatever else terrorism was, it was effective. People were milling around like children who had lost their parents. Fear had deprived them of direction. Old ladies were sitting on the benches clutching handkerchiefs and younger ones were asking everyone in sight what was happening now, what would they do. An angry man near Brooke was shouting at a member of the staff, demanding to know everything, while his wife stood by, lank and silent, her faith in a secure society probably shattered for ever. Four wealthy-looking Americans, two men and two women, were standing with their well-clad backs to the wall, astonished they could be as vulnerable as the poorer members of society.

As the Commander turned to leave a man in a black overcoat came striding towards him from the main entrance.

'Commander Brooke?' The voice had the polish of an authoritarian used to public speaking. It was vaguely familiar.

'Yes. Who are you?'

'Whiteside, Home Office. I spoke to you earlier on the telephone.'

'Oh, yes. How can I help you?'

'I want to talk. Right away. Where can we go?'

Brooke led the way outside and across to the co-ordination room. In the office Whiteside installed himself behind the desk and left Brooke to stand uncomfortably in the middle of the floor.

'Well, old bean, you've made a right muck-up of things so far.' It was said with the casual aplomb of a man remarking on a cricket score.

The dull weariness lifted suddenly, leaving Brooke sharp, aware of every problem. He moved closer to the desk, squinting at Whiteside. 'That's a little easy for you to say, isn't it? Let me have some constructive criticism and maybe I'll start listening to you.'

'You'll listen to me whatever I have to say.' The face was square, sure of itself. Precise wings of silver grey sat over each ear like a heraldic seal of authority. 'The position here is chaotic. There are people running right and left, doing what they please. I didn't see one sign of proper containment as I came in. Surely, while you're playing your waiting game, you could be addressing yourself to the problem of order, Commander? Simple, basic order. Is it too much to ask?'

'Some people are running about doing their own thing with your direct sanction,' Brooke snapped. 'That Israeli Colonel, for one. He's vanished and his deputy's making very hollow excuses. The CIA delegation's running its own show, too. It's all I can do to stop them taking over.'

Whiteside waved the outburst aside. 'They are not children, Commander. They won't do anything irresponsible, despite what you think of them. The disorder I'm talking about is in the terminal buildings, in the car parks and on the roads surrounding Heathrow. Do you realise that people are getting on planes, changing their minds and getting off again? And do you know that whole herds of them are collecting on walkways and aprons trying to see what's going on in the tower?'

'Look, we've been making every effort—'

'And are you aware there's a crowd-pleasing barrister swaying a chunk of the public in Terminal 1 with his revolutionary rhetoric? Customs is in a turmoil, PR and enquiry services are crippled, people waiting for relatives are setting up pockets of group hysteria, and the baggage-handling staff are refusing to drive out on to certain runways? I can go on and on. I've had a list as long as your arm over the phone, and a longer one since I got here.'

'Nobody could do any better than we're doing at present.'

'Nobody could do much now, I'll grant you. Because it's all been allowed to slip from the start.'

'Look, my report will go forward alongside your snap assessment, Mr Whiteside. We'll let the Home Secretary make up his own mind about who's telling it straight. Just what are you here for?'

Whiteside unbuttoned his coat and made a deliberately symbolic gesture of pushing the Commander's papers to one side of the desk. 'I'm taking over.'

'Good luck. What secret magic are you going to spring on us?'

'None. I'm simply going to get this show organised. We'll start by clearing the airport.'

Brooke almost jumped. 'What? Are you some kind of bloody nut case?'

'Your abuse will be noted, along with the rest of your manifest shortcomings. The Head of Security and the officer in charge of SPG will be instructed in what to do, and they'll do it. It's really quite straightforward when you get your thinking straight, Brooke.'

'But the terrorists have specifically demanded we let everything run as usual.'

For a moment some emotion flickered across Whiteside's face. 'They will have to be disappointed, then. I can't see it making much difference to the situation in the tower, anyway. We want this place clear of civilians. When that Washington plane lands, the runways and approaches and every inch of ground on the perimeter will be occupied by troops.'

'And how do they get in?'

'By the usual routes, of course.'

Brooke smiled grimly. 'Masterly thinking. Those buggering *routes*, as you call them, will be jammed for hours if you try to evacuate this place.'

The calm blue eyes wavered. 'Not necessarily . . .'

'And what about flights coming in? There'll be hundreds

of civilians coming tramping through the place in the next hour. We can't put out divert calls to all the craft, and even if we could the terrorists would start making their reprisals. No cancellations, they said. I happen to take these bastards seriously. They'll blow people to bits as soon as they get wind of your brilliant manoeuvres.'

'That is enough!' Whiteside shouted, and in the loss of temper Brooke saw the sudden uncertainty of a man losing his habitual confidence, too. 'I will not be talked to in that fashion!'

'Fair enough.' Brooke turned and made for the door. 'I'll await your orders, in silence.'

'Wait . . .' Whiteside flattened his hands on the desk and bit back his anger. 'Brooke, something drastic *has* to be done. We have to make big waves, don't you understand? The Prime Minister's up in arms, the Israelis are leaning on us, half the European press will be on to us in no time – it has to look like we're handling things the best possible way.'

'We have been, so far. There wasn't space for theatricals.'

'It's my neck on the line, Brooke!'

'I'm glad it's not mine, any longer.'

Whiteside suddenly looked stricken. 'I didn't choose to take over. I was ordered to. If I'm to succeed here I'll need your full co-operation.'

'You'll get it. But I won't make excuses for you. And I won't be your scapegoat, either. If you try to implement your high-definition plans, you'll be deeper in the shit than I was when you got here. Bear that in mind and take your precautions now.' Brooke opened the door. 'If you need me I'll be over at that bomb site. They're hauling the remains of two women out of the rubble. I want to try and get some identification organised.' He closed the door and left.

On the way to the scene of the explosion he was stopped by the aide who had been with him at the mortuary. 'Don't ask me for any instructions,' Brooke warned the young man. 'I'm not the guv'nor here any more.'

'It's Mr Malcolm, sir.'

'What about him?'

'We've had to put him in restraint.'

Brooke took out his pipe, looked at it, and stuck it back in his pocket. 'All right. Tell me.'

'He was in the cafeteria in Terminal 3. There's a lot of security over there, and I'd asked one of the SPG chaps to keep an eye on him. Well, he saw the officer watching him, apparently, and he tried to dodge off into the crowd. The officer caught up with him, and Mr Malcolm turned violent. Terribly violent.'

Brooke nodded thoughtfully, remembering the great sad eyes and the heart-tearing loss in the man's voice. 'Fine,' he said. 'Have him taken home when he settles down. I only hope the poor sod got the boot in before they nailed him.'

There had been a long delay in getting Abd Al-Adwan away from the co-ordination area. Lennox, the big, dour Detective Inspector from Scotland Yard, refused to leave before he had more details of the charge. One official had told him just to hold the man until he received further orders. Another said the same thing, but added that the charge would probably be serious and would require clearance with the Home Office before it could be laid. Lennox did not work that way. He had been lumbered before and left to carry the can when the authorities suddenly decided they did not want a suspect held. They had a way of pulling out completely and denying they ever asked to have someone detained, let alone charged with anything. A copper's career could be stunted by the kind of stink those arrangements produced.

'I'll go,' Lennox informed the SPG Inspector, 'when the charge is written down for me, and when I know I can place the charge. Otherwise, my arse stays on this chair.' The clipped Glaswegian delivery added force to his words.

'How can I spell out the charge to you?' the Inspector appealed. 'All I was told to do was see that the Arab was locked up, pending a charge and an appearance before a magistrate in the morning.'

'Which morning?' Lennox demanded, lowering his bushy eyebrows. 'This one? Or tomorrow? It's all very well for you lot to consign villains to custody right, left and centre. Some of us get roasted for acting on orders like that.'

'Oh, well . . .' The harassed officer looked about him, trying to see someone who might be able to help. He did not even recognise the people nearby. 'I'll get someone with top line authority to sign a chitty or something. Will that help?'

'It's better than nothing,' Lennox said grudgingly.

'Right. I won't be long.' He paused. 'Where's the Arab just now?'

'In my car. It's locked, and there's a uniformed officer standing right beside it. Listen, before you go, can you tell me what it was this character did?'

The SPG man threw up his hands. 'Who knows? I'm only a small cog round here. I gather it was something to do with encouraging the terrorists.'

'The bastard,' Lennox said glumly.

'Quite. Excuse me, I'll get the bit of paper you need.'

Lennox folded his arms and stared ahead of him, blind to the coming and going of a dozen people, all intent on getting the record straight. Arabs, he was thinking. Out in Port Said they had known how to handle those jokers. Fire was met with fire. You did not try to argue with them; that only made them think you were soft. You got them by the neck and banged them against every wall in sight until they told you what they knew. And if it was a simple matter of punishment you had only one restriction: do not kill the prisoner. This whole circus, with security units and anti-terrorist bods and police and SPG supported everything Lennox had always believed about official policy towards hoodlums. They bent over backwards to be fair. Fair! To garbage, trash, the dregs who went on flouting the law because they knew it was administered by a bunch of democrats with limp wrists. Ten boys from the old-time Glasgow Central Division would have cleared this mess up in minutes. Straight in, crash, straight out. Easy.

Adwan had been at pains to maintain his stolid dignity

behind the windscreen of the police car, but his patience was coming under strain. It had been an hour, easily, and still he was there, with that idiotic-looking constable standing outside like a waxwork. He had no fears about what they might do, and he did not mind the possible discomfort of a police cell for a while. That was all part of the game. But this. He was bored. He ached to be out stretching his legs or, better still, arguing with a stupid policeman.

Two men were approaching the car. They wore zippered green combat jackets and their hair was cut very short. In the faint morning light they looked like flat-footed reinforcements for the buffoon outside the door. As they drew closer Adwan's weary appraisal tightened to anxiety. There was no mistaking those faces, or for that matter the soft-soled boots and the coarse green denim trousers. They were Israelis. Ridiculous as it seemed, *they were definitely Israelis*!

Outside, the taller of the two men smiled courteously to the constable. 'You are the assistant of Detective Inspector Lennox?'

'That's right,' the policeman said stiffly.

'He wishes to see you.' The man pointed in the direction of the doorway Lennox had gone through so long ago. 'We have been instructed to keep watch on your prisoner until you return.'

'Oh. Well. Right. Thanks very much.' The constable turned and marched off without another word.

The Israelis stood by the car for a few seconds, looking round them carefully, then the tall one turned and stared grimly through the glass at Adwan. His companion took a long, slender strip of metal from his pocket and applied it to the edge of the door. Barely breathing, Adwan watched as the man slapped the end of the instrument a couple of times. With a soft click, the car door opened.

'Good morning, Mr Adwan,' the tall one said, showing his teeth in an unfriendly smile. 'We've come to take you for a walk.' He reached in and grabbed the expensive collar, pulling the Arab out of the car.

'Let go of me!'

'This way. And don't make any more sound, Mr Adwan, or we will hurt you quite badly.'

They marched him hastily across the open ground between two buildings and dragged him along a narrow passage behind a vehicle enclosure. At the end of the passage there was another building, used for storing bulk refuse bins. Adwan was pulled and pushed between the huge containers until he stood in a clear area of floor, illuminated by a single bulb high in the ceiling. Another Israeli was there, a man whose authority was obvious even though he was dressed the same as the other two.

'My name is Zalman,' he said, coming forward with his hands on his hips, his gaunt features emphasised into Old Testament severity by the sharp angle of the light. He was the Colonel's deputy, and he was acting on initiative. 'I have no hesitation in identifying myself to you in this way, Mr Adwan, for I am sure you will not want to repeat my name to anyone.'

Adwan was trembling, trying to muster enough of his dignity to dominate the gathering. 'You have made a mistake, doing this.'

'Threatening talk,' Zalman said. 'Empty talk. Try not to insult my credulity, please. You pose no threat to me.'

'Why have you brought me? I am in police custody—'

'No, you are in mine. Sit down, Mr Adwan.'

An oil drum was pushed forward by one of the men behind the Arab and he sat down sharply, keeping his eyes on Zalman. 'Tell me, what is it you want?'

'Two things. One: tell us what your young friend in the control tower is planning to do. Two: supply us with the names of all members of the Brotherhood of Zenima.'

'I will tell you nothing!' Adwan's cheek was jerking, as if someone held his lower eyelid by an invisible string. 'This is an outrage!'

'Of course,' Zalman said patiently. The other two men moved in close, one on either side of the Arab. 'And what your friend has done, that is civilised, I suppose?' He bent down, bringing his face in close. 'You will answer my questions, or my soldiers will show you what an outrage is really like.'

Adwan tried to stand up again and a hand came down on his shoulder, heavy and hard. As he resumed his uncomfortable seat a hand from the other side slapped him sharply on the back of the head. He howled, not meaning to, and Zalman moved back a few paces. 'I have no idea what Kalim is planning. I swear it.'

The tall soldier took a handful of the luxuriant hair and pulled it upwards swiftly.

'I swear!' Adwan roared, through tears of pain.

The other soldier caught his arm and held it fully extended, then began forcing it back and up.

'Make them stop! I cannot answer your question!'

Zalman shook his head. 'I have to be sure,' he said.

It took less than a minute of increasing torsion and pressure to dislocate Adwan's shoulder and tear the deltoid muscle. His screams were muffled behind a folded scarf, and when the arm was finally released he emitted a roar so loud it was necessary to push the material right into his mouth to deaden the noise.

After being allowed a few minutes to recover, he was asked the question again. 'I know nothing . . .' Saliva dribbled along his chin as he struggled to control the shuddering of his jaw. 'May I drink some water? I am feeling ill—'

'No.' Zalman withdrew to the far edge of the pool of light. 'I believe you know nothing of your friend's plans. So now I will ask you to answer my second question. You can give me an answer, so please don't put yourself to further pain by making a denial.'

Adwan touched his injured shoulder cautiously. The disorder of his face had changed him. He was a sweating, frightened man, older suddenly and bereft of resistance. 'Do you know what would happen to me?'

'I know what will happen if you don't talk,' Zalman said crisply. 'Your internal rules do not concern me.'

'But membership of the Brotherhood is secret – at the higher levels there are men who would ruin me if I disclosed their identity. Please, I ask you to consider . . .'

Zalman responded by nodding to his soldiers. Adwan's other arm was raised and folded behind his back. The tall soldier held the fingers and started to pull them towards the shoulder, buckling the wrist simultaneously.

'Very well! Please . . .' The arm was released and Adwan drew it across his eyes, clearing the droplets of sweat. 'Tell me, first, will it be known who told you?'

'We shall say nothing.' Zalman took a small notebook from his pocket and removed the pencil from its leather pocket. 'Please proceed.'

For five halting minutes Adwan reeled off the information, pausing sometimes to remember, at other times correcting himself. Finally, when Zalman had covered one page with names, he asked if the list was truly complete. 'We believe in being particularly thorough,' he explained. 'If we were to learn, one day, that you had protected anyone . . .'

'No, I swear to you, that is the entire list. What will you do to them?'

'Nothing too obvious, Mr Adwan. Shall we say they will be discouraged, strongly, from allowing their young men to play at warriors in future.'

When Adwan returned alone to the police car, Lennox and the constable both grabbed him at once. Their prisoner fainted from the onslaught before he could be ordered to explain. Something about the frightful change in him told Lennox there would be no point in trying to find out, anyway.

Zalman and the tall soldier remained in the small building for a time to examine the list.

'It will be a long operation,' the soldier observed. 'They will put up strong defences when they realise what is happening.'

'I know,' Zalman sighed, closing the notebook and pocketing it. 'But it will be done, nevertheless. I can see a hundred difficulties in our path already, and there are probably another hundred I can't see.'

'Will it really achieve very much?'

'Of course.' Zalman appeared surprised that such a question should be asked. 'It restores the balance, doesn't it? Our order, our law of procedure.' He went to the tiny window and wiped the dust from the glass. The sky was growing bright over in the east. 'Whatever happens here this morning,' he said, 'we can now be sure we will have the last word.'

SIXTEEN

Of the three hundred and twenty-four passengers on board Pan Am 898, only a handful had not joined in the uproar. Senior Steward Philip O'Malley was knocked out early in the furore and had to be given a large infusion of brandy before he would go back out amongst the milling, shouting, frightened mob who were filling passageways and refusing to return to their seats. David Mendel, assisted by Second Officer Bob Fields, began working on the people in groups of four and five, explaining there was no point in panicking, and pointing out the wisdom of sitting tight until the plane landed. Minute by minute, working from one end of the craft to the other, the two men reduced the number of resisting elements by half, and as more people sat down, more were inclined to follow their lead. The atmosphere in the Boeing changed gradually from anguished hysteria to controlled disquiet.

Stewardesses circulated with coffee, tea and free shots of spirits. Dan Bradley went round behind them, answering what questions he could and identifying himself as a peacemaker, one they could rely on. Apart from a few wild variations, most people had the same story: there was a fugitive on board, but he had been taken in hand. To tidy up their ruffled wits and restore the dignity that had left them for a while, a number of passengers talked aggressively about writing to their Congressmen, while others made harsh verbal drafts of letters and petitions to the airline, asking just where they got off, letting a thing like that happen. The little girl called Betsy began running around the cabin again, reminding everybody she was four. Mrs Ida Craig, who had been sick a few times already, was wondering if she could cope with one more bout.

Kay Morgan had been moved to a small cubicle with a bunk and basic medical facilities. A retired doctor had been found among the passengers, but he admitted he was hopeless when it came to trauma surgery, and apart from examining Kay thoroughly and declaring her to be in no immediate danger, he did no more than administer a pain-killing shot from the plane's emergency box.

'The bullet's still in there,' he said, 'but I reckon it's lodged in the sternum. Won't do too much harm for the time being. Bleeding's superficial, nothing vital's been hit.'

For minutes after the doctor had gone, David Mendel stood outside the cubicle, listening to the soothing voice of the stewardess assigned to sit with Kay. In there, he was thinking, was either a clear sign that he was bad luck for people, or just a terrible accident. Either way it had cut him deeply. The shock that landed on Mendel when Kay was hit had widened, touching the area of his uncertainty. He was a crazy man, doing a crazy job. It took an effort to quench the panic, and even when he did there was no peace in its place.

He was touching the handle, opening the door, when his resolve came back. The man in him had to be suppressed. It was no vanity to believe she would want to see him, but he could not do that, no matter how much they both wanted it. He closed the door again softly, telling himself she was wounded enough. As he moved away towards the galley something broke in him. It felt like a silent cry, or perhaps it was that last tiny hope, the one that had pushed him towards the girl in the first place, finally dying.

Paul Brent looked in on Kay for a few minutes. He found her alert, almost cheerful, but the trauma had put a grey pallor on her face and her eyes were sunken. 'If that idiot had known anything about gunplay, he'd have hit me,' Paul told her, smiling. 'I just thought I'd drop by and thank you, honey.'

'What for? Saving your life?' She tried to laugh, but it was too much of an effort.

'No. For getting me the publicity. I spent half the flight talking about a new campaign, and suddenly it's handed to me. Can you see the headline? A real beauty.' He moved his arm in an elaborate sweep, conjuring the banner. ' "Actor Runs to Rescue in Skyjack Drama", or some such.' He touched her hair gently. 'Seriously, I'd have been glad to take that bullet for you. Get some rest now, hear?'

When he had gone, Kay told the other stewardess she would try to sleep. Behind her eyelids she struggled to think of nothing, to accept what had happened and to simply wait. Above all, she would not dwell on the ruin of her hopes for the next few days. David Mendel would come and see her soon. That would help.

On the flight deck Harry Turner was trying to channel his anger. Sherman was leaning beside the door, providing no easy outlet for the Captain's wrath. When he spoke he confined himself to the shortest possible statements and answers.

'You damn nearly engineered a catastrophe,' Turner shouted. He was on his seat with his jacket off and shirt-sleeves rolled back. He looked like an irate foreman, brought to the limit of his wits by a sloppy work force. 'No use handing me that line about priority and necessity and all the rest of it. You blew your stack back there and it could have been the end, curtains. Have you any clue what it's like, piloting a plane with a stampede on board? These babies are delicate, you know. Forget all you heard about grenades going off and doing no damage. That's crap.' He paused and wiped the back of his hand across his mouth. 'You were sounding off about your report a while back. Let me tell you, my report on you is going to burn a hole right through the Head Office Investigator's desk.'

'Do what you think you have to do. I stand by my actions.'

That was the part that kept needling Harry Turner. Sherman was so damned *smug*. 'What is there to stand by? You fired off two shots, both of which missed the target and sent the passengers into a raging panic. You also punctured a section of fuselage that's created a problem in our pressurisation. And where's this weirdo you were chasing, this man who may have a bomb?' Harry threw his hands in the air. 'He's nowhere. You lost him. On a plane high up in the air, somebody's gotten away from the CIA. We're worse-off than when we started, aren't we? He's been activated now; he's like a hair trigger.'

'You're being alarmist,' Sherman said impatiently.

'Only a cretin wouldn't be! This whole flight has been one long series of alarms, and now we've got the big one.'

Sherman jerked his thumb upwards. 'If they hadn't been on board, none of it would have happened.'

'I'm not equipped to say that,' Harry retorted. 'And neither are you. Your anti-Semitism gets in the way of your thinking every time you open your mouth.'

Sherman stepped forward, a warning finger raised. 'Don't you use that kind of talk on me—'

'It fits. Now tell me, what's being done about locating this guy Turnbull? He has to be somewhere.'

'We're letting him lie low for a while. In cases of this sort it's been found best to let the fugitive catch his breath and take time to see how impossible his position is.'

Harry Turner was sneering. 'Fugitive! You live in a Hollywood dream, Sherman. The desperado is probably, at this moment, wiring the ass of this plane for the grand finale. And you stand around, applying your glib theory to the list of blunders you've already made.'

Bob Fields came back on to the deck and dropped into his seat by the Captain. 'It's not too bad out there, now. They're still rumbling, but they're being reasonable.'

'You might as well have saved yourself the trouble,' Harry said, without looking at Bob. 'Thanks to our friend here, they'll probably be charging up and down the aisles again any minute.'

Sherman turned and strode out through the door. He walked to the end of the short passage, then stopped, realising he had no destination in mind. He had only wanted to get off that deck.

'He really seems to have vanished,' Mendel's voice said.

Sherman spun round and saw the Israeli a few feet away, standing by the galley curtain, sipping water from a paper cup. 'This is your fault,' Sherman waded in. 'He's vanished and he's in a position to do more damage because you fluffed the preliminaries.' In retrospect it looked terrible. The idea of being handed an arrest with no trouble attached had seemed fine: now, the humiliation of agreeing to a thing like that, *and at gun point*, was crushing. 'I should have trusted my first instincts with you, Mendel.'

'I do wish you would leave personalities out of this,'

Mendel replied. 'We have a problem. It is a *joint* problem—'

'Oh, yeah, sure. Now you're in a fix you want to share the goodies.'

'Look at it any way you wish. But you failed to catch the man Turnbull, as I did. He is on the plane and probably armed. We have to find him, and soon.'

'We'll be landing soon. Maybe he'll stay under cover until then.'

'Have you lost your stomach for this one, Mr Sherman?'

A year ago he would have put one on the chin of anybody who said a thing like that. Now he just stood and stared, churning inside but finding no link between the urge and the ability to lash out.

Mendel crushed the paper cup and dropped it into a container on the wall. 'I am going to the rear of the plane to search for our man. Perhaps you and your associate could make a search of the toilets again. He may be moving forward without our knowledge.'

Sherman nodded and waited until the Israeli had gone before he leaned back against the panelling and rubbed his eyes. He had to face it, he was getting old. Too old for the job. The few bouts of temper he had expended were like holes in his energy pool. His legs felt as heavy as his mind, sluggish and slow to react. He had known before that he was into some kind of decline, but preferred to forget it. Now he could not, not after aiming a gun at nearly point blank range and missing. Twice. And not after finding, so many times in a few hours, that he could not dominate a situation the way he used to. The spite was about all he had left. The rest was a closing book.

He took his hands from his eyes and saw Dan Bradley standing in front of him. 'Yeah?'

'Nothing. I just got fed up comforting passengers. Thought I'd take a break.'

'No time for that.' The spectre of that desk job in Langley had loomed again, and it put movement into Sherman. He could still be his own man if he used the available time sensibly. Better he went down, if he had to, without a leash and collar on him. Better still if he managed to make a splash somewhere, big enough to cover the remainder of his professional decline. 'We have to search the toilets, the galleys, any nook where the guy might be hiding. There's still an emergency, don't forget that.'

They moved off towards the first cabin. On the way Dan Bradley noticed that his partner was walking with a stiffened spine. He had never seen that before. It looked odd. Like a man trying to appear much bigger than he really was.

Upstairs in the lounge, Avrum Maller returned from the wash room, accompanied by Yosef Mark. He took his seat among the others and rubbed his hands together briskly, demonstrating his confidence. 'It will not be long now,' he said. 'I am sure the situation can be contained until we have reached London. I have a good deal of faith in Mendel, and in Mark here, of course.'

Joel Singer went on looking depressed. 'If the man is after us, he will be determined. I shouldn't start feeling complacent.'

'I am not,' Maller snapped. 'But I am being positive, as we all should.'

'Until one of them gets you,' Abraham Glazer said, smiling. 'There will always be someone, from now on.'

'I suggest you hold your tongue,' Singer warned. 'I've no need to put up with your comments any more, now I'm convinced you're a traitor. Just close your mouth and keep your own counsel. You'll need all that breath when you're yapping to the press about what barbarians the rest of us are.'

Glazer complied, folding his hands on the table and narrowing his eyes against the brightness above the floor of cloud. How did someone like Sadat feel, he wondered, knowing the whole picture – as he must have done – before making a gesture of friendship towards his traditional enemies? Like the men at this table, the good President must have been aware of his danger, and the danger he was making for those around him. Did it increase his courage to know he was working for good? But they all thought they were working for good. The commissioners certainly did. The element of courage troubled Abraham Glazer. He had his share, but he sometimes wondered if there was a trace of the pathological crusader in him, a subconscious seeker after martyrdom. Were they all, perhaps, like that? No, he rejected the notion. They were all – Sadat and the arms commissioners and the other bodies working at odds with each other – basically good men, fervent in the support of what they believed, and pursuing their ends with a simple bravery born of determination. They were idealists.

'Just as I am,' he whispered under his breath. 'God preserve us all.'

Turnbull was freezing. There were no gaps in the wall of the chamber he was crouching in, but there was no insulation either, and no heating. He had been content, for a time, to accept the discovery of the trap door as a sign that all would yet be well. He was still in one piece, and although he might not see his luggage again, he had enough money on him to carry him to safety. But the feeling of salvation was slipping. He was cold, his plight was desperate, and for all he knew he was now a murderer, on top of all the rest.

With numb fingers he took the remaining ornamental gun from his pocket and set it ready. He could have used one more, always one more, just to offer that extra chance beyond the one pinning his hopes. There was nothing to be gained from thinking about any of this. He had to hold tight and wait, then act as the moment demanded.

Above him he heard a rumbling, the movement of some part of the navigation system perhaps, and for a few seconds he felt the whole chamber tremble. Then it stopped and everything was still again. The engines whined confidently and the wind slipped past. He was at least moving. There was a destination. Grasping the handle set into the wall beside him, he altered his position until he was lying almost flat, his gun pointing at the vent beneath the trap door. He was ready, it was enough to know that. He must not think; he must hold himself from despair. And he must drive every trace of Claire from his awareness, even though she loomed larger now than ever.

Shofal had withdrawn to the cover of the light inspection pit. Before he ducked down among the levers and switches, there had been time to see daylight on his handiwork. It looked good, because it seemed at first the detonators had vanished, they blended so well with the natural debris on the dull concrete.

He was tired. The cold had diminished his resistance to fatigue and pain, and away from the wind his injuries began to complain, like noisy children demanding attention. Shofal wondered what his face looked like; touching the wounds did not tell him much. Perhaps he looked ferocious, bloodied and stiff-faced from the wind, or maybe the effect was comic. He longed to be in a warm bed, curled close to Leila, the mission over and his aches seeping away into sleep. It was curious how his tiredness dulled everything in the spirit and energised the nerves. The thought of the forthcoming holocaust barely fired him at all now. He would much rather dwell on the prospect of rest.

The sound came to Shofal slowly, through all the others. The increase of overhead traffic had become a tune to him, the notes and rhythms spread out and complicated, with an underlying tempo of whining and rumbling to give them cohesion. The new sound started so faintly at first that he had not noticed, until it was near, threatening. He turned his head and strained to listen. Boots. The steady tramping of boots on concrete.

Carefully he raised his head until he could just see over the edge of the pit. He found he was staring at an empty runway, then realised he was looking the wrong way. Turning, he saw an Israeli, probably the partner of the one he had killed, striding across the strip from the other side, his dull black combat boots striking the ground like hammers. He was several feet away from the nearest staggered line of detonators. Shofal watched until the man cleared the runway and stepped on to the grass. He took a few steps in the direction of the pit, then he stopped and began scanning the ground on either side.

Shofal wanted to shout, scare him away, shoot him dead, anything to remove him from that place. In daylight anyone could find the dog or the dead soldier, and if the Israeli found either he would raise the alarm. The place would be swarming with security troops.

The breath whistled through Shofal's teeth as the man started moving closer. It was obvious what he intended. He was going to look into the pit. A natural thing to do, inevitable as any other detail of surveillance. Shofal reached for his pistol, lacking space to manoeuvre the submachine gun. The surprise alone would provide the opportunity: he would look, stiffen, and in that instant he would receive a bullet between the eyes.

But the man did not examine the pit. He stopped a few feet away and blew on his hands, stamping his feet as he revolved steadily and faced across the runway again. Shofal raised his head a fraction and wondered if there was a chance of shooting him, calculating the possible outcome of firing a shot in that open space. It had to be heard. The pistol was lowered but still gripped tightly. The soldier remained motionless for an endless ten seconds, then he moved forward and on to the runway again, directly towards an oblique line of detonators.

Shofal saw it all in a flash – a foot landing on one tiny pyramid, an ear-splitting explosion, the mission in ruins. He was climbing out of the pit before he knew it. His gun struck the metal rim as he surfaced and the soldier stopped. He saw Shofal as he turned but he did not freeze. He kept moving, changing from a walk to a run as he came back to the verge, his gun levelled.

Conscious action was suspended as Shofal found himself leaping in the air and swinging his gun hand. The muzzle of the pistol struck the Israeli on the bridge of the nose, leaving a scarlet groove as it passed. The man dropped to one knee and Shofal's gun hit him again on the back of the head. He rolled over on his back, stunned, and Shofal dropped astride him, pounding at the face with his pistol butt.

In a few seconds it was over. The soldier was dead, and killing him had taken every last reserve of Shofal's strength.

He squatted on the twisted legs and gulped air painfully, seeing fresh blood of his own mingle and spread through the mashed skin and shredded bone that clung to his gun. The wound on his palm had been opened again. He could feel no triumph in this killing. It had been more a matter of luck than skill and it had reduced him to a feeble, exhausted, pain-racked inertia. He barely had the strength or the sense of immediacy to stand up, and when someone shouted at him he did not turn. He just sat there on the dead Israeli, watching the blood run from his hand.

'You! What are you doing?' The SPG officer was young, attuned to certainties, so far, and rather afraid of his gun. He moved cautiously across the grass, closing on the two motionless figures, trying to make sense of the picture. At ten feet he could understand what had happened, but he was wondering who was the enemy.

Shofal turned his head wearily. His chin and nose were caked with dried blood. He did not look dangerous at all.

'What happened?' The young officer came nearer, his features twisted with disgust at the sight of the dead man's face. 'Who is he?'

With great effort Shofal managed to stand. Blood dripped from his hand and spattered the toes of his boots. He was seeing the new intruder only faintly; something in his head had stopped working and consciousness was slipping away. He should not have been in the cold so long, he thought, and realised he was swaying.

'What the hell is going on?' The young man looked like a student, his polo neck pulled up to his chin, denim jacket buttoned against the wind. 'Come on now, explain this.'

Without knowing if his hand was up or down, Shofal pulled the trigger of his pistol. The bullet hit the ground inches to the side of the officer and he yelped, raising his own gun. He did not shoot but took an agitated step forward and kicked the pistol out of Shofal's hand, then grabbed the collar of his jacket. Instinct, worn down to simple reaction, made Shofal pull away and he spun, freeing himself, and began to run. The SPG man gaped at the stumbling, retreating figure, then at the dead one on the ground with a face like chopped beef. He could understand none of it. For another couple of seconds he stayed motionless, then took off after Shofal, who was several yards across the runway.

'Kalim! Please, Kalim . . .' Shofal had the little radio in his hand, calling breathlessly into it. He must have help; there was too much to cope with on his own. He wanted to stop, lie down and accept darkness, but his legs pumped on. He knew the radio had only a short range but ignored the fact, grunting into it steadily as he jolted forward. The young man was behind him now, closing, but in that instant, Shofal also realised he was on the runway. He tried to stop himself, gaping down at the concrete as it passed under his feet. One leg stiffened, then the other, but he was still moving, and as he leaned back, tearing at his will to arrest himself, his right heel came down sharply on a detonator.

The explosion brought a Land Rover of anti-terrorist soldiers to the spot within two minutes. Commander Brooke, who had taken the wheel himself, brought the vehicle to a skidding halt twenty feet from the edge of the runway, and for a long time he was only able to stand on the grass and stare at the devastation, surrounded by his silent, nervous men.

'What kind of a bloody bomb did that?'

Chunks of concrete lay in piles all around them. On the runway there was a crater almost fifty feet across, lipped with crazed blocks and twisted steel reinforcements. White dust and powdered earth hung in a cloud over the centre of the hole and drifted gently out across the ground.

'Look, sir.' One of the soldiers was pointing behind him. The dog's carcase was lying beside two embedded blocks of concrete, the hind legs pushed up around its head.

'Maybe it set the blast off,' Brooke murmured, then winced as he saw a human hand a few feet further away. He pulled open the door of the vehicle and picked up the handset from the dashboard, flipping the switch. 'Brooke here. Can we have the bomb disposal wallah over to Runway 16?' He waited for the crackling acknowledgment, then dropped the mike and started walking out towards the ruptured airstrip. Captain Hughes, the officer in command of the eight-man unit, fell in step beside him. 'So why did they mine this strip?' Brooke asked him, not expecting any reply.

'Maybe the bomb was being transported when it went off,' Hughes suggested. He was not a man who liked mysteries. He had a pair of field glasses around his neck, and as they neared the edge of the runway he raised them and started scanning to right and left. 'Oh, Lord,' he murmured.

'What is it?'

'Take a look, sir.'

Brooke peered into the glasses, adjusting the focus, then groaned. 'An organised bunch,' he said, and looked again. 'I've only ever seen those little bastards in photographs.'

'So have I.' Hughes frowned, then came up with the data, extracted from his precise mental file. 'Kolnig detonators. Reckoned to be manufactured in Latin America. The specification's German, with Russian and American refinements. We can't touch them.'

'Why not?'

'Epoxy-based adhesive on the backside. Sets in minutes. You'd need a chisel to shift it. One tap of the hammer and boom, good night everybody.'

'But what are they doing here? This strip's an emergency item, and a pretty rough one at that. I'd see the sense—' Then it dawned on Brooke, as it would have done sooner if he had not been so very tired. 'They've diverted the Washington plane here,' he said. 'Mother of God, all those bloody things planted there . . .'

'And that hole,' Hughes pointed out.

'And we can't tell them.' Brooke was suddenly angry. 'We should have guessed some of this. It makes sense. They work away from the area of obvious concern, where surveillance is nil, and they take the tower, so they can divert the plane. Why didn't any of us come up with that, even as an outside possibility?'

'Wisdom after the event . . .'

'Don't give me that patter! It looks obvious now, but I'm not saying it should have been obvious before. What I'm saying is we didn't consider it, and it's not exactly an unfathomable, is it? Christ, they must have been working here during the night . . .'

Hughes was looking through the glasses again. He extended his arm and waggled a fingertip. 'Out there, sir. By the edge of the hole.'

Brooke peered again and saw a gun, an American 180, its strap wound around an arm with some fragments of cloth adhering to the wrist. 'The hardware survives very well,' he mumbled. 'I wonder if this means the terrorists in the tower are the only ones left?'

'Very likely,' Hughes said at once. He favoured optimism in combat. 'Just the two of them, now.'

Brooke returned the glasses and turned away from the airstrip. He looked at the tower in the distance, its lights still bright against the sky. 'Might as well be fifty, for all the chance we stand against them.'

'Couldn't something be done, sir? I mean, we know now what they're up to—'

'Oh yes, we know. But wisdom isn't always strength, is it?' He looked up at the sky and across to the horizon beyond the start of Runway 16. Within minutes, unless some miracle had occurred in the meantime, Pan Am 898 would be coming down out of the clouds over there. Computers would be ticking, sophisticated anti-shock mechanisms would be at the ready, the craft would be in perfect alignment with the runway and nobody would be looking out of the window. 'I suppose we could form a chain across the strip and wave at the pilot. Come on, Hughes. Let's get the word to Whiteside.' He shivered and put up two fingers in a vee of peace. 'Thank the Lord I'm out of his chair.' He kicked a small stone, Shofal's lucky charm, and sent it flying into a pile of rubble.

SEVENTEEN

Dyson was sitting hunched in on himself, stroking the wrist of his injured hand. Mike Evans, watching, started to realise something. The biggest lie had not been about his family. It had been before that, when Kalim gave his assurance that they would soon be rid of him. The statement was a playful ambiguity, definitely intended to deceive. No doubt Kalim and Leila would go when their mission, whatever it was, had been completed. But they would kill everybody in the room before they went. That was terrorism, after all. Its point had to be made at every opportunity. Society must tremble.

Pan Am 898 had just been on the radio, confirming the landing co-ordinates and receiving clearance for the approach. In fifteen minutes they would touch down. Understanding now that he was under sentence of death, Mike began to see that time as a precious gap between his plan and Kalim's, with a closing speed that was unreasonably swift. He had just looked away from Dyson when the explosion occurred over on Runway 16. For one ghastly moment it looked as if Kalim would carry out the sentence there and then.

'Carry on working! Everybody!'

Leila's startled eyes made an inventory of the room, as if the source of the explosion might be there. Kalim was by the window, his gun jabbed against the leg of the woman on the ledge as he craned his neck to see. There was little to detect beyond a blurring of the air in the distance. Kalim muttered something and returned to the centre of the room.

'Do not looked so pleased!' No one, in fact, was looking more than mystified. 'We shall still prevail!' The wildness was back on his face, a frothing beneath the surface that hinted at dwindling control. 'If there is one irregular movement in this room I will kill the woman!'

Mike was calculating the risk. So much depended on

Leila. Kalim had alienated her, and her adherence to the cause had slackened visibly in the past couple of hours. But she was scared. Scared, and with a weapon in her hands. That had to be weighed against Kalim's unravelling, the likelihood of his using the gun at any minute, and the certainty that he would use it anyway, sooner or later.

'Tell me, Kalim.' Leila had lowered her gun and was walking slow-footed towards him. 'What is it? What has happened out there?'

'Get back to the door!'

'I must know!'

Kalim swung his hand and struck her on the side of the face, knocking her down. 'Return to the door and keep your gun pointed there! That is an order!'

Anger was showing as she stood up, rubbing her cheek, the gun dangling by its strap from her other hand. 'Shofal has been killed!' Leila said it harshly, and the accusation was clear. 'He had too much to do!'

'We do not know what has happened!' Kalim screamed back at her. 'We will carry on according to plan. There is no reason to do anything else. Now go to the door.'

She was resisting him. Mike gauged it and set himself ready.

'I do not want to go on with this. Not now.'

Kalim took her arm and squeezed it. 'Your mind is like jelly, Leila. It collapses under the smallest pressure. Don't you see, even if part of the runway has gone, we still win? That plane will still come down there. It will crash, Leila . . .'

Mike Evans heard himself gasp, a constriction of the throat that echoed his shock. He had been frantically wondering and guessing in the realms of hijacking, missile attacks, gun battles – a mined runway wasn't something he had considered. It was diabolical. He could imagine it, see it, and if that explosion had really meant that a segment of Runway 16 was gone, the result would be the same. And within minutes . . .

Kalim put his fist up before Leila's face. 'Get yourself

under control,' he warned, 'or I will beat some sense into you . . .'

She was backing away from him, her face drawn with anger and bewilderment. Her grip mechanically adjusted itself on the gun. Kalim took one step in her direction to speed her obedience, and in three long strides Mike Evans was there, bringing the heavy punch down on Kalim's head with a sound like a brick hitting a cabbage. Unbelieving, Leila stared at the crumpling figure, then up again at Mike as the others began whimpering and groaning their fear.

'Don't do it, Leila. I've done you a favour.'

She had the red dot on his shirt, her finger hooked on the trigger. Mike did not move. His hands were out from his sides and he was no longer holding the punch. Leila took in his vulnerability and the moment of reaction passed. Her finger slackened on the trigger and she motioned for him to get back.

'Let me save that plane,' he said, walking backwards carefully to his console. 'Your mission's in ruins. Where's the point anymore?'

'The mission will succeed. Nothing has changed.' Leila's voice was much calmer than her face, which showed confusion, wariness. 'I am dedicated to the mission and so you will stay in your chair until the Washington plane is down. The mission ends there.'

'And so will you.'

'They will not take me.'

'But you know they will. One girl with a gun. What odds are those against what's waiting for you outside? If you give yourself up . . .'

'My life would not be worth living, then. Sit down, Mr Evans. Rest assured I will kill you if you try to interfere.'

Mike lowered himself into the chair, keeping his eyes on her. There could be no more than ten minutes to go, now. He could not believe the girl would end the exercise in the way her companion would have, but he believed she might use the gun on him. He glanced along the floor at Kalim, who was lying doubled over, blood oozing from a tear on the back of his scalp. His gun was on the floor beside him, just where it had dropped when he was hit. Perhaps there was an avenue of salvation there, but it was slender and urgency was taking the edge of Mike's confidence.

Keeping her gun angled towards Mike, with the dot wobbling on his abdomen, Leila climbed on to the nearest chair, giving herself a strong vantage point and ensuring a clear line of fire whatever happened. She had gone very pale, and her lips were parched. 'We will just wait, now,' she said. 'Everyone will carry on working. Please do not make me shoot.'

A feeble hope surfaced in Mike's brain. 'Kalim is bleeding badly,' he said, inching forward, half ready to leave his chair. 'We should do something—'

'Sit!' Leila screamed. Her knuckles whitened around the gun. 'Let him lie there. There is nothing you can do.' She glanced once in the fallen man's direction, then back at Mike, steadying her gun. 'He is probably dying,' she said. 'Move, and you will join him.'

When Commander Brooke had delivered his news to Whiteside and the assembled unit leaders, there was a small outbreak of disorder as voices fought for priority.

'Please, this is no way to tackle our problems,' Whiteside shouted. 'I must have order! Please!'

'Then what in hell are you going to do?' The CIA man was at the front of the throng, confronting Whiteside with spread feet and hands cowboy-style on his hips. 'You're the new broom, friend. What's the drill?' He looked at his watch. 'We got less than fifteen minutes.'

'We can only line up the rescue services as near to the runway as possible. Always assuming, of course, that the plane has been diverted to the emergency strip.'

'What? Are you kidding?'

'I'm not in the habit of joking about matters as serious as this . . .' Whiteside was flustered, his grey wings drooping on his ears, his waistcoat rumpled with the constant raising and lowering of his arms.

'You're condemning hundreds of innocent people to death! We have to get up in that tower and gun those bastards down! Now!'

'Out of the question,' Whiteside snapped.

The noise broke out again. While everyone was shouting, a policeman in a heavy greatcoat came in and passed a slip of paper to Whiteside. He snatched it and read it twice, then put up his hands again for quiet. 'Gentlemen, listen. Please.' He waited for the riot to subside, then delivered the message. 'The observers on the roof opposite the tower have noticed a disturbance. It's difficult for them to see anything too clearly, because of the sky's reflections on the glass, but it appears that one of the terrorists has been put out of action.'

'Big deal,' the CIA man yelled. 'That leaves one. One's enough to run that show, Whiteside.'

'And one person can kill everybody in there, too,' Whiteside countered, without much conviction.

'Weigh the thing, for Jesus's sake.' The American was almost coughing his words. 'A plane load, or a handful.'

He had touched Whiteside's dilemma, one he had been plagued with for some time now. Outcomes were what he had to think about, appearances and the subsequent weight of public and political opinion. He might conceivably take a course of action that would save the plane, but that in itself could be a disaster. The thing sat in his head like an ugly equation: America plus Israel set up against the Arabs, *on British soil*, and the explosive situation is defused by a British civil servant, *sacrificing British citizens in the process*. He would be beheaded, professionally. No amount of logic would sway opinion. This was not Britain's fight, and as innocents in the squabble they did not stand liable for casualties on the American, Israeli or Arab sides.

'We will not rush that tower,' he declared again. 'Apart from anything else, if the control centre is knocked out, we run the risk of endangering several other craft.'

Relations would be strained, of course. America and Israel would want to know why it was made so easy for the Arabs to carry out their plans. Relations had been strained before, and Whiteside had survived, simply because he had put his own, or rather his country's, interests first.

'I think it's time we stopped listening to you,' the CIA man roared. The Israeli, Zalman, was bellowing too. Whiteside stared back at the pair, feeling like telling them how lucky they were to be allowed a say in matters at all. The British Government had agreed to their presence out of courtesy. No British agents would ever be allowed to shout the odds in Washington or Tel Aviv.

'We will set up as large a rescue operation as we can.'

'Shove it, Whiteside. I'm ordering my men up to that tower right now.'

'If you do,' Whiteside said, 'I will order the anti-terrorist troops to stop them.'

'You bastard!'

Sticks and stones, Whiteside thought. The government would back his action as long as he played the right game. He remembered the stern directive fed to him by a senior colleague in his early days with the department: accommodate the foreigners, but never let them scratch the paintwork. He also recalled that the Israeli colonel was missing. If he did anything off his own bat, that was fine. Whiteside could not be blamed. 'I suggest we concentrate our efforts on the rescue programme, as fast as we can. If the people in the tower can do anything to help, they will. I'm sure they're trying.'

As the red-faced CIA operative went striding out of the room, Commander Brooke edged in and touched Whiteside's sleeve. 'That runway,' he muttered. 'We can't make it safe. The only way is to blow it up. There are still a lot of detonators out there. If we have rescue services anywhere close when the plane comes down, they'll get blown to buggery as well.'

Whiteside took a long, deep sigh. 'I've clearly done you a great service by allowing myself to be put in this position, Brooke. Can't you reciprocate? Is there no good news anywhere?'

'Not that I know of. All we can do is start foaming the runway and putting shields around the rescue vehicles. In the time we have, that won't do much good.'

In his heart, Whiteside knew that the short warning would be one way for Britain to argue her way out of this mess. No time to do anything. Regrettable, but there it was. 'No chance at all of alerting the pilot, I suppose?'

Brooke shook his head. 'None. Unless the control people have managed to do it already.'

'Well then, let's put our prayers at the disposal of Air Traffic Control, shall we?' And let's spend the remaining minutes, he said to himself, keeping ourselves clear of the quicksand.

In the Boeing, John Mitchell was making adjustments to the flight path, preparatory to taking the landing approach. The inertial navigation system allowed for minimum drift, in this case less than a mile, and he re-set the co-ordinates at the same time as he checked the rate of drop. They were in dense cloud, descending into weather that was forecast cold and wet. All his memories of London had a cold, damp backdrop, even the summer ones. He sometimes wondered if English people could understand what a long, hot Florida day was like. Maybe, like some Mexican Indians he knew of, they were programmed not to want or understand what they would never have.

'And you said you were bored,' Bob Fields ribbed the Captain. They were in their seats, dutifully watching their instruments. 'I bet you'll never say that out loud again.'

'Don't joke,' Harry Turner warned him. 'They still haven't found that bimbo Turnbull yet. My stomach's been edging my heart out of the way for the last twenty minutes.'

'He won't do anything now,' Bob said, trying for an authority of tone he did not possess. 'Probably scared himself half to death. Sit tight and chew your digitalis pills. We're on the home stretch.'

'Thank the Lord,' Turner murmured, then pulled on his headset as the radio light flickered on. It was Heathrow Control.

'Speedbird 898,' Mike Evans's voice said clearly, 'you are thirty miles south-west of our south perimeter.'

'Confirmed,' Harry said, checking the dials. 'We're starting our descent, on a heading three zero one.' John Mitchell passed descent and air speed details and Harry fed them to London. 'We've had some high drama on board,' he added, smiling at the microphone. 'Read all about it in the tabloids.' Mike Evans said he would, and they closed radio contact. A moment later, Turner activated the landing gear.

Nick Turnbull, huddled and numb in his little chamber, squirmed round in fright as the noise behind him grew to a sudden roar. The panel at his back had swung aside and a huge wheel bogie was filling the space, moving back towards him.

'No . . . Oh hell, no . . .'

He watched two sharp, grooved wheels roll back a foot and he jumped, flattening himself on the opposite panel. The thing was still moving, and there was a wind like nothing he had ever felt, slicing in on either side. He looked up into the darkness of the vent he had shinned down earlier. That way lay arrest, years of incarceration and despair. Where he stood, so far as he could tell, he would be a dead man within seconds. As the bogie continued to trundle back towards him, its grim girder work menacing as a guillotine, he tried to chose. The bullet would be the swift way, in his mouth and angled upwards. It had been on the cards, anyway. Pushed to it like that, he did not want to die. He did not want to be caught, either. The giant wheeled a few inches closer and he leapt, catching the metal ladder and pulling himself up. There was no room to crouch, no way he could hang there on those narrow spars. He had to keep moving. The plate above his head did not respond as easily to his push as it had to his desperate tug. Nick strained and cursed and suddenly it lifted. With one hand he gripped the rim of the hole and pulled himself back into the warmth of the tail storage bay.

There was no one about. That was something. Maybe he was on a current of luck. He pushed aside a stack of cartons and found a two-by-two space behind them. That would do. He would have settled for less. Slipping into the gap he drew the cartons into place in front of him, then leaned back against the panel and wondered, in a surge of fright, what he had done with the gun. It had become as much a lucky piece as anything he had ever owned. He patted his chest, fumbled inside his jacket, then found it in the left outside pocket, where he must have dropped it without thinking. Nick took it out carefully and handled it, passing the bright cylinder from hand to hand. Baby, he thought, we could make it yet. He could feel the plane going lower, down to solid ground, where a man could at least run and get somewhere.

Elsewhere in the plane passengers were fastening their seat belts, putting out cigarettes and steadily grumbling their displeasure. The Israeli commissioners moved down from the lounge and took their reserved seats in the first-class cabin. David Mendel and Yosef Mark, having failed to locate the man with the gun, stayed close to their superiors, guns tucked discreetly in their laps. A special anchor strap had been placed across Kay Morgan. The stewardess sitting with her fastened her own belt and kept watching Kay anxiously: in the past five minutes she had changed, her lips were tinged with blue and dark circles shrouded her eyes. Twice the girl had tried to rouse her, just to ask if Kay was all right, but there had been no response. Sleep had given way to a deeper unconsciousness. The stewardess chewed her nails and prayed for a quick, uncomplicated landing.

Dan Bradley and Lou Sherman hung on until the last minute before getting into their seats. Twice in ten minutes Sherman had been given the cold shoulder on the flight deck and now he was leaning on the panelling of the galley, scribbling moodily in his notebook.

'What are you doing?'

He glared at his partner. 'What do you think? Getting the facts down while they're still fresh.'

'They're printed on my brain,' Bradley said. 'Any way up, we catch a cold, I think.'

Sherman closed the book and put it away. 'That's the old fighting spirit,' he grunted. 'Don't give in until it's inevitable. Christ.'

'They'll slam us for botching the passenger check, Lou. No way out of that one.'

'Just wait and see. We've had enough in the way of harassment, obstruction, gunpoint threats—'

'I still think we'll get the hammer,' Bradley said. 'Nothing mitigates our shortcomings with the department. They see clean through smokescreens.'

'You're beginning to bore me, Bradley. Why don't you go and sit down? Your little black cloud's raining all over me.'

'Sure. Glad to oblige.'

When Bradley had gone Sherman moved to one of the windows and looked out. He could see land below, grey and dark green, irregular shapes with clean margins. Between landing there and going back to Washington, he would have it all hardened in his mind, rehearsed and ready to lay out before the boss man. If they had fault to find, let them do what the book told them. Depending on how much Israeli flak they pulled, it would either be a reprimand or instant removal to the desk job. Turnbull had vanished, so there was not much chance of saving face with him as the trophy. Assuming the worst, Sherman was already prepared to tell administration to shove their desk job. Again, two possibilities. Either they let him resign, or they forget the foul-up on this flight and ask him not to. Resignation was a move he wanted to avoid, but if it had to be, well, he would go to New York and take the security job he had poo-pooed a year ago. Any way it went, he was not going to beg anybody for anything. Dependence was a curse. It took away every shred of dignity. He only had to think of his wife.

'Would you go to your seat now, please? We'll be landing shortly.'

He turned and saw Jo Hampton. For a moment it was hard to understand what she had said, his mind was so packed with other things. He frowned at her.

'Are you all right, Mr Sherman?'

'Huh? Me? Of course I'm all right. What's up?'

'I asked you to sit down and fasten your belt. We'll be on the ground soon.'

'Yeah, sure.' He moved past her, trying to put some spring into his step as he went towards the cabin. Lou Sherman was always all right, he reminded himself. Even if it meant the rest of the world being all wrong, sometimes.

Closing on Heathrow, Harry Turner radioed the tower and confirmed his approach position, in accordance with procedure for security flights. There was a delay in answering, and when Mike Evans eventually came on he sounded different, less confident than before.

'Heathrow Control acknowledging, Speedbird 898. Over.'

'You OK down there?'

Bob Fields looked across at the Captain, then shrugged at the engineer.

'Yes, fine,' Evans replied.

'Right. Be dropping in on you soon. Over and out.'

'What did you think was wrong?' Bob Fields asked.

'Who knows?' Harry shrugged. 'He just sounded kind of, well, limp.'

'You're getting spooked. Your nervous system is going tapioca with all the stress. Wouldn't you say so, John?'

Mitchell said nothing. This was the one part of the flight when he got some real work to do, and he was not going to miss any of it playing games with Bob Fields.

Leila had focused the red dot on Mike Evans's head when he acknowledged the Boeing's last call. The thing had flashed on his eye for a moment, letting him look into the laser path and reflect, unwillingly, on what that gun could do. The girl was going to pieces, but not in the way Mike had hoped. She was holding only one thought at a time, and until the plane was down on Runway 16 she would not be swerved along any other channel.

Feeling his heart bunch in his chest, Mike looked out of the window and saw the beautiful bird coming down out of the cloud. Silhouetted black against dark blue it seemed to move in exaggerated slow motion. In a minute, he knew, that would change, the plane would sweep into the end of its approach turn and its true speed would be seen. The enormity of the situation crowded in on him as he stared out: they were all up there, safe, alive, being brought down with deliberate grace, yet in three minutes, four at most . . .

He felt his hands hit the floor and he was rolling sideways towards Kalim's body before he caught one breath. Leila's warning shout was beyond the desks and consoles. Mike was out of her line and grabbing the other gun. He pushed himself up, squatting with the stock in his armpit and his finger on the trigger. Then he saw the dot on his chest. She was on the bench, feet wide apart, her eyes narrow with intent.

'Don't, Leila!' He yelled. 'Those people can't die!'

She was not hearing him, he could tell from the hunching, the readiness to fire. Paralysed, Mike watched her finger curl, then heard a distant crack and saw Leila's head explode. Her body fell down off the bench, revealing the neat hole in the glass where she had stood.

For seconds the room was silent. Nobody moved until the woman on the ledge behind Mike started to howl with relief. Then they were talking, rushing to windows, trying telephones and opening the door. Mike was on his feet, tripping on chairs and the gun he had dropped, his arms out ahead of him as he made for the radio.

The call came through as Harry Turner was altering pitch, reversing the thrust to arrest the 747's speed as it dropped towards the runway.

'Don't land! For Christ's sake don't land! The runway's mined! Don't land!'

The reflex was ingrained. Turner pushed maximum thrust to the engines and struggled to bring the nose up. The jumbo shuddered and keeled, dipping to starboard as it fought to obey. The vibration along the wings transmitted itself to the cabins, shaking fittings loose and popping one window as people screamed and saw bottles, hand baggage, life jackets and trays float through the air and crash against panelling.

'Come on!' Harry Turner was shouting. 'Lift, you bitch!' Battling the controls, he could feel the weight beginning to prevail, the sheer tonnage of something too big to change its course so swiftly.

As they closed on the runway Nick Turnbull kicked himself free of his hiding place and was slammed hard against the door. He was babbling, tears and saliva and sweat covering his face as he crouched and reached out for the silver pencil. Fate, bastard fate had conned him, let him run straight to his own destruction.

'Claire!' He howled her name against the wall and fumbled, trying to get the pencil to his lips. All the plans, deceits, tricks and cunning – all for *this*! He did not want to die, but most of all he did not want to die in a crashing plane. Whimpering, he braced the top of his head against the door and pushed the end of the little gun to the back of his throat. His finger was slippery on the trigger and for one second hope surged again, a belief in salvation, even now. Then the plane lurched and roared and he shut his eyes and it was over. The tiny explosion was nothing against the tortured scream of the engines.

Before he died an old woman in the forward cabin had time to see her sister fly, unbelievably, across the aisle and land on her side against a seat. A moment later an attaché case came spinning the length of the cabin and hit the old lady in the face, smashing her glasses. People throughout the plane were on the floor, grasping the seat supports, while others, dizzy and hoarse from screaming, tried to fight their way out of their seat belts. The child called Betsy was face-down under a fallen service trolley. She was crying over and over for her governess, who was several yards away across the back of a seat, her legs and one of her arms broken. A fat businessman who had fouled himself now sat braced between a seat and the floor, gaping through his shock at all the howling, writhing humanity around him, wondering at how little sound they seemed to make in that roaring, shuddering prison.

Harry Turner brought the plane level at twenty feet above the runway. The vibration set off the remaining detonators seconds after they passed and the blast lifted the tail. He could see through the window and reacted immediately to the dictates of eyes and instinct, cutting the power and flailing his controls to keep the craft skimming as long as he could.

'Keep going, you whore!' He saw the end of the runway, then land falling away, a dip into fields and a wood dead ahead. Height was down to twelve feet when the tops of clustered firs brushed the plane's belly and chewed its skin, simultaneously cutting the speed and aiming the nose into the lip of a wide sand pit.

From his speeding Land Rover Commander Brooke saw the giant lop trees and vanish from sight. He flattened the accelerator and worked the four-wheel drive to its limit as the sound of the landing came to him, a crash like the rending of distant hills.

Behind the Commander, Whiteside goaded him on and cursed the slower, heavier appliances that trundled down the dirt track in their wake. 'Damned bloody dinosaurs! If that plane burns I'll have their hides, every last bloody one . . .'

They rounded a bend and saw the jumbo down to their right. Smoke was rising in swirling black plumes from the undercarriage and engines. All emergency doors appeared to be open and people were already on the ground, lying, staggering, helping each other away from the tilted wreck. Getting nearer, Brooke could hear the terrible wailing as injured men and women clambered from the canvas chutes.

He was out of the vehicle before it stopped. With Whiteside running behind him he panted his way to a man in uniform, sitting on the ground twenty feet from the plane, rubbing his leg.

'Are you the Captain?'

The man nodded. His forehead was bleeding and one eye was already closing from a massive bruise on his cheek. 'It's a mess on board,' he said weakly. 'I don't know if anybody's dead, but there are some near shots.' He looked up beyond the Commander and Whiteside as the convoy of fire appliances and ambulances came over the hill. 'Thank God. They'll be busy.'

As more security men began to arrive in cars and Whiteside started alternating questions and apologies at Harry Turner, Commander Brooke moved closer to the plane and finally saw what he was looking for. A cluster of four men, badly shaken, with blood and grime on their torn clothing, guarded by two younger men openly holding guns.

Sternly, Brooke said, 'You can put those away.' He showed his identification to the taller guard. 'The terrorists are dead. All but one, and he's damned near dead.'

Avrum Maller stepped forward and told Brooke who he was. 'There were terrorists, you say?' He jumped aside as an arc of foam swept directly over his head and began spattering the plane. 'Do you know who they were? Is our Foreign Minister safe?'

'He stayed at home,' Brooke said. 'There's been a blood-bath at the airport, though.' He turned and pointed to the Land Rover. 'Look, I want you all to get in there. Not quite the limousine that was planned, but it'll have to do. We'll get you patched up in the medical room.'

David Mendel stepped to one side and beckoned to the Commander. He explained about the gunman and how he had disappeared. 'He has not come out of the plane,' Mendel added. 'I have looked carefully.'

'Leave it to me,' Brooke told him.

Ambulance crews were removing the injured on stretchers as the fire teams began smothering the plane with foam. Brooke delegated a driver to take the Israelis back to the airport and watched as Whiteside climbed in beside them, his lips framing condolences and regrets as the door closed on him and they moved away. Security troops were on the side of the hill overlooking the pit and others were down among the passengers, questioning, helping, doing their job. Brooke was starting to feel the recoil of events when a limping, haggard individual came across to him, waving his ID card.

'You some kind of security?'

'Yes, I am.' Brooke read the card. More CIA, he thought. A man could spend years wondering about them, half believing they were a myth, then in one five-hour span he could not turn sideways without bumping into one of them.

Sherman started to tell him about the gunman called Turnbull. Brooke said he had already heard. He would handle it. Sherman was not so sure about that, and said so. Brooke excused himself curtly and walked away.

One of the three doctors attending the scene approached the Commander, walking through the pale haze fanning up from two sprinklers trained on the engines. He was carrying a clipboard and used it to signal. Brooke stopped in his tracks and waited, hoping he was not going to be bombarded with any more depressing statistics.

'I think you should come over here,' the doctor said, pointing to a small ambulance at the end of the dirt path. 'It's a security thing, I fancy.'

Brooke nodded and followed the man. Nowadays, it only had to get around that you were security and everybody assumed that meant police, army, MI5 and, for all he knew, the Water Board, rolled into one.

There was a girl on the wheeled stretcher inside the ambulance. A white-coated attendant was monitoring a drip in her right arm and another of the doctors was gingerly examining a wound on her chest. The girl looked terribly ill, but she was conscious.

'Shot,' the first doctor said. 'She might have died, if it hadn't been for one of those Israeli chaps. He dug her out of the busted remains of the cubicle she was in and brought her down the chute himself.' He smiled faintly. 'Bit like the Lone Ranger, really. He waited to hear she was OK, then cleared off before anybody could thank him properly or ask his name.'

Brooke moved closer to the stretcher. 'How do you feel, my dear?'

'Sore,' Kay said. There was morphine in her veins now and she was having trouble fighting it. Then to the doctor examining her she said: 'I'm going to be all right, am I?'

He nodded. 'It'll take time. The bullet's no danger to you, but you've been in pretty bad shock by the look of things. Give it a couple of weeks, say, then you can fly back home.'

'No way,' she said dreamily, her dry lips curling in a smile. 'I'll hop a ship.'

By the door, Brooke noted down the details, then found himself an armed security soldier and explained they had to go on board the plane and find themselves a gunman.

As they stood a few yards from the forward emergency door, waiting for clearance from the fire team, a battered but happy-looking coloured man went limping by on the arm of a pretty blonde. A little girl with large, frightened eyes walked behind them, led by an ambulance driver who told her everything was fine, she was not to be upset. A moment later a stretcher came by, carrying the Flight Engineer, who had severe concussion. The Second Officer walked alongside, white-faced, exhausted. He bumped into Brooke and apologised.

'You've had a rough time,' Brooke murmured, patting his shoulder.

'The roughest,' Bob Fields admitted. Then he turned and raised a thumb at the plane. 'But she held. She damn well held.'

The signal came from the Senior Fire Officer, and Brooke walked over to the ladder set up by the forward door. 'Let's get it over with,' he mumbled to the soldier, then paused for a moment, looking up at the foam-shrouded nose of the plane.

'Something wrong, sir?'

'No, I was just being poetic. It struck me how outraged this thing looks.' He took his pistol from the pocket of his coat and set his foot on the bottom rung. 'Any way you look at it, it's been a bloody outrageous night. Come on.'

In the tower, Mike Evans was trying to drive some order into a traffic situation that was getting more chaotic as the minutes ticked past. With a fresh crew and some auxiliaries, he was yelling instructions, taking calls and refusing to rest or answer police questions until he knew his territory was in shape again.

He paused for a minute and watched as men drew chalk marks around Leila's sheet-covered body, down in the shadows where she had landed. There was an odd sense of loss. It could have been different. Then a light jabbed on the edge of his vision and he turned, snatching up the microphone and running his tongue across flaking lips.

'Sorry, Papa Whisky Delta. Your landing clearance will be passed in a few minutes. Apologies for the delays.' He looked around the room, warming to the slow return of order, the safe pattern overlaying the disruption. He put his mouth to the microphone again, suppressing a painful yawn. 'We've had a spot of bother, you see. Heathrow over and out.'

TWILIGHT'S LAST GLEAMING

Walter Wager

HE'S GOING TO WIPE OUT THE WHOLE WORLD.

The Ultimate Threat . . . five men with nothing to lose, convicted murderers escaped from a prison death cell and led by a former Air Force Major, take over command of the underground control centre of an ICBM launch site.

They want five million dollars in cash, safe conduct out of the country and a hostage – the President of the United States.

If they don't get what they want, the world gets . . . WORLD WAR THREE.

THE DEFECTOR

Donald Seaman

'EXPERTLY CONSTRUCTED THRILLER' *Daily Express*

From the author of THE BOMB THAT COULD LIP-READ, a second brilliantly realistic thriller – THE DEFECTOR.

A vital Russian scientist leaves the Soviet Union in order to save his wife from torture and imprisonment. In Britain their faces are changed by plastic surgery and they learn to play the roles of Mr. and Mrs. John Stevens. It is the perfect defection, until John Stevens shoots and kills a housekeeper and becomes the pawn in a deadly struggle between the English courts of law, British Intelligence and the KGB.

'A slow-fuse thriller that GRIPS FIERCELY' *Birmingham Post*

The Minotaur Factor

Stuart Stern

The cause:
THE BIRTH PILL

The symptoms:
LETHAL CATATONIA

The result:
CERTAIN DEATH

A young woman goes berserk at a party and mutilates three people with a knife before collapsing into a coma. She dies and acute lethal catatonia is diagnosed as the cause of death, an unstoppable and incurable chemical malfunction of the brain.

Sir George Upton, head of the medical team investigating the epidemic, discovers that it is linked with a brand of birth pill. But what is the link? In desperation the team selects a group of human guinea pigs for a series of experiments as deadly as the disease itself.

THE MINOTAUR FACTOR is a terrifying extrapolation on the theme of the possible long term effects of the birth pill – effects which are still not wholly known.